Barnaby Brown
and the Time Machine

By Michael A. Gordon

For Sean, William and Lucy

Cover illustration by Ludmila Gazdova.

Huge thanks to my editor Sharon McLean for
Sharonifying the text. Also massive thanks to the guys at
POZA Publishing for helping a newbie reach for the stars.

Prologue

"Mathias! You need to come and see this!"

Professor Mathias Finch, a particle physicist, looks up from his copy of *A Brief History of Time* that he is reading under the dig tarpaulin. He lowers his reading glasses enough to be able to focus on his colleague, Professor Peter Lansdowne, whose face is beaming with excitement.

It's been three weeks since he first arrived at the dig in Pompeii and while the first couple of days had been exciting, looking around at the recently found artefacts, his interest has waned since then. Not being an archaeologist, he has been refused permission to be hands-on involved in the dig for fear that he may break something or overlook something of historical importance, and when Mathias Finch has nothing to do, he loses interest completely.

At first, he stopped traversing down the steps to the dig site, opting to stand above and oversee progress.

Eventually he didn't even bother turning up at all, instead favouring to sit in his comfy wicker chair with his feet up on the map table, re-reading his favourite science novels and pondering the endless possibilities if their dig actually produces fruit. In all honesty, it's not their dig, they've merely latched on to the ongoing archaeological excavation at the site, a favour granted by the head of the project, Professor Marco Bianchi.

"What is it Peter?" asks Mathias, as his feet drop to the ground allowing the blood to flow back into them.

"I think we've found it!" replies Peter, giggling with excitement and dancing on the spot like a hyperactive toddler.

"Well, old man, about bloody time!" bellows a grinning Mathias as he leaps from the chair, pops his reading glasses into his shirt pocket and rushes past packing cases and equipment towards his old friend. "Argh, oops, nearly forgot!" he announces, and at the same time snags his big toe on a tent pole. Hobbling back to the desk, he slips his bare feet into a pair of tattered sandals and throws his canvas work bag over his shoulder. "Right, come on, no point standing around here all day. There's work to be done!" Mathias dashes past Peter, a slightly eccentric, sixty-two-year-old stocky, diminutive chap with glasses and short curly greying hair. Even in these temperatures, he prefers to wear a tweed waistcoat and a cravat.

"Uh, um, wait up, old chap!" calls out the ageing British professor with his finger raised in the air like an exclamation mark. He's not as mobile as he used to be, certainly not as much as the younger Mathias Finch. So he does his best to canter along after him, dabbing his forehead with a pocket-square handkerchief. All the while he steadies himself on his walking stick as it kicks up dust, much to the amusement of the Italian workforce who have stopped for lunch.

Mathias gets there first and stops for a moment to cast his eye over the scene. It's not immediately clear as the overhead tarpaulin is blocking out most of the light, but below him, an area some fifteen square metres wide begins to present itself. The hole, formerly the lower room of a house in one of the city streets, contains five members of the archaeological team, who are now all gathered around one object in the corner of the site. After a moment, a sweaty and out-of-breath Professor Lansdowne reaches Mathias' side and, with a sigh, rests his hand on his shoulder for support.

Digging into his work bag, Mathias pulls out a yellow and black handheld optical power meter which he switches on and points in the direction of the assembled excavators. The device gives an audible crackle, like that of a Geiger counter.

"Incredible!" exclaims Mathias. "It's even stronger than it was."

"Wait," says Peter as he grabs Mathias' arm, preventing him from rushing down the steps to the dig. "Is it safe? I mean, is it radioactive?"

"No, it doesn't emit any radiation at all! But look, look at the reading." Mathias holds the power meter up to Peter's face.

"Good God, 24.7 megawatts. That's impossible!" Peter holds the device steady in front of his face and peers over the top of his glasses.

"No, no, dear boy. These aren't megawatts. These are gigawatts!" replies Mathias, grinning like a Cheshire cat. Peter's jaw hangs agape as Mathias turns and hurries down the steps into the dig site. He bolts over to the five excavators brushing them aside and drops down to his knees to examine what lies before him, the power meter still crackling away in his hands. Peter soon joins him, and there is an audible gasp as his eyes fall upon the object. There before them, buried up to its waist in the ash soil, is the petrified remains of a person. The face is contorted in pain, the arms pinned to its side with the hands raised, clasping on to a black rock through which pokes a segment of blue crystal. The body has been frozen in time at the moment when the pyroclastic superheated ash cloud from Mount Vesuvius struck the ill-fated city, encapsulating its victims in this hellish mould, their tortured poses captured for all time. The bodies are not actually made of stone. They are resin casts of the space left behind after the body has decomposed, the resin having been carefully poured into the moulded space by the excavation team, who located them using sonic scanners.

"Incredible!" announces Peter, crouching beside Mathias. "It's as if he's holding the stone up as some form of protection. As if the Gods would spare him if he offered it to them."

"Perhaps he thought the stone had magical powers," grins Mathias as he turns to face Peter, who shrugs at the suggestion. "Come on, Peter, look at the power reading! You know what this stone is, you've been searching for them all of your life."

"Well, I guess it possibly could be," mumbles the professor. "I just don't want us to get our hopes up prematurely."

"Of course it is! What other stones from antiquity could have yielded such power? Hmm? The one at Delphi! Carthage! Mount Cassius! All lost, but somehow one of them has made its way here. To Pompeii!"

"Didn't do this chap much good, did it?" Peter points out with a bemused look.

"I need to get this back to my laboratory," continues Mathias Finch in whispered tones to his old friend. "Something with this much power can't fall into the wrong hands. Hmm? It must come directly to me. I'm not allowed to touch it, but you can. Make sure you personally remove it, wrap it in tin foil and ship it to my address on Long Island. It must be marked as a geological sample. Customs won't query it as there's no radiation being produced. It'll appear like a normal rock sample as it goes through the scanners."

"Yes, yes, old boy, I can arrange that with Marco. We can use the diplomatic channels, no problem, but what will you do with it once you've analysed it?" asks Professor Lansdowne, getting to his feet with a combination of groans and the clicks of popping knees.

"Oh," replies Mathias as he turns once more to stare at the mysterious black rock clasped in the hands of the nearly two-thousand-year-old corpse. "I have BIG plans for it!"

Chapter 1

Welcome to long island

Barnaby Brown likes toast. Lots of it.

When he lived in England he had his favourite brand of bread, McNortons, and wouldn't accept any other substitute. Toppings varied from just butter to jam, marmalade to chocolate spread, even tuna mayonnaise, but always on McNortons.

Now living in New York with his mother, fifteen-year-old Barnaby is quite settled. At nearly six feet tall, he towers above most of the other children in his class, a gift from his equally tall father. They both have the same dark hair, parted to the side, and the same natural skinniness. Barnaby looks mildly less goofy than his father, bordering on handsome, the looks coming very much from his Mother.

Sitting in his uncle's kitchen staring at a buttered bagel, he still misses his old life, his old friends and, of course, McNorton's bread. It reminds him of his first day at school after the move when he was thirteen. Again, bagels were on offer and were entirely new to him. It was also the day he first met his best friend, Jack Warner, his sister Polly and their friend, the breathtaking Marsha Moon. Closing his eyes he remembers the day well. He had been woken early by his mother, Elizabeth, to make extra sure he didn't miss his school bus. "First impressions are so important," she was always telling him. Staring at the non-McNorton's breakfast, thirteen-year-old Barnaby sits motionless, the grumpiness rising within him.

"Stupid bagel!" he shouts, as he folds his arms in defiance.

"Come on Barnaby, how do you know it's stupid if you don't try it?" replies Mum.

With a deep sigh, he picks up the bagel and nibbles on its outer rim, warm butter now running between his fingers. It tastes fantastic, but he's not going to let his mum know that. As far as she is concerned, he is in misery, having been dragged across the Atlantic Ocean to live with 'Mad Uncle Finch', his mother's brother and, to his embarrassment, an actual mad scientist.

Mum's family are all a bit crazy, to be honest. Maybe that's what drove dad away? Barnaby's father left them when he was only a year old, and mum had been forced out to work to make ends meet. The whole family is stinking rich, but mum is a very proud lady and would not accept charity from any of the family. That money can go to Barnaby when he is older, and she wants to earn her own money.

Barnaby has since, only recently, met his father once more. It wasn't a good meeting as Barnaby was carrying around so much resentment, but it did get a lot off of his chest. Since then, he's been a delightful soul to be around, his demons put to rest.

Uncle Finch's house, in which they are now staying, is vast. It's a typical New England style, ten-bedroom house, with lots of garden space and an enormous basement, which Uncle Finch uses as his workshop/laboratory.

The good thing is, Uncle Finch spends most of his time down there. When he does come up for air, his interaction is minimal as he always looks like he's on the verge of solving a problem and doesn't really have the spare brain capacity for idle chatter, or indeed, ANY kind of chatter.

"Come on Barnaby, get it eaten, the school bus is coming in ten minutes!!" shouts Elizabeth, as she runs around the kitchen preparing his lunch and sealing it inside a Tupperware box.

"I don't want to go to school!"

"Oh come on darling, it won't be that bad. First days are always a bit scary, but you're bound to make friends quickly. Americans love English accents, so you're guaranteed to be super-popular," continues Elizabeth, trying to inject some positivity into the proceedings.

"Mum, do you know anything? They're not going to love my accent. They're going to say I sound stupid or call me 'Gaylord the third' or something.

Barnaby is joining in ninth grade, and his school is a ten-minute bus ride away, just a little bit too far to walk in an area he's unfamiliar with. He's dreading that first bus ride. EVERYONE is going to be staring at him. They'll pick on him and call him names, he's sure of it. The doors will open, he'll walk on, and it'll be like one of those cowboy movies where everyone stops talking and the pianist stops playing, and they'll all turn and look at him and he will feel simply AWFUL!

"I don't know why we had to come to this stupid country in the first place!" screams Barnaby, the textbook teenager.

"Darling, we've been over this a million times. I was headhunted by DDent Industries. They have offered me an excellent salary to head up their finance department. It was too good an offer to resist! Besides, this is New York, one of the greatest cities in the world and you, my boy, are going to love it here."

"I won't, it'll be rubbish and I will hate it!"

Mum gives a little sigh and decides to leave this battle for another time.

DDent Industries is one of the world's biggest arms manufacturers. Mum doesn't really like the fact that they make weapons and wrestled with her own conscience for a couple of weeks before accepting the offer. The opportunity for both she and Barnaby was the deciding factor. He's been stuck in an English village for most of his life, and this will help him to become more worldly-wise. At least, that's the hope.

Their CEO, Darius Dent (pronounced DAR-EYE-US) is a self-made billionaire. Not a particularly pleasant man to be around, according to the web research she did on him. He has business connections with some seriously awful people around the world, but to counteract this, he has set-up several global charities to aid victims in war-torn countries, perhaps to ease his own conscience. He also has a particular love of the natural world and has charities that look out for the well-being of endangered species. He especially donates heavily to all charities dog-related. Anyway, she'll find out what kind of character he is for herself if she gets a chance to speak to him at the annual summer ball next Saturday. An opportunity for her to mingle and make some friends for herself. She hopes.

"Come now darling, you need to get your coat on."

"Mum, it's twenty-two degrees outside! I'll melt."

"Well, go put a hoodie on or something. At least you don't have to wear a school uniform here, unlike your last school."

His last school was a typical public school. Three hundred years old, dusty, the children crammed into over-starched uniforms, with an emphasis on boring homework and etiquette. Barnaby, as a result, is a well educated and polite boy although not particularly streetwise.

All of his old friends were exact copies of him, except perhaps Colin. Even though his father was a renowned archaeologist, Colin came from a less-privileged background and always fooled around to make himself popular, and to make up for the fact he wasn't wearing designer clothes in his spare time, an instant admission to the club of posh kids.

For just that reason, Barnaby had actually quite liked him.

Barnaby had the family name and the breeding, but no access to the kind of funds the other kids did. He was accepted because of his father's connection to the school, gaining instant access to what is commonly referred to as 'The Old Boys Network'. Simply put, if your family had a history at the school, you were part of the club. This followed on in later life when they would still look out for each other, sharing business tips on the golf course. The mere sight of a school tie, worn strategically, could swing things in your favour at business meetings or in court.

He and Colin had spent lots of time together, having adventures in the woods, discovering pretend ancient temples and building 'Gang huts'. They were both very outward bound and didn't spend much time with their faces buried in an iPad or similar.

He misses Colin dreadfully. At least he still has his big blonde Golden Retriever, Momo for company.

Momo came into Barnaby's life when he was only four. A spritely little puppy who took to him straight away. Momo was part of the gang, chasing sticks in the woods and swimming in the rivers. At the time of moving to New York, he was eight years old and still a little dazed from the flight, but soon joined in with the stick game and his favourite, the tennis ball game.

"Bus!" shouts Mum.

"I've got a headache!" yells Barnaby.

"Nonsense. Here's your bag. I've packed your lunch in it and put in an extra top in case the classroom is cold."

"Why would the classroom be cold Mum? I already said that…"

"Aircon darling, now get a move on."

"Oh, alright," mutters Barnaby, conceding that he just won't be able to avoid school.

Mum puts his bag on his shoulders and kisses him on the head.

"Have a great day darling!"

'Hmph!" replies Barnaby, as he flaps his arms. He storms out of the door secretly patting Momo on the head, and meanders his way down the drive to the gate where the dreaded school bus awaits him.

He looks around and sees mum waving from the door.

"Oh God! Go back inside you silly woman", thinks Barnaby to himself while walking the final few paces of shame to the bus door. It opens with an unwelcoming hydraulic hiss.

"Ok, here we go," thinks Barnaby, as he takes the first couple of steep steps up to his doom.

The driver seems nice. He has a broad welcoming smile and invites him to take a seat.

"I'm Chester," grins the driver.

"Barnaby."

"First day, huh?"

"Yeah."

"Well, go park your behind. Gotta lotta others to pick up."

At this, Barnaby finally looks up and realises he's one of the first pickups of the day! Yes!! Brilliant! He instantly feels better. There are only two other kids on the bus. One small skinny boy who looks like he should be in fourth grade and…

Oh...

My...

God.

Barnaby trembles a little and sits down quickly at the next available seat, eyes forward, not daring to turn around.

Three rows behind him, caught in the morning sunlight, is the most beautiful girl he has ever seen. As their eyes met, she had given him a welcoming smile and he had responded by almost vomiting and stumbling into the seat he now occupies.

How awful! He hadn't been attracted to any of the girls at his last school. Well, not his exact school, as it was boys only, but the sister school across the road, where all of the girls were sent. He had known them all since he was five and they had all been a bit stuck-up.

In his mind, he can still see her. That smile, those gorgeous Asian, light brown eyes, almost green in the sun, the voluminous dark hair, the dimples. Noooooooo. This is the worst thing that could have happened. Now, gripped with fear, he is dying for other kids to fill the gap between them. She's bound to be staring right at him.

The bus pulls off down the tree-lined street in search of its next pickup.

At the next stop, two kids get on. One girl and one boy. Probably brother and sister. The girl sets off down the bus aisle and calls out "Morning Marsha!"

So, she's called Marsha.

"Hey, new kid, you look terrified".

Huh?" says Barnaby.

"I said, you look terrified. First day nerves or is it Marsha?"

"Uh, no, I um…"

"Yeah, I figured", says the brother who is now sitting in the opposite row of seats.

"No, it's just that…"

"You all pull the same face. Like God just spoke to you or something." The brother raises his eyebrows and sighs.

"No, really, I…"

"From England, yeah?"

"Um, yesss?"

"Cool. Chicks dig an English accent."

Damn you, Mum, are you ever wrong?

"I'm Jack," grins the boy.

"Barnaby. Pleased to…"

"So, wanna have a farting competition?"

Not what Barnaby expected. Jack is a very forward boy, handsome, like a young Harrison Ford. He may even be modelling himself on him.

"A farting competition?"

"Yeah, we mark on volume and strength."

"On the bus?"

"Sure, you go first."

"I don't think so," remarks Barnaby, half looking over his shoulder.

"Ah, you trying to tell me Marsha doesn't fart?"

"No, but somehow I can really imagine that now, thanks!!"

"Come on. If you don't, I'll do one and blame it on you!"

"Look, Jack was it? I can't just fart at will, and it's not the kind of behaviour I want to entertain on the…"

Paaaarrrrrrpppppp!

Jack lets a very impressive pump roar.

"Oh God! Ewwww, new kid, what the hell?" says Jack standing up, holding his nose and gagging.

Barnaby stands up to protest his innocence.

"No, no, that wasn't…"

"You need to see a doctor about that, new kid."

"The name's Barnaby and I don't need to see a... ah, this is stupid. I did not FART!"

He takes the opportunity to check out Marsha again. She's still smiling but now has her eyebrows raised. "Oh God, she still looks cute. Even with a fart in the bus!" thinks Barnaby to himself. Or did he just say that out loud? Ah, this is all too confusing.

"Ah, sit down you big goofball, I'm just playin' with ya," exclaims Jack.

Barnaby slowly sits down and re-composes himself.

"So, what sport are you into?"

"We used to play a fair bit of cricket and rugby at my last school."

"Well, you're halfway there. Here it's baseball and football, so you'll get by," replies Jack.

Barnaby almost responds with "They're nothing like each other! You pansies wear all this gear and helmets," but he thinks better of it and stops himself.

"You played baseball before?"

"We have a similar game in our country called 'Rounders'. Basically the same idea."

"Rounders? Sounds lame."

Is this kid trying to be annoying?

"Okay, maybe I can teach you to fart properly and play baseball?"

"How kind," murmurs Barnaby, wondering if sarcasm has landed on the American shores yet.

The bus continues on its way, picking up more children. Barnaby is oblivious to who gets on as he and Jack are now deep in conversation.

"So how long have you been at this school?" enquires Barnaby.

"Came here in third grade. We used to stay in the City."

"Which city?" asks Barnaby.

"THE city. N to the Y to the C! Well, Manhattan."

"Aren't we in New York now?"

"God, limeys! We refer to Manhattan as 'The City'."

"Okay. I've got lots to learn, obviously".

"You do that my friend. You do that."

"So do you have any brothers or sisters?"

"That's my sis up the back with Marsha. Polly. She hates me though."

"Let me guess, you fart on her lots?"

"Yeah, usually. I grab her head, stick it under my bed sheets and let one go."

"That would do it. In the UK, we call that the 'Dutch oven'."

"What about you? You got siblings?"

"No, my dad left before getting around to another one. Just me and my mum left now."

"Is your mom hot?"

"What sort of question is that??"

"My dad is divorced, could do with a lady friend instead of moping around the house all day."

"Doesn't he work?"

"Nah, he co-wrote a hit song back in the 80s and just lives off the royalties."

"I see."

"So, are you guys renting?"

"Huh? Oh, the house? No, it's my Uncle Finch's."

"Sweet. What does he do?"

"Um, it's kind of embarrassing."

"Come on dude, tell me!"

"He's, um, he's a scientist."

"What's weird about that?"

"He invents crazy stuff."

"Yeah, like what?"

"Um, well, it's all quantum mechanics stuff. He's…
he's working on a teleportation system," Barnaby ventures
sheepishly.

"What? Oh, that is hilarious. Like *Star Trek*? Beaming
people around the world stuff?"

"Yeah. He's bonkers though, all he's managed to do is
microwave a watermelon. To be honest we've hardly
spoken a word since I arrived. Mum filled me in on what
he's been doing, or at least was doing a few years ago.
Who knows, maybe the crackpot has gone and done it!
Impossible to know as he keeps the basement locked."

"I think you'd know. If he gets up in the morning and
comes back with authentic warm Parisienne bread."

"Hahaha, yeah."

"Okay, this is us, North Woodward High School!"

It's not very attractive. Nothing like his old school,
with its Gothic spires and faux battlements. This reminds
Barnaby more of a mall, a crumbling mall from the 1970s,
with no shops.

"That is one turd of a building," remarks Barnaby.

At that, Polly and Marsha walk past, with Marsha
giving a little chuckle on the way.

Sigh.

Since that day, Barnaby and Jack have been
inseparable. Jack's other friends such as Ed and Ranjit
have been pretty much sidelined by the duo. Each thinks
of the other as the brother they never had. Of course,
Barnaby is an only child, but Jack has Polly, his twin, who
is almost like a boy were it not for the fact that, no matter

what she wears, she looks incredibly cute. Still, as cute as Polly is, Barnaby can't see past Marsha. In over a year, he's rarely said a word to her, due to his fear of vomiting on her.

Today is like every other day. Barnaby polishes off his yummy bagel, gets on the bus, freezes when he sees Marsha, holds back the urge to vomit, waves to Polly as she passes, and then dives deep into conversation with Jack.

This will be the last normal day of his life.

Chapter 2

Strange goings-on at night

Barnaby arrives home from school and throws his bag onto the kitchen table. Picking up an apple, he plops himself in a chair and starts to crunch away.

"Mum?"

"Yes, darling?"

"Would it be okay if Jack stayed over on Friday?"

"I don't mind, we're not doing anything. It's Independence Day on Friday, so he'll need to get his dad to phone and confirm they've nothing planned."

"Thanks, Mum!"

Barnaby rushes off in the direction of his room.

"Momo?" he shouts for his canine friend as he goes.

Nothing. That's weird. He always sleeps upstairs on the bed and when called, comes clattering down the stairs with his big tail wagging furiously and a ball in his mouth. Licks about the face usually follow.

"Momo!"

WOOF!

Wait. That's coming from downstairs.

"Momo!"

WOOF, WOOF!!

"Come here, good boy!"

Barnaby now hears the creaking of wooden steps.

"Uncle Finch?"

The sound of a door unlocking and a security bolt sliding open alerts him to the fact that Uncle Finch is approaching. As he opens the door, Momo pushes past and runs to greet Barnaby.

"Hello boy, who's a good boy, who's a vewy, wewy good boy then? Huh?"

Momo is all over Barnaby.

"Hey, you're cold! Uncle Finch, don't you have the heating on down there?"

"Eh, no, I have to keep a controlled temperature," replies Uncle Finch from a gap in the door, which has now almost closed.

"What was he doing down there with you?"

"Ah, you see, I uh, I heard a scratching at the door earlier. He, uh, must have been lonely and wanting company. He's been down here with me all afternoon."

"Wowwwww, who's a good boy making friends?" says Barnaby, ruffling Momo's fur.

"Yuh, he's a, uh, very good, uh, boy," Uncle Finch nods in agreement, but not quite sounding sincere.

Uncle Finch is a tall, thin and very shifty looking man. He wears glasses that exaggerate his crazy looking eyes. His hair has a sizeable amount of grey through it but doesn't yet have the full head of white 'mad scientist' hair. Although, if he's not careful, that is certainly the direction in which it could head.

Click. The basement door shuts, locks and then the bolt draws back over.

"Nice, talking to you," says Barnaby with a truck-load of sarcasm.

"Come on Momo, let's go upstairs and play ball!"

WOOF, WOOF WOOF! Yelps Momo in complete agreement.

***

After dinner, Barnaby is dead tired. Usually, he would have an hour of reading/study time, but tonight he feels really beat. Deciding to have a pop at reading anyway, he doesn't make it to the end of the first page before nodding off. The book he was holding plops onto the bed and closes itself.

Nothing now but the tick-tocking of Uncle Finch's Grandfather clock in the hall. Uncle Finch is quite the horologist and has an extensive collection of antique clocks.

Momo has curled up next to Barnaby and plonked his head onto his chest as if to stand guard.

Now only the rumble of very distant traffic on the Expressway and the odd car in the street exist.

A cat screeches. A dog howls.

Time passes.

A delivery motorbike is bringing someone a hard-earned pizza.

A slight rumble.

A dog barks.

Momo has now curiously lifted his head.

He stares long and hard at the door and then begins to make muffled woofs, a kind of pre-woof.

Woowoowoowoowoo! A barrage of woofs expels from him as he leaps from the bed and skids to a halt at Barnaby's door.

Those were some loud woofs, which stir Barnaby from his slumber.

"Momo! Really?"

Rumble.

"It's just a dump truck or something, come back to bed."

Then the rumble seems to pass like a wave through the house. Everything on the shelves leaps into the air by one centimetre and drops back down again, a couple of items falling to the floor.

"Wowwwwww! What was that?"

Woowoowoowoowoo! Momo repeats himself.

Barnaby slides out of bed and crosses the room, opening the door to the hallway. There's a strange smell. Like an electrical discharge, the kind you would smell during a lightning storm.

He creeps to the edge of the hallway bannister and looks over. It's dark.

"Mum?" whispers Barnaby.

No answer.

He creeps downstairs, followed closely by Momo.

There's a light flickering in the living room. It's the T.V. Mum is lying fast asleep on the couch, a half-drunk glass of wine in front of her. He decides to leave her be and sneak off down the hallway to the basement door. Maybe this is Uncle Finch's doing.

There's no light coming from under the basement door, which remains locked.

"Uncle Finch?"

"Uncle Finch??"

Nothing.

"Ah, it's a wild goose chase," says Barnaby, as he pats Momo and heads back along the corridor.

Then, the same rumble. A small one, followed by a louder noise.

This time Barnaby can see a light coming from under the basement door.

"Uncle Finch? Uncle Finch??" He bangs on the door. More electrical smells.

"Uncle Finch??" He's now shouting, fearing that something may have happened.

This wakes mum.

"What on earth is going on here, Barnaby?" She always uses 'Barnaby' when he's in trouble and 'Darling' when he's not.

"Mum, it was like an earthquake, two big rumbles. It's Uncle Finch, I just know it. He must be doing experiments or something. What if the house burns down with Momo and us in it!!?"

"Calm down dear. Get back up to bed and I'll speak to Uncle Finch. I'm sure he's fine. Back to bed now."

Reluctantly, Barnaby heads back up the stairs with the ever-faithful Momo at his side.

Mum taps on Uncle Finch's door.

"Mathias? Mathias Finch?" Ooh, he must be in trouble too.

Creaking and then the bolt sliding and then the lock.

"How can I help you Elizabeth, I'm very busy?"

"What's going on down there? What's that smell?"

"Ah, uh, a fuse blew. Used a little bit too much power. Won't happen again."

"Look, I know this is your house, but as long as my son is under your roof, I want assurances he'll come to no harm."

"No harm, no harm at all. I have circuit breakers in place for this, it's quite safe, I can assure you. Now, I have so much work to do and I must bid you goodnight."

"Mathias…"

"Goodnight Elizabeth," says Uncle Finch, sliding back into the crack of the door and bolting it.

Mum stands, a little dazed and confused in the hallway.

He had always been an odd-ball that one. They were thick as thieves when they were younger and played well together, but after their parents died he grew ever and ever more reclusive. Now she only sees him when he sneaks past with bundles of circuitry and the like. Yesterday he crept past with a dishevelled copy of *App Building for Dummies*.

As Mum flops back down onto the couch, she picks up her half-finished wine glass and starts to reminisce of happier days before their parents died. The Christmas gatherings in England, flying off to the Long Island house for Thanksgiving. Such happy days.

Connor and Eleanor Finch had both died in a car crash in heavy snow in the south-east of England. Although no-one was to blame, Mathias always blamed his father for even going out in such conditions. Eleanor had some last-minute birthday gifts to pick up, as Christmas day was also Mathias' birthday, and was insistent that they go.

It was Christmas Eve 1977. Elizabeth was nine and Mathias was almost eight. The knock came at the door and the maid answered it to two British Bobbies, their helmets in their hands as a sign of respect. The maid had burst into tears and turned to the two children and hugged them. They both knew what had happened with no explanation. Mathias just turned, ran upstairs and locked himself in his room. Nothing much has changed since then.

Upstairs, devilment is being planned.

"I just have to get into the basement Momo. I need to know what Uncle Finch is up to. This is very peculiar."

Momo gives a little grunt, happy that the rumbling has stopped and he has now curled up again and is drifting back off to sleep.

"How am I going to do it though Momo? How can I get access to his keys? I need to do it while he is out on one of his big shopping sprees. Maybe Jack can help me formulate a plan on Friday. Yes, I'm sure he'll have some fab ideas."

Barnaby kisses Momo on the head and turns out his nightlight.

"See you in the morning good boy."

"Mmmmmm," sighs a content Momo.

Chapter 3

The basement

The week passes quickly. By Wednesday, they had gotten the thumbs up for Jack to come over on Friday. His dad, for once, was dropping him off.

"Hi, I'm Walter." Jack's father outstretches his hand toward Elizabeth.

"Elizabeth," replies Mum, with a childlike grin on her face.

It is obvious where Jack gets his good looks from and mum, Barnaby could swear, is blushing.

"Noooooo," thinks Barnaby, as he grabs Jack and drags him away.

"Dude," says Jack, "have I ever told you your Mom is smoking hot?"

"Every time you come over!" Barnaby declares, starting to increase speed.

"She had you young right? So there's not a HUGE age gap between her and me?"

Barnaby puts his fingers in his ears.

"Bleh-la-le-lah, Bleh-la-le-lah, I can't hear you."

"No denying it buddy."

Barnaby continues to trail Jack up the stairs and into his bedroom.

"Dude, how can you live in a house with that hottie? That must drive you crazy!"

"Are you serious?" cries Barnaby. Elizabeth has retained her youthful looks well. She has naturally pretty blue eyes, always wears her hair up leaving a few strands suggestively dangling down and she has looked after her body, never letting age run away with it. At five foot seven, she's significantly smaller than Barnaby, a feature that seems to encourage Jack.

"Well…"

"Anyway, shut up and listen to me."

Jack shuts up. For a change.

"Dude, I think my Uncle may have finally finished his teleport device."

"Dude! You've started saying dude. Cool!!"

"Are you even listening to me?"

"I hear ya," says Jack, as he wanders across the room and lifts up a Kylo Ren doll.

Barnaby hurries over and takes the doll from his grasp.

"My uncle... may have finished… his tel-eee-port."

"You've lost it dude. You've been going on about that thing for months. He's never even mentioned it to you or hinted that it's being worked on. It's all been made up in your mind!"

"No, I'm being serious. There have been these weird rumblings coming from the basement and burning smells, and he's acting very strange."

"Dude, it sounds more like you have a faulty washing machine."

"I can prove it!"

"How?"

"Well, that's where you come in. We need to get down there and take a look, do some investigating. Only thing is, he keeps it locked and he always has the key with him. He wears this big long coat when he goes out, and I've seen him put the key in his inside pocket. We need to figure out a way of getting that key without him knowing."

Jack looks at Barnaby for a while, as if trying to figure out if he too was crazy.

"Okay, I'm in."

"Sweet, so how do we do it?"

"Easy. Tomato soup."

"Huh? Tomato... soup?"

"Yeah. When he comes out of the basement, you walk into him carrying a bowl of tomato soup."

Barnaby looks bewildered.

"You spill it on his shirt, he has to take off his jacket to get cleaned up, and WE steal the key."

"Oh my God! You're a genius!!" exclaims Barnaby, grabbing Jack's shoulders.

"Meh, I have my moments," says Jack, flicking imaginary dust from his shoulder.

"Come on, let's go see if we have tomato soup!"

"Dude, you do realise ANY kind of soup will do?"

"Alright then, let's go find some soup!"

The pair rush off down the stairs to the kitchen, past Elizabeth and Walter, who are DEEP in conversation.

"You check these cupboards, I'll do these ones," says Barnaby.

For the next thirty seconds, the house is filled with the sound of slamming kitchen cupboard doors.

"Bingo!"

"Tomato soup?"

"Heinz. THE tomato soup!" exclaims Barnaby.

"Wow. You crazy Brits! Only you could get so excited about soup."

"Remember, my Yankee friend, this tin of tomato soup could be the key to a world of adventure!"

"That is NOT a phrase I ever expected to hear in my life," replies Jack, shaking his head in disbelief.

Barnaby quickly produces a soup bowl from another cupboard. He proceeds to pull off the ring-pull top and pour the contents into it.

"What wonders lie in a bowl of soup?" Barnaby imagines. "This could really be the start of an incredible adventure, no matter how much Jack mocks me. What if Uncle Finch really has invented a teleport machine? What if we could travel anywhere in the world in an instant? Maybe even the Moon!? Or Mars!? What a wondrous adventure that would be."

Barnaby continues to stare at the bowl of soup for a bit longer as he continues his internal dialogue.

"Should we heat it up?" asks Jack, as he joins Barnaby in what seems to be an international soup-staring contest.

"Huh? Sorry, I was miles away," Barnaby mutters.

"The soup. Do you want to add to the effect by scalding your uncle with boiling hot soup, perhaps disfiguring him permanently, or would you rather just warm it slightly?"

Barnaby thinks for a few seconds.

"I think just above room temperature would be fine. We needn't scald him without good reason."

"Good call, my friend, good call."

"Are you sure this will work?" enquires Barnaby.

"Of course, my plans always work, they NEVER fail! Now, it's just a question of how long we have to wait before..."

No time at all. The familiar sound of the basement door bolt being withdrawn ends Jack's question abruptly.

Any moment now.

Uncle Finch turns and locks the basement door. Barnaby knows this is all going to be about timing, and that timing is now.

"No Jack, get your own soup!"

As Uncle Finch turns around, Barnaby charges, soup first, into him, delivering the package directly on target in the middle of Uncle Finch's starched white shirt.

"W-w-w-what the bloody hell are you doing?!!!!!!" shrieks Uncle Finch, looking down in horror at the mess now dripping from his shirt onto the wooden flooring. Not quite speechless, but almost.

"Sorry Uncle Finch," replies Barnaby, "but Jack was trying to…"

"Stupid, stupid boy!!" screams Uncle Finch, barging his way past Barnaby and into the downstairs bathroom, slamming the door shut and locking it behind him.

"Damn it!" whispers Jack. "He's locked the door!"

The boys can hear a fair amount of ranting coming from the bathroom. He sounds quite furious.

"What do we do now? What if…"

Suddenly, the bathroom door flies open and out storms Uncle Finch, still wearing his long coat, but with only a white vest on underneath it (and underwear of course). His shirt and trousers are bundled under his arm like a big tomato filled rugby ball, as he proceeds to barge past them and upstairs towards his bedroom.

"Oh no! He's still wearing it!" shrieks Barnaby.

"Looks like tomato soup does not equal adventure today, huh?" replies Jack, patting him on the back and walking toward the bathroom.

"Where are you going?"

"To the John!"

Barnaby looks quizzical.

"The bathroom?" says Jack, not quite believing that Barnaby has never heard the American term for toilet.

"Unless you want to know WHY I'm going to the bathroom?"

"No, no, you're fine, no need to divulge that much information, no thank you!"

Jack enters the bathroom, closes and locks the door behind him.

Barnaby sits down on the chair next to the landline, dejection starting to pull his shoulders down to his knees.

"My plans never fail!" whispers Barnaby to himself in an American accent, mocking Jack's own voice, "I'm a big stupid American… clutz!"

Suddenly, the bathroom door unlocks and out walks Jack, dangling Uncle Finch's keys from the end of his finger. Barnaby is clearly amazed.

"How? What? When? Who? Where? Which? Eh, huh? How did you do that?" exclaims a confused Barnaby.

"I told you, my plans never fail!"

"But I don't understand." Barnaby has never been more mystified. He's imagining some sort of crazy scenario, where Jack has rigged a drone to fly in and grab the keys. Nope, that's ridiculous.

"Well?" shrieks Barnaby, awaiting the details of the cunning plan.

"In all the excitement, he had to take off his coat to get his shirt off, right?"

"Right."

"When he did, he threw it onto the edge of the bath. Keys must have slipped out. Found them sitting right next to the plughole." Jack, clearly impressed with himself, starts to imitate the sound of a cheering crowd. He high-fives a bunch of invisible admirers before finally awaiting one from Barnaby.

"So that was part of your plan, right?" Barnaby is not convinced.

"Right from the start," says Jack, as he continues his victory lap.

"Genius or buffoon?" thinks Barnaby.

"Anyway, it doesn't matter, we have them now, let's go lay low somewhere until he has gone out."

The pair rush outside and pick up their bikes before racing off down the road with Momo in hot pursuit.

"Come on boy, keep up!" shouts Barnaby over his shoulder to Momo.

"Woof, woof!" responds Momo, as if to say "It's not a problem!"

Momo's keen little smiling face follows the two boys all the way down to the local park where they spill their bikes and rush over to an ageing climbing frame, whose paint now makes climbing a hazard.

"That was so cool," remarks Jack.

"Totally," replies Barnaby, picking up a stick and throwing it with all his might. Momo rushes off to retrieve it.

"So what now?" Jack enquires.

"Let's give him ten minutes, then we'll go back and make sure the coast is clear."

"And what if he has invented a teleport device? Do we take it for a whirl?" asks Jack cautiously.

Barnaby really hadn't thought that far ahead.

"I'm not sure. I guess we need to know it's safe first."

"Hey! What are you two losers up to?"

Jack and Barnaby spin round to see Jack's sister Polly walking up to them with Marsha at her side. Barnaby feels his knees go a little weak.

"None of your business," replies Jack.

"We're going to sneak into my basement and find my mad uncle's teleport machine!"

All three kids turn to look at Barnaby. Jack is mouthing "Shut up," to him.

"You're going to what?" questions Polly.

"Um, my mad uncle. We think he's built a teleport machine and we're going to… owww!"

Jack has kicked Barnaby on the leg.

"Nothing, he's just having an episode, don't listen to a word he…." Jack is forcibly silenced as Polly steps towards Barnaby, putting her hand firmly over Jack's mouth in the process.

"The truth now boy and don't lie, coz' I'll know!"

Polly is actually very pretty. Shoulder-length dark red hair with a straight fringe, blue eyes and a light dusting of freckles across her nose, all wrapped up in a grungy-tomboy outfit of black dungarees and a shocking pink polo-neck. She is also directly in Barnaby's face and chewing on a piece of gum. It's at this point that he finally notices just how beautiful her eyes are. "Don't vomit, don't vomit."

"Yeah, he built a teleport device… we think… and, you know, we've stolen his basement lab keys and... we're going to... go… have a peep!"

Polly continues to be right up in Barnaby's face. She is looking at him from left eye to right eye and back again, trying to suss him out. She pulls a slightly bemused look and then steps back.

"Cool. Let's go," insists Polly.

"Go? Where?" asks Barnaby nervously.

"I want to see a teleport machine," replies Polly, as if it was an everyday occurrence. "Marsha?"

"Hello?" Marsha responds sheepishly.

"Wanna go see a teleport machine?"

"Sure, sounds like…"

"Yeah, we're coming to see your teleport machine," says Polly, throwing a fresh piece of chewing gum into her mouth.

"Woof!" Momo is waiting patiently with his stick.

"Is this your dog?" enquires Marsha.

"Yeah, this is Momo," Barnaby responds, still shaking a little at the knees.

"He's beautiful!" Marsha bends down and gives Momo a big kiss on his nose.

In turn, Momo licks Marsha directly across her face.

"Pffffft!" she shrieks, wiping the dog spit from her face, but maintaining a smile. Barnaby offers his hand so she can get up, but Jack pulls him away briskly before she can accept the offer.

41

"What are you doing?" whispers Jack through gritted teeth.

"I was just going to help Marsha up…"

"No, idiot, telling my sister, MY sister anything! Secrets to her are things she posts on Facebook. She's never kept a secret in her life! She's the *New York Times* for God's sake!"

"I just thought…"

"YOU thought, oh, hi Marsha, wanna come on an adventure and then maybe WE'LL KISS!"

"Keep your voice down Jack!" whispers Barnaby, trying to get the volumes lowered a bit.

"Come on losers!" shouts Polly, who is now exiting the park with Marsha and her new best friend, Momo.

"Coming," cries Barnaby, as he picks up his bike and rushes off after the girls. He leaves behind a shrugging, bewildered and annoyed Jack.

"Yeesh!" Jack grabs his bike and races after the rest of the group.

"So, Marsha, my name's Barnaby," says Barnaby, trying to introduce himself while pushing a bike with one hand and attempting to offer his hand with the other.

"Yes, I know." Marsha smiles and nods.

'God, she even knows who I am!' thinks Barnaby.

"So where are you from?" asks Barnaby.

"Em, New York!" she replies, her eyebrows raised.

"No, I meant originally?" he continues, starting to grimace a little.

"New York," she reiterates, becoming serious.

"Oh, it's just…"

"Haha," laughs Marsha, "I'm playing with you. My parents are from Singapore, but I was born here."

"Oh, sorry, I didn't mean to assume…"

Marsha grabs Barnaby's arm. "It's okay, I get it."

'You big klutz!' he inwardly screams.

"So do your parents live here also? Ignore me, of course they do!"

'What are you saying you idiot?' Barnaby continues to chastise himself.

"Yes, they're both here. My father is a banker and is originally from Hong Kong and my Mother is a good-old-fashioned house Mom, from Germany."

"Ah, is that why your eyes are so green?"

Marsha stops walking and stares at Barnaby.

Barnaby, in turn, freaks.

"I just meant that Germans, you know, blue eyes, plus Chinese…"

Marsha leans closer and smiles.

"I think you can stop with the racial stereotyping now Barnaby."

Barnaby stutters and splutters.

"Of course, forgive me, I didn't mean to…"

"You're cute!" smiles Marsha, and she walks off to catch up with Jack and Polly.

'Idiot!'

***

"Hello?" Barnaby calls out as he enters the front door, still blushing from his faux-pas.

"Uncle Finch?" he shouts again, already knowing that his car is no longer in the drive.

Silence.

"Hola?" comes a voice from upstairs.

"Hola Consuela!" Barnaby hollers to their housemaid, who is preparing to vacuum all nine bedrooms upstairs.

"Come on in guys," whispers Barnaby, ushering his chums through the door.

"Why are we sneaking around your house? You live here!" remarks Polly.

"Fair point," replies Barnaby, raising his eyebrows.

The four of them gather around the basement door as Momo trots off upstairs to find a comfy bed.

Barnaby pulls out the key and inserts it into the lock.

"Here goes!"

The lock opens up and the four chums stare down into the darkness.

"Go on then," says Jack, pushing at Barnaby's shoulder.

"Oh for goodness sake," mutters Polly, as she pushes past them and flicks the basement stair light on. The other three follow behind her as she confidently trots down the stairs and into the basement.

"Wooooh!" Barnaby and Jack exclaim, as they get their first look at the basement.

It is a HUGE space, with several divider bookcases, filled with textbooks and reading material. Barnaby recognises a couple of books by Stephen Hawking, Brian Greene and the grubby copy of *App Building for Dummies*.

There are also several tables in various states of chaos around the room. Each looks like it has its own unique little project going on, with heaps of components, wires, cables and tools scattered around. The most noticeable table contains a vice that is holding an odd-looking blue crystal, from which segments seem to have been removed. Next to it, there is a neat little device that looks like an iPad has been bolted to a meat griller with two handles and an extended inverse cone that looks like one of those 'ball popper' toys.

"Is this it?" asks Jack, as he picks it up.

Barnaby looks at it with great interest.

"Don't know," replies Barnaby. He hits the power button of the iPad, which then proceeds to boot up. As it does, a thin blue light emerges around the circumference of the 'meat griller' part. It holds like that for a few seconds and then turns green.

Jack moves the device around in his hands checking the underside and staring into the cone section.

"This looks promising," states Polly, pointing at a pair of snow boots.

"Huh? How is a pair of boots promising?" asks Jack.

"They're sitting in a puddle of water," she responds, clearly noticing something that no one else is. "They've been used in snow, and it's the middle of summer!!" Polly finally has to explain.

'Ahhhhh," exclaims the group collectively.

"Hey, Barnaby," says Jack, tugging at his sleeve. "We need the iPad password."

Barnaby thinks for a second.

"Try, 25… 12… 69. His date of birth. He was born on Christmas Day," replies Barnaby.

"Nope," says a dejected Jack.

"No wait, try 24… 12… 77," Barnaby suggests as an alternative.

"What's that date?"

"The date his parents, my grandparents, died."

"They died on Xmas eve?" asks Marsha.

"Yeah, car crash," Barnaby replies with a sombre tone.

"Bingo! We're in!!" announces an elated Jack, brightening the mood somewhat.

The group moves closer together to look at the contents of the iPad. It contains the usual Apple-supplied apps, weather apps, BBC News, Google Maps and one other called 'Leaper'. Jack taps it and it begins to launch.

"Has to be this one," he says, excitement gathering in his voice.

The screen goes black.

"Did it break?" enquires Polly.

"No look, there's a very thin red line at the bottom of the page, progressing toward the right. It's loading something," Jack explains.

They watch in anticipation as the line completes its journey to the opposite side of the screen.

Then more black.

A few more seconds pass and then two circles appear on the screen. One contains a picture of Uncle Finch and the other has one of Momo!

"Wait, why is your dog in here?" asks Polly.

"I don't know!" replies Barnaby.

Jack taps the photo of Momo and the screen is replaced with some data:

Last journey:
Name: **Momo trial.**
Latitude: **77.004298** • Longitude: **107.218237**
Elevation: **24.6m**
Date: **01.07.2014 - 15:47**
Target date: **01.01.1970 - 12:00**
Return date: **01.07.2014 - 15:52**
Outcome: **Successful**.'
Then two buttons. 'View map' and 'Return'.

"Look at that! Son of a gun! He's used your dog as part of the experiment!!"

"When was that? That was Monday! He had Momo downstairs that day!!" cries Barnaby, realising the truth.

"What are those coordinates?" queries Marsha.

"GPS, longitude and latitude," replies Barnaby.

"Yeah, I know, I meant where are they?"

"Hit the 'View map' button," insists Barnaby.

Jack complies, and a Google-Map-type screen pops up showing a rugged satellite view of a piece of unrecognisable coastline somewhere.

"Zoom out," advises Barnaby.

Jack continues to click the 'zoom out' icon until the first words appear.

"Severnaya Zemlya." Barnaby reads the map aloud.

"Holy moly," shrieks Jack, as he continues to pull the image back. "Look at that! Right in the very north of Russia! Siberia!!"

"That's why Momo was cold when he came out of the basement. He'd just been to bloomin' Siberia!!" says Barnaby, the truth unfolding before his eyes.

"That's why we have wet snow boots here!" declares Polly, pointing over her shoulder.

"Why take my dog to Siberia?" enquires Barnaby.

"Well, let's just say you're not going to get any passers-by there!" replies Marsha.

"Wait, go back to the journey page will you?" Barnaby is curious.

"Sure," says Jack, clicking the 'Back' icon.

"Why does it say, 'Target date: **01.01.1970 - 12:00**'? Why would you put an old date into a teleport device?" queries Barnaby.

"Because it's not just a teleport device!" comes a voice from the back of the room, cloaked in darkness.

"Uncle Finch!!" shouts a surprised Barnaby, as the group all spin around in unison. Uncle Finch walks towards them, the one basement light casting long shadows across his face.

"What do you mean, 'It's not just a teleport device?'" asks Jack.

"My dear boy, you are holding in your hands the world's first, working time machine."

Chapter 4

Proof

"What?" yelps Jack as he rolls the device around in his hands. "An actual time machine?! There's no way this actually works!"

"Oh, it works alright," replies Uncle Finch.

"You used this on Momo!" announces Barnaby.

"Actually, I used it on both of us. I wanted to make sure it would take two passengers. So I took Momo for a walk. In Siberia. In 1970."

"My dog is a time traveller!"

"Yes, and a good one," Uncle Finch responds. "He wasn't scared and actually quite liked the Siberian coast. Lots of dead fish you see."

"I thought his breath was worse than usual," remarks Barnaby.

"How did you even build this? It's an iPad velcroed to a George Foreman grill!" exclaims Jack in disbelief.

"Well initially I wasn't building a time machine. I was building a teleport device. I thought rather than disintegrating and reassembling a living organism it would be much safer to warp the space around them. But as I started to test the device, I discovered that it is also able to warp the fabric of time."

"How does it work?" enquires Marsha.

"Never mind how it works. Can we have a shot?" asks Polly.

"Yeah, I'm not convinced here," presses Jack. "You're going to have to give us a demonstration!"

"I don't know," says Uncle Finch. "I'm not so sure that's such a good idea."

"Oh please Uncle Finch!" pleads Barnaby. "It would be such an adventure!"

"You were fine doing it to the dog!" Polly points out.

"Yes, but he's...."

"Expendable?" says Barnaby.

Uncle Finch is still looking uneasy, shuffling from foot to foot, trying to decide what best to do.

"Do I just hit this?" announces Jack, pointing to the 'Return' button.

"Don't touch it!" barks Uncle Finch. "I've not finished calibrating everything."

"Calibrating? What do you still need to do?" enquires Barnaby.

51

"Well, as we leap, the computer needs to be able to accurately assess its surroundings and place you on the ground out of harm's way."

"It can do that?" asks Marsha.

"Yes! Let me explain why. Assume you go back to a nice field in England in the year 1066. As you land, you look up and there are ten thousand arrows screaming towards you. Or let's say you go to have a look at Mount Everest and it's not in the same position it was, because the date you input is one million years prior to today. Well then you could end up inside the mountain. That is why I always aim for safe, secluded areas where we can't be seen."

"How many can travel at one time?" questions Jack.

"As long as we're all touching, it will take the entire combined organic mass. The sensor at the front knows not to take the floor with us or the desk you are leaning on."

"So where do we go first?" asks Barnaby.

"I want to see Nirvana!" shouts Polly.

"Just be patient young ones. Any decision about where to go has to be carefully planned."

"So you'll take us?" presses Barnaby.

Uncle Finch sighs. Now that the cat's out of the bag, perhaps it's not such a bad idea.

"Alright," he mutters.

"Awesome!" yells Jack as the group collectively yelps with delight.

"But first, you have to decide where to go and be prepared. You need to be ready for the weather and dressed for the occasion. There's no point turning up for the birth of Christ in jeans. You also need to be prepared for some shocking truths and to keep your mouth zipped!"

"Shocking truths?" Barnaby nervously enquires.

"Dear boy, time has a way of distorting truth. Let's assume you go back and witness the death of Jesus Christ? What if he doesn't rise from the grave? Hmm? Announcing this to the world could start a religious war! Everything the time traveller does can have far-reaching consequences."

"I see," says Marsha.

"And the most important thing of all is not to interact with anyone. It's fine to be in a crowd at one of your Nirvana concerts, but you couldn't try to save Kurt Cobain or warn John F. Kennedy that he will be shot. Acting on the past in such a way could erase you from existence!"

"Erase us?" gasps Jack.

"Sure. Directly impacting a world event such as the Kennedy assassination would irreparably change the course of history. In many cases your parents would never meet!"

"So time travellers have to be 'time tourists' effectively?" asks Barnaby.

"Exactly!" Uncle Finch nods in agreement, "As much as I would love to go back to 1977 and warn my parents, there's nothing I can do. My only option is to go back and see them alive again from a distance."

"So where then? What would be the ideal event to watch from a distance?"

Uncle Finch suddenly has an idea and smiles.

"How about July 16, 1969?"

Barnaby's eyes widen.

"The moon launch?"

Uncle Finch winks and takes the device from Jack.

"Wait, THEEEE moon launch. Neil Armstrong, Buzz Aldrin, Michael Collins? You mean THEEEEE moon launch??" quizzes a very excited Jack.

"The very same," confirms Uncle Finch as he starts to tap away on the iPad.

The kids all gather around to watch the process in its entirety.

"Okay, first we find a safe place. Somewhere away from the flames but close and secluded. Ah, how about here? There's an area of swampland near to the access road. Let me just copy and paste these coordinates: 28.604775, -80.597039. Time is July 16, 1969, 09:30 in the AM. Boom. Done. The only thing we may need is this," says Uncle Finch, reaching for a broomstick.

"Um, why do we need a broomstick?" asks Marsha.

"To shoo off the alligators," comes the casual response from Uncle Finch.

The group all look at each other with a worried expression.

"Alligators?" gasps Marsha.

"Come now you two, put your hands on my shoulders and link hands with everyone else," orders Uncle Finch corralling the children together.

"Alligators?" repeats Marsha, as Barnaby takes her hand.

"Ready everyone?" asks Uncle Finch.

"Real alligators??" continues Marsha.

"I'm more worried about the armed patrol guards, personally," says Uncle Finch, as he taps the iPad one last time.

"What?" shrieks Marsha, as the room lights dim and the show begins.

For Barnaby, it's an odd experience, like being forced to duck slightly. There is a slight breeze that catches his hair and then a feeling of extreme dizziness, before being plonked down into cold water up to his knees. His head still spinning, he falls the rest of the way into the water. A second later, he is aware that one other person has joined him in the cold swamp.

"Oh my God!" cries Marsha pulling herself from the water. "I'm soaking!"

"We bloomin' did it!" shouts Jack.

"Oh wow," cries Barnaby as he stands up and looks around.

There, about four hundred metres in front of them, is the Apollo 11, Saturn V rocket. It sparkles white as the morning sun contrasts it against the pure blue sky surrounding it. Towering some thirty-six stories, it clings to the familiar orangey-red frame of the launch tower.

Barnaby stands, dripping into the swamp, dumbstruck by this most beautiful of views, oblivious to the shouting going on around him.

"Barnaby! Get down!!"

Then suddenly he is being pulled through the water by persons unknown. Around him, the world is a complete haze. He could be on fire right now and wouldn't notice, as his eyes remain transfixed on the glistening white tower.

"It's beautiful!" he finally manages to whisper.

"Barnaby! Get down, they'll see you!"

Finally, Barnaby regains his senses and looks around him. Uncle Finch and Jack are pulling him towards a bush as Polly helps Marsha to the same location.

"Everybody get ready. It's going to get a bit smokey soon!" shouts Uncle Finch.

"Are we far enough away?" hollers Marsha.

"Oh yes, quite far enough!"

Marsha is not convinced.

"I dunno, we look pretty close!"

"That's the actual moon rocket! Oh my God!!!" Polly laughs.

"This is 1969!!" cries Jack "Can you believe this?!"

"We're witnessing ACTUAL history!" shouts Uncle Finch.

Then smoke starts to appear from a couple of the dividing sections of the rocket.

"Is it supposed to do that?" asks Polly.

"Yes, all part of the launch sequence, get ready!"

Suddenly there is an intense flash, as tonnes of rocket fuel begins to be burned and ejects itself from the five engines at the base of the ship. The noise is deafening as billows of smoke blast out from underneath the launch pad.

The retaining arms of the launch tower retract and the mighty Saturn V lifts off into the sky, enveloping the excited travellers in an ever expanding light grey cloud.

"Bleh!" coughs Marsha.

Through the mist, they get their first glimpse of the rocket as it clears the tower.

"Oh my God! Look at that!! Look at how fast it's going!!!" yells Jack.

"Holy cow, I've only ever seen footage of this in slow motion! I can't believe how quickly it's travelling!" yells Barnaby above the noise.

The group now stand, mouths agape while they watch the rocket. Its fiery heat warms their faces in the cold morning air, as it slips away from the Earth's gravity and into the history books. In four days its occupants will step foot on the Moon for the first time.

"It's so beautiful," gasps an astonished Marsha.

"Damn it, why didn't we film it?" asks Jack.

"No, we can't do that," explains Uncle Finch. "Evidence that we've been here. No, there's enough footage of this launch without us adding to it."

The group can't take their eyes off of the ship, which is now just a fiery dot in the morning sky.

"Right, time to head home. We can't hang around for much longer," announces Uncle Finch.

"Awwwww, it's all over so quickly!" grumbles Barnaby.

"It has to be!" Uncle Finch continues. "We have to arrive at the last minute and leave as quickly as possible, otherwise we may be detected by NASA security!"

The group begins to assemble again as Uncle Finch waves them towards him.

"So now all we have to do is tap 'Return', and it will take us to our last position, which was 04 July 2014 at 14:46. But, just to be on the safe side, I've set it up so we always jump back five seconds later. So we don't slam into ourselves travelling here at the same time," says Uncle Finch with an almost comical tone.

"Yeah, if we could avoid slamming into ourselves, that would be great," smirks Jack.

Uncle Finch taps the iPad, and the group are plopped back into his basement at exactly 14:46 and five seconds.

Once more, Barnaby spills over onto the ground. Everybody else has managed to stay on their feet.

"Haha, Barney. You are the world's worst time traveller!" laughs Jack.

"Hey, my clothes are dry!" announces Marsha, looking down and feeling her jacket.

"Mine too," Barnaby announces as he gets to his feet and wobbles slightly.

"A helpful addition to the software! I've made some modifications so we don't bring back anything unwanted."

"But your snow boots are still wet?" remarks Polly.

"Yes, those very boots made me ask the question. I've made the adjustments since then. The machine will only bring back what it took. No rogue organic material, like viruses from the Cretaceous!"

"So you can't bring back souvenirs?" queries Barnaby.

"Absolutely not. The policy should always be 'Touch nothing!'"

"Okay, we get it. So where next?"

"Nowhere. I think we've all had enough excitement for one day," is Uncle Finch's response.

"Awwwwww," sighs the group collectively.

"Besides, I want the device to cool down after a couple of jumps. I have to be super careful until I know that the power source is definitely stabilised."

"What does power it?" quizzes Barnaby.

"This," says Uncle Finch, picking up the light blue crystal from the vice.

"What is it?" enquires Jack.

"The honest answer? I'm not quite sure. It harnesses an incredible amount of power though. I call it 'Adionium' after the Roman deity Adiona, the Goddess of Safe Return. It is composed of only fifty percent of elements from the periodic table. The other elements are brand new to us, so I can only assume that it's extra-terrestrial in nature," replies Uncle Finch, gazing into the crystal.

"You built a time machine out of an alien crystal? That is beyond cool!" gasps Jack turning to the group, who chuckle at his response.

"So when can we go again, Uncle Finch?"

Turning to face the group, he examines them and ponders the question. He's obviously warmed to the idea of having some human guinea pigs, even if one of them is his own nephew.

"Okay, here's an idea. We won't just be leaping around the universe willy-nilly. I want you to all go away and come back with a valid destination. Somewhere you can honestly discover something. It may be part of a school project, a history lesson perhaps, something you can genuinely gain from, but it must be conducted with the utmost professionalism. This isn't a joy ride; this is a serious scientific tool and must be treated with respect. Furthermore, we must plan ahead. If you choose to go back to the Jurassic era, you must be prepared for the consequences. We may need oxygen, which will be lighter in content in prehistory. For sure we would need a tranquiliser gun for any larger predators we may encounter. All considerations must be met, so you MUST do your homework and approach this in a methodical fashion. Otherwise, it ends right here!"

The group nod in agreement.

"Okay, so let's meet back here tomorrow with some ideas then," announces Uncle Finch.

An excited quartet of grins beams back at him.

"And Barnaby!" says Uncle Finch.

"Yes, sir?"

"No more tomato soup shenanigans."

"Yes Uncle Finch," mutters Barnaby, as he and the rest of the group slowly begin to walk away.

Uncle Finch smiles as he watches them wander over to the basement stairs and begin the ascent back to the real world. He's surprised at how much he's enjoyed their company. Perhaps he has fed off of their sense of wonder and curiosity, something he feels he was robbed of at an early age when his parents died.

He lays the mysterious crystal on the table and sits down at his workstation. Stretching his arms out and yawning, he then begins to upload the data he has collected from the 'Leaper' app. He's spent weeks examining all of this information, which has helped him to perfect the software. Rubbing his eyes, he feels it's almost time for a rest. But before he retires for the day, he's got to perform a full backup and then download it all into his original prototype time machine. Yes, there are two!

Chapter 5

Homework

"Dudes, did that really just happen?" asks Jack, as he sits neatly, for a change, on Barnaby's bed.

"Yup," replies Polly, nonchalantly, like it was an everyday occurrence.

Aside from Polly, the group are unsurprisingly in a bit of a daze.

"It was soooo surreal," says Barnaby. "Like when you visit a famous building or something. You're looking at it, you know, like the Eiffel Tower or the Taj Mahal, and it just doesn't seem like you're there. Like you have to pinch yourself."

"Can't comment, dude, I've only ever seen New York," admits Jack.

"I don't think we had enough time to get properly excited," adds Marsha. "It's not like going on holiday where you're excited for months. You're just in and out. Maybe, it'll always be like that. No time to hang around and get a buzz. Which kinda sucks."

"Yeah, but that's only because of NASA security," Barnaby responds. "What if we could go visit something that we could observe at our leisure. Like the twin towers or something."

"Now that would be cool! I never got to see them," replies Jack. "I was born in December 2001. All my life, it's been a building site."

"Yeah but the next thing we visit has to be a project, remember?" states Marsha.

"All Uncle Finch said was that it has to be a valid destination," Barnaby reminds them. "Something we're interested in. He said it 'could' be a school project, but he didn't say it HAD to be."

"Okay, let's write a list then," announces Marsha, who is a hugely organised girl. 'The Spreadsheet Queen' being one of the many names used by her school chums.

Barnaby tosses her a note pad, which she catches awkwardly near her face. He instantly apologises and blushes slightly.

"Okay," says Marsha grabbing a pen from Barnaby's desk and propping herself on the edge of his office chair. "Number one. Twin Towers."

"On September 11th?" asks Jack with a grimace.

"No, no way. We do NOT need to see that!" declares Marsha, waving her pen.

"Yeah, we're not disaster tourists here," remarks Barnaby. "We're just a bunch of kids looking at cool stuff. Stuff we can't see any more. In fact, if we want, we COULD go see stuff that we CAN still see!"

"Huh?" Polly looks up from an encyclopedia she has been toying with.

"I mean, it's still also a teleport device! We could go look at stuff that's just hard to get to! Doesn't have to be in the past."

"Such as?" enquires Polly.

"I dunno, em, the… what's the place in Peru?"

The group shrug and look around.

"The place up in the mountains. The old city with the…"

"Machu Picchu!" blurts out Marsha.

"That's the one! It's just massively hard to get to from New York. We could be there like THAT," says Barnaby, clicking his fingers.

Marsha scribbles 'Number two, Machu Picchu' in the notepad.

"Number three, Machu Picchu five hundred years ago!" adds Jack.

"Didn't they perform human sacrifices and stuff?" Polly pipes up, flicking through the encyclopedia looking for the ancient city.

"Well, yeah, possibly, but we wouldn't enter the city, that would just be asking for trouble. We could just place ourselves on a nearby mountain and view it with binoculars. That's what I think a good time tourist would do."

"A good time tourist who wants to end up on someone's plate! Nom, nom, nom," replies Jack, nibbling on his arm.

"Oh come on, I'm sure they weren't that bad!" states Marsha. "Anyway, we're in and out quickly, remember?"

"Yeah, but we gotta spend a good bit of time observing! Uncle Finch would approve, coz then it's more like a project. Noting down all of the things they do, for our own historical records," explains Barnaby, now on his feet.

"Okay, Richard Leakey, sit down!" says Polly.

"Richard who?"

"Leakey. It says here he's a 'pay-leo-an-thrap-ologist'," Polly reads from the encyclopedia. "Studied old dead folk."

Barnaby sits back down.

"How about the pyramids?" asks Jack.

"Now THAT would be awesome," replies Polly.

"Still dangerous though," adds Marsha.

"Oh come on Marsh, where's your sense of adventure?" screeches Polly.

"I'm just saying, turning up there in a land full of crocodiles and guys with spears and swords, might not be such a good idea!"

"We'd be real careful!" continues Polly.

"Yeah, and we could disguise the time machine as a bundle of reeds!" adds Jack.

The group turn to look at him, eyebrows raised. Silence.

"Okay, maybe not reeds, but we'd stick out like a sore thumb carrying around a piece of metal technology!"

"He's right, wherever we go, the time machine needs a disguise. We don't want to be burned for witchcraft or have it fall into the hands of Nazis or something," Barnaby points out.

"Ooooooh, Nazis. We could go watch them get their asses kicked in Normandy!" yells an excited Jack.

"Again, too dangerous!" says Marsha. 'Can we not just go to nice places?"

"Oh, you are so boring!" replies Jack, who consequently receives a punch on the arm from his sister.

"We just have to be SUPER careful," Marsha comments. "For starters, we can't end up influencing events, and we certainly don't want to end up over a bonfire. So let's just plan out seeing safe things that can still excite us!"

"Oooh, like Justin Bieber!" smirks Jack, mocking Marsha.

"Okay, more ideas please," Barnaby commands, as Marsha stares menacingly at Jack.

"How about the launch of the *Titanic*?" suggests Marsha, releasing her stern gaze from Jack.

"Good one! Write it down!" replies Barnaby.

"Oooh, good one, MY SWEET LOVE", teases Jack, throwing his arms in a cuddle around his OWN waist and making kissy faces.

Barnaby blushes redder than a rose and gives Jack a long hard stare, which Jack returns with a wink. Marsha, also blushing, is adding in entry number four.

"*Titanic*," notes Marsha, dotting the end of the sentence. "What else?"

"The dinosaur asteroid!" shouts Jack.

Marsha gives Jack a look, as if to say "Enough with the dangerous destinations!!"

"No, hear me out," says Jack, waving his hands. "I mean, how cool would it be to see that in the sky, to feel it hit, to feel the cloud and stuff coming towards you, only to leap away at the last minute! What a rush that would be!!"

"It would be pretty cool," adds Polly.

"And if the time machine failed?" asks Marsha.

"Duck and cover?" offers Jack.

"Riiiiiiight," replies Marsha with a comical look on her face.

"I take it we're still looking for number five?" Barnaby observes.

"We sure are," nods Marsha.

"How about a big open-air concert? Something legendary like Woodstock?" suggests Jack, finally finding something safe to recommend.

"Yeah, that could work! There's no seating at open-air concerts, so we're not robbing a seat and changing history, and we'd get to see some cool legendary performances!"

67

"Who played at Woodstock then?" questions Marsha.

"Jimi, Janis, Creedence, you name it!" Jack plucks from the air.

"How do you know all of these people? You're fifteen!! And are you forgetting something? We're fifteen!" adds Marsha, pointing around the room. "They wouldn't let us in!"

"I don't think there was an age limit at Woodstock. There are definitely kids in the photos. Or the Isle of Wight. That would be cool also."

"I still want to see Nirvana!" declares Polly.

"Okay, I'll put down 'Music'. We can decide later which concert best suits us," says Marsha, jotting down point number five.

"So. We have a time machine. It must go forward too, right?" queries Barnaby.

"Jump into the future?" asks Marsha, with another stern look.

"What? What could possibly be wrong… actually, yeah, I can already think of reasons why that would be stupendously bad," ponders Barnaby.

"Such as?" Jack questions.

"Well, next week might not be a problem, but what if we jumped forward a thousand years? Who knows where we would find ourselves. We could end up in some kind of post-nuclear apocalyptic, radioactive wasteland."

"But if that was going to be the case, we could do something about that! Warn people," exclaims Marsha.

"I thought we couldn't go changing stuff?" Jack points out, shrugging.

"Changing stuff in the past! Doing it in the future won't affect us!" replies Barnaby.

"It'll affect somebody though, surely?" Marsha takes great pains to clarify.

"Yeah, but who cares!?" adds Jack. "So some future guys don't have to survive a nuclear war! I think that's a fairly Christian approach, wouldn't you say?"

"I think this is more about the far-reaching implications of adjusting space-time. Have you guys never seen *Back to the Future*?" says Barnaby. "Couldn't it all unravel or something?"

"I dunno. I doubt even Stephen Hawking would know the answer to that one!"

"I think that is one for Uncle Finch."

"Yeah, he can make the call! Let's just stick to cool destinations. SAFE ONES!" states Marsha, as the group moan and huff.

"The birth of Jesus?" Barnaby puts forward.

"I thought Uncle Finch said that would be a bad idea?" comments Jack.

"No, he said we couldn't film it or turn up in jeans," replies Barnaby.

"Wait. Jesus was born in a stable," points out Marsha.

"And your point, caller?" Jack adds sarcastically.

"Well, think about it! There were only five people there! Mary, Joseph and the Three Wise Men! It didn't say anything about four kids and a dog, did it? That would change nativity plays around the globe somewhat! Imagine the scene, "Okay, who wants to be the donkey and who wants to be the kid from New York City with the dog?" That would be silly!"

"Sheep outfits?" suggests Barnaby.

"Maybe we could go to the 'Sermon on the Mount' instead?" says Marsha.

"What's that?" asks Jack, the atheist.

"It's the whole 'Blessed are the meek' bit. Basically where Jesus lays down the law about morality. The whole central proposition of Christianity," explains Marsha.

"And where did that occur?" Jack enquires.

"Not sure," replies Marsha, "but we could research it."

"The 'Mount of Beatitudes'," chips in Barnaby, who has been tapping away on his phone.

"And who can understand Hebrew?" asks Jack.

"We don't need to hear what he has to say, we just need to see him!" answers Marsha.

"And if it turns out it never happened? Wouldn't that completely destroy your faith?"

"I would take solace that perhaps Matthew or someone down the years got a few of the facts wrong along the way," Marsha continues.

"I dunno," Jack grins. "Sounds kinda dangerous!"

"Oh, haha!" replies Marsha, shoving him off the bed and onto the floor.

"Look, if we're going to dig into the past," Barnaby remarks, trying to defuse the tension. "Then we have to be prepared for a few truths that might, well, hurt a bit."

"I agree," adds Marsha. "History has a way of adding 'rose-tinted glasses' to things. Maybe history is less interesting in real life. Maybe Jesus is boring. Maybe once you've seen the *Titanic* plop ceremoniously into the water after her launch, it's just like any other ship. A bit dull."

"Sounds like you need a trip to the D-Day beaches to liven you up!" exclaims Jack.

"Yeah, come on M, you're even boring me now," teases Polly, flapping her arms.

Marsha goes into a little madame huff and folds her arms. Frowning, she flips her head round to look out of the window.

"Okay," Barnaby chips in. "I say we call it a day and regroup tomorrow."

"Yeah, let's sleep on it," replies Jack, as he stands up and gives Polly a nudge.

"I'll speak to Uncle Finch, see if he can spare some time for us to run some ideas past him," says Barnaby, as he walks his three friends down the stairs to the front door.

As they are about to leave, Jack pauses and turns to Barnaby.

"Is outer space out of the question?"

"Come on loser!" Polly jests, grabbing Jack by the collar and leading him away.

Marsha follows behind but stops halfway down the drive, turns, smiles and gives a cute little wave to Barnaby.

He returns the gesture with a similar tinkle of the fingers, which is met with giggles from Jack.

"Oh man, he has it soooooo bad…" mutters Jack as his voice trails off down the path and into the distance.

Barnaby stands at the door, listening to fragments of far off conversations and laughs until he can hear them no more. With that, the day's excitement is over.

Later that night, Barnaby lies in bed with Momo faithfully stretched across one side, as if to lay some sort of claim to 'his part of the bed'.

As he drifts off to sleep, he has a little chuckle to himself. Tomato soup. Hehe.

Chapter 6
The attic of adventure

Yummy bagels! Barnaby's new favourite.

"How are the bagels?" asks Mum, placing a glass of fresh orange juice next to him.

"Alright, I suppose," is the typical, teenage response.

"And here you go young man," continues Mum. She places a bowl of kibble on the floor for Momo, who, not being one to savour a dish, proceeds to inhale ninety per cent of them, while the remaining ten per cent is scattered across the floor. Don't worry, he'll see to them in time. About ten seconds time.

"So what have you got planned for today?" enquires Mum.

"Jack's coming over with Polly and Marsha," replies Barnaby.

"Oh, what are you guys going to do with your time?"

Barnaby almost sniggers at the word 'time'.

"We're going to plan our next trip."

Oops.

"Trip? What trip?" asks a puzzled Mum.

"Em, to theeeee, uh, Museum or something, yeah the Museum. Or maybe the beach. Yeah, probably the beach."

"Okay, sounds like fun," replies Mum, putting her breakfast dishes into the dishwasher and only half-listening to him.

Barnaby takes a large bite of bagel, again, warm butter runs between his fingers.

"Miz, Unkwul Finf awound todayf?" mumbles Barnaby.

"Honey, I've told you not to talk with your mouth full!"

Barnaby inhales and chews the food quickly, resulting in it lasting even longer. Mum stands motionless, eyebrows raised, awaiting these words of wisdom.

After an agonising thirty seconds of chewing, swallowing, nodding and gesticulating to 'hang on' with his hands, his palette is finally cleansed of bagel matter.

"Is Uncle Finch around today?"

Mum's eyebrows remain raised.

"I'm not sure darling, I've not seen him this morning. Nothing new there though," is the response as the eyebrows drop back down again.

"Oh," Barnaby inadvertently blurts out as he breaks off a piece of bagel for Momo, who gulps it down and begins to lick Barnaby's fingers.

"Why?" quizzes Mum, with eyebrows back up.

"Emmmm, no reason. Just thought it would be nice to finally get to know him."

"Well, I'm sure you two will have plenty of time to chat tonight," replies Mum.

Barnaby looks perplexed. What does she know? Again, the word 'time' sticks out like a sore thumb. "Did she emphasise that? Or am I going crazy," considers Barnaby.

"My summer ball darling. Remember?"

Barnaby shrugs.

"My work summer ball! It's tonight. Uncle Finch is babysitting you."

"Oh Mum, I'm not a baby!"

"It's a term of phrase darling. I'm not overly happy about leaving Mathias in charge, but I couldn't find a babysitter so he will have to do. I am not missing this ball. Darius Dent will be there in person and I've missed him at all the other balls!"

"Who?" asks Barnaby.

Mum sighs. He never listens.

"Our CEO darling. He's the top guy."

"Oh, yeah, right, him," mutters Barnaby with total disinterest.

"Anyway, I'm heading off around seven o'clock, so make sure you're back home in time for dinner".

There she goes again! Time! Is that all she ever talks about?

"Yes, Mum."

Then, an odd thing happens.

Whistling.

Not from a whistle or an old kettle, but from an uncle!

As Barnaby turns around with a bemused look on his face, Uncle Finch saunters into the kitchen and ruffles Barnaby's hair on the way past.

Mum stands motionless in disbelief with one hand inside a pot she's been drying. Her mouth agape, she is still like stone, as if caught in Medusa's gaze.

The whistling continues.

"Good morning Uncle Finch," chirps Barnaby.

"Good morning my young nephew, and how are you this fine morning?"

"Em, very good thank you!"

Barnaby shrugs at Elizabeth. Uncle Finch is perfectly aware that all eyes are on him and that this is not in his normal behaviour. Still he chooses to carry on about his business, opening the fridge, looking for nibbles, without making eye contact with mum.

'Well I never!" Mum gasps.

"Hmm, what's that Elizabeth?" asks Uncle Finch, popping his head around the fridge door to look at her.

"Well, you look, I don't know, positively… happy?"

"Me? Oh, just woke up this morning with a little spring in my step dear sister! Was up like a rocket!" Uncle Finch retorts, giving Barnaby a sideways look and a little smirk at the 'rocket' reference.

Barnaby grins back.

"So what are you up to today, now that you've found happiness?"

"Oh, I thought I might go on a trip somewhere, get out and about, see some sights."

"Well, that IS a coincidence. Barnaby and his friends were looking to plan a trip today. Maybe you could take them somewhere interesting?"

Barnaby nearly chokes on his last bit of bagel.

"I don't see why not," replies Uncle Finch. "I'm sure, given time, we could find somewhere that would be of interest to us all."

Another sideways grin.

"Okay, but remember, as I was telling Barnaby, I'm going out tonight at seven, so you all need to be home sharp.

"Not a problem. We'll be home in plenty of time."

Alright, Unc, enough with the time references.

"Okay, I'm going to be out all day, so you'll have to fend for yourself today for lunch and dinner. I've got to go find a dress and then I'm getting my hair done at Marge's, before going directly to the ball with Karen," continues Mum. She starts fussing around the kitchen, putting things in drawers before finally slipping a denim jacket on, followed by a handbag. "You have my phone number, but in case there's no signal, I've left the address on a post-it on the fridge."

"We'll manage Mum, go spoil yourself!"

Mum pauses.

"What is with this family today? Have you been on the happy pills?"

"Just looking forward to a bit of adventure!" says Barnaby, winking at Uncle Finch.

Mum pauses again, thinking she saw a wink, but isn't quite sure. She looks bemused and confused at the same time, before finally shaking her head and walking to the front door.

"Remember, be home in plenty of…"

"Yes Mum!" shouts Barnaby, avoiding yet another time reference.

As the door closes behind her, Barnaby spins around to face Uncle Finch.

"You can never be late with a time machine!" shrieks Barnaby with delight.

"And that would be the advertising slogan!" laughs Uncle Finch, spinning a banana on the kitchen table.

"So what's the plan for today, Uncle Finch?"

"Well, when are your friends arriving?"

"Should be here any minute. They said they'd come after breakfast," replies Barnaby.

"Good, because I have a plan I think you'll all get a kick out of."

Ten minutes later, there is a knock at the door.

Barnaby dashes from the kitchen and opens it to find Marsha dressed in a silky camisole top and grey sweatpants. Her hair is cascading down onto her shoulders in streams of auburn. The image of her, surrounded by Uncle Finch's well-kept garden, rays of sunshine and the sound of birds tweeting, leaves Barnaby quite speechless. 'Mona Lisa, eat your heart out,' he thinks to himself.

"Well?" asks Marsha.

"Huh?" Is the clumsy response from Barnaby.

Marsha shrugs a little.

"Aren't you going to let me in?"

"Of course! Come this way, please do!" replies Barnaby, perfectly pronouncing all of the words like a proper little butler.

Barnaby turns and trots after her like a well-trained dog.

"Good morning young lady," beams Uncle Finch, as they walk into the kitchen.

"Good morning," murmurs Marsha sheepishly.

"We were never properly introduced yesterday," he remarks, holding out his hand, "I'm Mathias Finch, Barnaby's uncle."

"Marsha, Marsha Moon."

"Ah, so yesterday's excursion was particularly relevant to you with that surname!?"

Marsha blushes a little and allows herself to be guided to a kitchen table chair being offered up by Uncle Finch.

"Why thank you kind sir." She bows slightly, as if pretending to be a lady of a distinguished and wealthy family.

"Enchanté," replies Uncle Finch, as he too gently bows and plays along with the act.

"Would Ma'am care for a cup of tea?" Barnaby interrupts in his best privately educated English school voice.

"One would be beside oneself with joy. Does one have Darjeeling?"

"One does," says Barnaby, bowing.

"Oh, how simply divine," continues Marsha, revelling in this game of upper-middle-class, drawing room comedy-style tomfoolery.

There is another knock at the door.

"Excuse me m' lady, I shall be but a moment," says Barnaby, bowing further and backing towards the kitchen door.

"Oh, consider it no trouble," responds Marsha.

Barnaby trots off towards the door, with a virtual skip in his step and a feeling of happiness at the game being played out with this delightful princess. He floats down the corridor, almost waltzing to the music of Strauss in his head. Finally, he gracefully breezes toward the front door, grabbing its handle as he comes to rest in a cotton wool world of sweet dreams and kittens and flowers.

"Morning loser," belches Jack, as he pushes his way past him, bringing Barnaby back to reality with a thud.

Polly struts past, popping a gum bubble as she comes alongside him.

"Well, I can see Marsha's already here," Polly observes, looking into Barnaby's eyes as she breezes past him with an air of superiority.

"Eh, yeah, just arrived," says Barnaby, stumbling like an idiot, as he runs after the two siblings.

Jack is wearing his favourite black t-shirt and jeans. Polly, by total coincidence, is wearing a black camisole top, as if in stark contrast to Marsha, plus a plaid skirt with knee-high black socks that neatly glide into a pair of Dr Martens boots.

"Ah! So the gang are all here!" announces Uncle Finch.

"Ta-dah!" shouts Jack, his arms outstretched.

"Yo!" says Polly, perching herself on the edge of the kitchen table.

"Mathias Finch, at your service," heralds Uncle Finch, bowing slightly and still playing the posh game.

Jack and Polly are clearly not about to join in the pageantry.

"This is Jack and his sister Polly," explains Barnaby, pointing in their general direction.

"Ah good, lovely to finally put names to the faces," replies Uncle Finch.

"So, are we going to do dinosaurs or what?" asks Jack.

"Em, not quite my dear boy, we'd need a bit more preparation for a trip like that," answers Uncle Finch, much to Jack's dismay.

"No, I have other plans for today, and it starts in the attic!" Uncle Finch looks around the group for a response but is met with a sea of bewildered faces.

"When I was your age, attics were where all adventures started." Still nothing, not even a blink.

"Oh I can see you've never experienced the joys of an attic in a big old house like this, so why don't you all follow me and let the adventure begin?"

"Did you want your cup of tea?" Barnaby asks Marsha.

"No, I'm suitably curious enough now to pass on that," she responds.

The group climb the stairs to the first floor. About halfway along there is a door, which looks like it should contain a vacuum cleaner or an ironing board. Uncle Finch reaches into his pocket for the set of keys, so skillfully stolen from him by Jack only yesterday. He turns the key and the door creaks ajar. Then he swings around to the group, stopping them from pushing their way past and adopting the bowed hunch of an evil henchman. In his best spooky voice, he says:

"What lies beyond this door is the gateway to a WORLD of adventure. Only the brave should step through, else they suffer the fate of mere mortals."

Jack, who is closest to Uncle Finch, is clearly the most impatient and keen to be the first to sprint through the door. He turns to the group with a look of distaste, his glare finally resting on Barnaby as if to say, "Who's your crazy friend?"

"Shall I just drop the theatrics?" says Uncle Finch, straightening up.

"Probably best," Jack confirms, as the group all look at each other and murmur in approval.

"Alright, onwards and upwards brave soldiers," declares Uncle Finch, still not dropping said theatrics.

Jack races up the stairs as the others ascend at a reasonable pace.

"Hey! I can hardly see a thing up here!!" shouts Jack.

"Some sort of lighting is required then?" quips a sarcastic Uncle Finch, flicking the light switch as he climbs the staircase.

The attic is the ultimate hoarder's paradise. A vast space, filled to the brim with chests and boxes, old gramophones, stacks of gilded picture frames, coat hangers full of dusty jackets and coats, furniture now regarded too old to sit within a modern, or at least twentieth-century home.

"Jeeeeeez!" gasps Jack, "Look at all this stuff!"

"The combined haul of centuries of accumulation," adds Uncle Finch. "Generations of belongings dating back some four hundred years, perhaps even older."

"Even without a time machine, this would be an adventure," thinks Barnaby to himself.

"So, my young adventurers," announces Uncle Finch with arms outstretched, again not dropping the theatrics. "The time has come to unveil today's plan!"

Curiosity spurs the group to gather around him like disciples.

"When I was a child, my sister and I would spend our weekends lifting the lids of these boxes and marvelling at the treasures within. We'd spend our time 'dressing up' and transporting ourselves to different worlds. A pirate's cove, an Edwardian palace, the trenches of the Somme and the beaches of Normandy, the Battle of Trafalgar or the canals of Venice. An almost infinite collection from my family's journeys awaits you. Now, my rather nostalgic trip down memory lane is our key to travelling incognito. These precious items that would take us to far off places in our minds, will allow us to neatly blend into whichever society we decide to visit. Let the clothes we choose be our guides, for when we look the part, we live the part!"

"Okay, where do we start?" asks Jack.

"Every chest or box has a date. Each contains clothing and apparel from that period. Go find the shoe that fits!"

The group begin to slowly fan out as Uncle Finch plops himself down in an old rocking chair and observes, nostalgically reminding him of past adventures. After a while his eyes grow heavy and he closes them for a few seconds.

Polly and Marsha instantly team up and head for the nearest chest.

Jack has wandered over to a bookshelf crammed with trinkets and begins picking up and examining various curiosities made of metal and wood.

"Hey, what do you think this is?" queries Jack, picking up an ebony, brass and ivory object.

Barnaby wanders over to take a look.

"It's a sextant."

"A what now?"

"A sextant. Sailors used it for navigation," explains Barnaby.

Jack nods and places it back on the shelf.

Polly observes Marsha as she opens a chest and rummages through it.

Meanwhile, Uncle Finch is gently rocking and starting to feel drowsy. His sleep patterns are erratic and he grabs the opportunity for a siesta whenever he can. He slowly drifts off to the sounds of girl's giggles and boy's shouting. "Come look at this, hahahahaha, OMG! I am not wearing that! En garde! Geronimo!" etc.

He finally comes around, being gently shaken on the shoulder.

"Uncle Finch," Barnaby is whispering.

Slowly he sits up and rubs his eyes.

As the group come into focus, he realises they are all lined up in front of him, as if for approval. They are wearing a collection of clothes from the 1930's chest. The boys are in pressed trousers and white shirts, the girls in knee-length dresses tapered above the waist, one lemon and one white, each with delicate pink flowers.

"We want to see the war!" says Polly, still chewing on gum.

"From a distance!!" Marsha clarifies.

"I want to see Nazis," Jack adds.

"Spitfires. I want to see Spitfires," announces Barnaby, holding up a pair of binoculars that are hanging around his neck.

Uncle Finch stands up and contemplates the request.

"Somewhere safe with Nazis and Spitfires?"

"Yup!" says Jack.

"That's a tall order!" replies Uncle Finch.

He stands, deep in thought.

"Maybe even…"

"At-cha-cha!" interrupts Uncle Finch, stopping Jack in his tracks and tapping the side of his head, as if to say "I'm thinking."

For at least five minutes Uncle Finch stares off into space, intermittently nodding, shaking his head, nodding again, shaking his head again, until finally he awakes from his trance and turns to face the group.

"I've got it!"

A nervous shuffle ripples through them, as the tension starts to grow.

"There isn't anywhere safe with Nazis AND Spitfires. So, I should say it's two trips!"

Silence.

"Well?" questions Barnaby.

"Biggin Hill. Battle of Britain. As many Spitfires as you care to view from a safe distance."

"And the Nazis?" asks an impatient Jack.

"Well, there's no safe place to view REAL Nazis, but if you want to get a feel for German occupation, I think the Channel Islands are the safest place to be."

"Why the channel islands?" Barnaby quizzes.

"Well, it was a kind of soft occupation compared to the rest of Europe. I'm not saying they had it easy, there were some unspeakable crimes committed there. Still, we could come and go with relative ease, while freely speaking English. Anywhere else and I'd probably be arrested as a spy!"

"Okay, which one first?" enquires Marsha.

"Spitfires, Spitfires, Spitfires!!!" pleads Barnaby.

Uncle Finch looks at the gang, who stare at him, awaiting his next words.

"Alright, let's go see a war!" declares Uncle Finch after allowing them to stew for a few seconds.

There's a collective shriek of "woohoo!" as they run toward the attic steps.

Uncle Finch follows, rubbing his hands and grinning.

In the basement the group huddles around Uncle Finch as he searches the web for info on Biggin Hill, an RAF air force base in England, home to squadrons of Spitfires.

"Here we are! Biggin Hill. It was one of the busiest airfields in England during the Battle of Britain."

"The Battle of Britain?" questions Polly.

"Ah yes, better give you some background on where we're heading to. You see, the only thing that stood between Hitler and a conquered Britain, was the skill of the RAF pilots and the machines they flew. The Brits had the Hurricane and the Spitfire and the Germans had the Messerschmitt ME109. The Brits were marginally outnumbered, so it came down to the skill of these incredibly brave pilots to gain the upper hand. Britain also had a radar net that covered the east coast and gave them advanced warning of any approaching enemy aircraft. Those two factors ended Hitler's campaign, called *Operation Sea Lion,* and would eventually turn the tide of the war."

"So will we see any air battles?" asks Jack.

"Possibly. It's hard to determine exactly where they will be, but we'll make sure we can observe the aircraft take-off and then we'll just see what we can see. Remember, this isn't just about watching air battles or planes, it's also about getting a feeling for what life was like."

"I'm there for the air battles," replies Jack.

"Yes, I know," Uncle Finch confirms.

A few more taps on the iPad and he has chosen his date.

"Friday, August 30th, 1940. A very busy day for Biggin Hill!"

"I'm getting nervous!" shrieks Marsha.

"You don't have to come my dear, you can always stay here. Remember, we'll be back seconds after we leave," replies Uncle Finch.

"Hmm. No, I'm coming. I'll be kicking myself in a few seconds when you guys come back whooping and hollering!"

"Okay, let's have a look for a good landing spot. Aha! This looks perfect! It's a nature reserve and golf course. Look! Right next to the home of Charles Darwin!!"

The kids lean in closer for a better look.

"The golf course dates back to 1912, so the landscape is unlikely to have changed much. I'll set the time to 5 am, so we're arriving when nobody else is around."

"Cool. This is soooooo exciting," announces Barnaby.

"Okay, if anyone asks, we are plane spotting and we come from Barking," Uncle Finch states, emphasising the whole sentence.

"Barking? That's soooo apt," says Jack.

"Why is that apt?" enquires Barnaby.

"Coz we're all barking mad to be doing this!" grins Jack.

Uncle Finch gives a little chuckle and nods his head.

"Okay, here we go then. Hands on each other's shoulders please. Do NOT break contact or you'll be left behind. Some golden rules are that if we do have to interact with anyone, at NO point can we say who we are or where we're from. Make NO references to future events. We cannot tell anyone how the war will end or ANYTHING that will happen after this day. I need you all to swear!"

"Shitbuckets," says Jack after a few seconds of silence.

Uncle Finch raises an eyebrow.

"You said to swear!" chuckles Jack.

The group shake their heads and return to the business at hand.

"Okay, are we all touching?" asks Uncle Finch.

The group look at each other and nod.

"Okay, here we go!"

Uncle Finch taps the iPad, and the show begins.

Chapter 7

Biggin Hill

Barnaby once more feels the sensation of being forced to crouch slightly, before a blast of air hits him in the face, forcing him to close his eyes. Suddenly his head is spinning and, as he opens his eyes, the dizziness takes over. Swaying from side-to-side, he proceeds to stumble and fall over onto damp grass.

"Woohoo," shouts Jack.

"Quiet boy!" whispers Uncle Finch.

"That was freakin awesome!!" Jack half whispers, half shouts.

"I don't feel so good," groans Barnaby, attempting to get to his feet but falling back onto the grass.

"Just stay sitting until the dizziness stops!" explains Uncle Finch.

Polly is lying, star-shaped on the ground next to Marsha who is trying to focus on one thing to stop her head from spinning.

"You lot are sooooo lame," teases Jack, who seems to be immune to the effects of time travel.

The queasiness starts to pass and Barnaby can finally focus on his surroundings. It's dark, but there is a distinct orange glow in the sky as the sun begins to crest a horizon, hidden by dense woods. Some of the light is starting to cast long shadows across the golf course, which is now glistening with morning dew.

"I am freezing!" moans Polly.

"Ah, yes, I guess we should have brought some coats or something," replies Uncle Finch.

Uncle Finch taps the iPad and disappears, as though he has shrunk into a pinhole. The action leaves a sonic ripple rumbling across the golf course.

"What? He left us!!" screams Marsha.

"Um, guys, what happens if the machine breaks? Are we stuck here?" asks Jack.

"Maybe it's just…" Barnaby is interrupted by the reappearance of Uncle Finch out of the same pinhole. Around him the scenery seems to visually vibrate for a couple of seconds to complement the rumble that carries off into the distance.

"Ta-dah!" says Uncle Finch, holding up two girls' coats, one navy, one khaki.

"Jeez Uncle Finch! We panicked for a second there! What if the machine had broken, we'd have been stuck here!" yells Barnaby, flapping his arms and pacing.

"If the machine had broken, it would maybe take me days or weeks to fix, but that would be of no consequence to you, as I've only been gone an instant," Uncle Finch calmly explains, as he hands the coats to the girls and places his reassuring hands on Barnaby's shoulders.

"I guess," replies Barnaby, who has stopped pacing.

"That's the spirit! Alright, let's go see what we can see!" continues Uncle Finch, as he walks off down the golf course, stuffing the time machine into a haversack slung over his shoulder. The four teenagers dutifully trot along behind him.

"I guess we should try and use some historical phrases or something," announces Barnaby.

"Such as?" asks Jack.

"I dunno, maybe I should call you 'old chap', or something like that?"

"Oh, I get it. Sound like some posh kid," Jack replies.

"No, not necessarily posh, just, I dunno, relative to the time we're in?"

"Good use of the word 'relative' Barnaby," remarks Uncle Finch. "Relativity is key here. All of our observers cannot see what we actually are. That's a fantastic idea to use some relevant phrases. 'Old bean', 'Old chap' and so on. Not so much for our American friends here, but certainly for you Barnaby."

"Why not so much for us?" asks Marsha.

"Because locals here won't have encountered many Americans, so much of what you say will sound alien to them anyway."

"Ahhhhh, yeah, that makes sense," Marsha agrees.

The group picks up a small trail that starts to meander through the woods, heading downwards to what Uncle Finch hopes is the airbase.

After about five minutes walking, the group finally begin to see through the trees. They can just make out a couple of huts on the other side of a vast expanse of open, level ground.

"Look, over there!" hollers Barnaby, raising his binoculars.

"I see them!" Jack responds.

In the distance the group can see a little cluster of squat objects, their noses pointing up at about fifteen degrees.

"Spitfires!" screams an excited Barnaby.

"C'mon, let's get a better look!" whispers Uncle Finch.

As the group move toward a wire fence separating them from the airfield, they spot a neat little place where a tree has fallen. As a result, it has left behind a large crater which is now flanked by wild bushes and the circular vertical canopy of the tree's root system.

Uncle Finch motions for them to stay put while he goes over to check out the potential viewing point.

"This is sooo surreal!" exclaims Barnaby to the group.

"You're telling me," replies Jack. "We're looking at planes that will either be shot to bits or will end up in museums years from now! But there they are! Large as life, ready to shoot down Nazis!"

Uncle Finch returns to the group.

"No, it's not Nazis they're shooting down, it's the Luftwaffe, the German equivalent of the RAF."

"Aren't they all Nazis?"

"Nazis were, sorry, ARE the politicians. The pilots in those fighters and bombers that will very soon be up in those skies are soldiers, doing their governments bidding," Uncle Finch explains, trying to educate the kids.

"They're still all bad guys though!" says Jack, starting to feel a little let down that he's not getting the Nazis he was promised.

"Come on, this little spot will allow us to see the action, hopefully without being spotted ourselves," continues Uncle Finch, directing the group to the upturned tree.

In the crater are various items of junk, a wooden packing case with the words 'Tonbridge Apples' along the side, an old tea towel and an upturned ceramic pot.

"Look at this stuff. Even this long ago folks were just dumping rubbish," remarks Jack, suddenly becoming an eco-warrior.

"Hmmm," says Uncle Finch, "I'm not so sure."

Uncle Finch picks up the tea towel. Sitting the wooden crate on its end, he then spreads out the towel over the top and finally sets his bottom down.

"Nice little impromptu seat, don't you think?"

"So somebody else has been viewing planes from this spot?" enquires Jack.

Finch nods.

Barnaby suddenly grabs Jack's arm.

"Nazi spies!!"

Jack turns to Barnaby as his eyebrows slowly raise to almost the top of his head.

"Yes! Yes! That's it!! Nazi spies!!! Maybe we can catch him and interrogate him?"

"Nope," replies Uncle Finch. "Interrogating Nazi spies could alter the course of history."

"Oh God, this time travelling stuff is so boring!!"

Barnaby turns to Jack.

"Remember, we're 'tourists' and this is NOT Disneyland!"

"Yeah, I know, but come on, this is the stuff heroes are made of!"

"Wrong again," reiterates Uncle Finch. "The real heroes are over there in the huts, awaiting the call to get in those planes and face an uncertain future. Remember, the people here don't know they are going to be triumphant. For all they know, the German invasion could land on their shores any day now."

Then a noise in the distance makes them all stop and look at each other.

A snapping twig.

Then another.

The group all duck down.

"Nazi spy!" whispers Jack, his excitement turning to fear.

More snapping twigs.

"He's getting closer!" murmurs Marsha.

"It could just be a squirrel or something," replies Uncle Finch.

"If it is, it's a big squirrel walking on two legs!" exclaims Polly, who is cottoning on to the fact that there is now a rhythm to the snapping twigs. Left, right, left, right.

"Okay, we'll have to grab him when he arrives!" whispers Uncle Finch, realising they have nowhere to run.

"Then what?" shrieks Marsha in a hushed tone.

"When I say 'now', we all grab him and get him down on the ground, okay?"

The gang nods.

"Okay, ready?"

More nodding and crouching.

The footsteps are now directly on the other side of the upturned tree.

"Now!" yells Uncle Finch, leaping up just as the figure enters the clearing.

"Aggggggghhhhhhhh!!!!!!!!!" comes the response from the shocked visitor.

To everyone's surprise and the disappointment of Jack, the Nazi spy is actually a terrified boy, who is now reeling backwards in complete fear. As he stumbles, he trips over a broken branch and plunges into a bramble bush.

"Hey, it's a kid!" exclaims Jack.

Barnaby rushes forward and begins to extract the boy from the thorny bush.

"Hey, it's okay, we won't hurt you," says Barnaby, pulling the boy out carefully.

He's clearly very shaken and overwhelmed at the number of people now staring at him.

"Hey, what's your name?" asks Barnaby, as the boy stands upright and looks on sheepishly.

"G-Graham," mutters the terrified boy, trembling.

"Hi Graham, I'm Barnaby," says Barnaby, shaking the boy's hand.

"How old are you Graham?" enquires Uncle Finch.

"I'm ten."

"Is this your stool?"

Graham nods.

"Did you come here to watch the planes take off?"

More nodding.

"Well," continues Uncle Finch, "that's what my nephews, nieces and I have come here to do also."

Graham looks around the group, taking in all of their faces, but still shaking a little.

"Would it be okay if we joined you?"

Graham fails to respond but is clearly thinking things through.

"What's your favourite? The Spitfire or the Hurricane?" asks Uncle Finch.

"Spitfire," comes the quiet, muffled response.

"That's my favourite too!" says Barnaby.

"Is this a good time to see them?" Uncle Finch quizzes.

Graham nods.

"That's good. We've travelled a long way to view these wonderful aircraft. Have you seen much action?"

"Yes," says Graham, "bombing."

"Bombing? Here?" presses Finch.

"Yes."

"Was it scary?"

Again, Graham nods.

"I'll bet it was."

Behind them, the sound of an engine sputtering to life interrupts the conversation.

In the distance, the group can see pilots scrambling into their aircraft. Some begin to turn and make their way towards the runway, while others start up their engines, as engineers rush back to the barracks

"Oh my God, look! Wooo-hoo, this is so exciting!!" shrieks Barnaby with delight, as he raises his binoculars to get a better look.

"That's 72 Squadron! The Spitfires!" shrieks Graham, bursting into life and rushing forward to get a better view. "And over there, that's 79, those are Hurricanes. See, their ground crew are preparing them now."

"Wow Graham, you are remarkably well informed!" remarks Uncle Finch.

"Wouldn't you be without the internet?" Polly blurts out.

"Shhhhhhh," whispers Uncle Finch, as Polly realises she's broken the first rule of time travel.

"Oh, oops," she mumbles, putting her hand to her mouth.

Fortunately Graham is too engrossed watching the scrambling aircraft to notice the reference to the yet-to-be-invented technology.

"Where do you think they are heading Graham?" asks Uncle Finch.

"Incoming bombers over the Dover Strait and the North Sea. They come from Holland, Belgium, Germany, thousands of them. Our boys will see them off though!"

"I bet they will," replies Uncle Finch, ruffling Graham's hair.

"Say Graham, what's your second name?"

"Ogilvie."

"Pleased to meet you Graham Ogilvie, I am Mathias Finch and these are my nephews Barnaby and Jack, and my nieces Marsha and Polly."

"Pleased to meet you!" smiles Graham in response.

Then the first group of Spitfires begin to take off, one after the other in quick succession, ready to assemble into formations in the sky. The sound is incredible and continues as each aircraft takes to the air, wheels retracting as they go.

"This is fantastic!" roars Barnaby over the noise of the departing aircraft.

After a while, the sound of Rolls Royce Merlin engines vanishes to reveal the sound of the English countryside once more. Birds tweet and chirp in the trees overhead, safe once again from their noisy metallic cousins.

"That was so much better than a crumby air show!" says Barnaby.

Uncle Finch coughs and directs Barnaby's eyes towards Graham.

"What's an air show?" queries Graham.

"Ah, it's something we have in the States," interjects a fast-thinking Jack. "Folks come from miles around to see old planes from the First World War and stuff. You know, Tiger Moths and the like."

Behind Graham's back, Uncle Finch gives Jack the 'thumbs up'.

Then behind them, more spluttering as the Hurricane's Merlin engines burst into life. Again, in quick succession, every remaining Hurricane takes to the sky to intercept the incoming German bombers.

"They might not be as beautiful or as graceful as the Spitfire, but those guys are absolute beasts. You know they shoot down more enemy planes than Spitfires by the end of the war?" announces Barnaby, a real WW2 plane enthusiast.

"I hope so!" nods Graham, not noticing Barnaby's 'past tense' reference to the figures.

Barnaby cringes, realising he almost messed up again. He moves up alongside Uncle Finch and whispers into his ear.

"Let's get out of here before we completely slip up. Not talking about the war in the past tense is so difficult!"

"I completely agree," replies Uncle Finch.

"Well Graham, it has certainly been a pleasure to meet you, even though our introduction may have been a tad frightening. We've got to be going now as we have tea with the vicar in our village this afternoon."

Jack looks as baffled as ever.

"Come along children, off we go!"

"Goodbye," Graham waves.

"Goodbye Graham, take care old chap!" adds Barnaby patting him on the back as he heads off.

The group disappears on up the path as Graham takes his rightful place on the apple crate. He reaches down and lifts up the upturned ceramic pot to reveal a set of cardboard playing cards wrapped in brown paper. He begins to leaf through them, sorting them into order, Ace of Hearts, Two of Hearts, when suddenly the ground rumbles beneath him in a rippling fashion.

"Wow, Gerry bombers are early this morning!"

Of course, it has nothing to do with German bombers.

Chapter 8

Preparing for occupation

"That was a real bucket-list moment!" declares Barnaby, as he shakily stumbles to the floor of Uncle Finch's basement.

Jack is helping Marsha and Polly to their feet.

"We have got to work on our dialogue though. Fortunately that kid was far too distracted by Spitfires and Hurricanes to notice the number of times we put our foot in it!" remarks Marsha, leaning on the workbench.

"Graham was it?" asks Polly.

"Yeah," confirms Barnaby.

Uncle Finch lays his haversack on the workbench next to Marsha, who proceeds to pull the time machine out of it.

"What was his surname?" enquires Marsha.

"Ogilvie," replies Barnaby, who had been paying attention.

Marsha types the password into the iPad and does a search for 'Graham Ogilvie, Kent, 1930'.

"Oh my God guys, look at this!"

"What is it?" asks Uncle Finch.

"That's him, isn't it?" Marsha points to a black and white picture of a child.

"God, yes it is! What site is that?" Polly joins in.

"Hang on, I'm looking at the picture results. Here we go. The bombing of Biggin Hill, Battle of Britain website!!"

"What does it say?"

"It's a post. His recollections of the day Biggin Hill was bombed. Oh my God, it says here that thirty-nine people were killed in a bombing raid later that day. He saw it all."

"Read it then Marsh!" prompts Polly.

"I recall it was a pleasant morning. I had gotten down early to watch the first of the crews take off to meet Gerry. Not early enough as others were also there to watch." That's us!!!! "Then I spent the morning playing cards before nipping home for lunch. Arrived back after lunch with my notepad to start recording the planes aircraft letters, when suddenly a couple of Junkers 88's came in and dropped their load over the field. The damage didn't look too bad but some houses in the village took hits. Later on in the day the real damage came, when some more JU88's flew over, roughly ten of them, and decimated the airfield. The engineer's hut took a direct hit and killed many of the chaps inside. The girls' hut was also hit and the fire crews spent hours digging them out. We so often talk about the pilots turning the tide of the war. The few. But they weren't as few as we think. The boys and girls on the ground were as much in harm's way and gave their all to get those lads up in the air quickly. We should never forget them. Graham Ogilvie."

"Is he still alive?" asks Barnaby.

"It doesn't say. That was posted back in 2013. He would have been eighty-three."

"This is soooo freaky! We were just talking to him!" Polly declares.

"AND we featured in his recollections. That's the first instance of our interaction changing the future!" Uncle Finch takes great pain to point out.

"You're right! Nothing that would make a big impact, but it shows you how even the mildest interaction can change things," Barnaby adds.

"We get it. No future chat," states Polly, still looking every bit the rebel, even in her 1940's clothes.

"Uncle Finch?" says Barnaby, changing the subject.

"Yes, Barnaby?"

"Remember when you went back to get the girls' coats?"

"Yes?"

"Well, it got me thinking about what happens if the time machine should break or should be discovered. How would we get home?"

"Hmmm. That is an excellent point, Barnaby. Tell you what, why don't I take an hour or so to update the software on the original prototype, that way we have a backup. Okay?"

"Original prototype?" quizzes Jack.

"Yes, this one is an adaptation of the original I have over here," continues Uncle Finch climbing a small step ladder and taking down a suitcase from the top shelf of one of his cabinets. "It's a bit more cumbersome, but it will still work."

Barnaby takes the case from Uncle Finch, but its weight nearly pulls him down onto the floor.

"Jeez Uncle Finch, that weighs a tonne!"

"Yes, my next task is to try to get the next version down to a more manageable size. Something you could fit in your pocket."

"That would be good! This one isn't really working out for me!" announces Barnaby, placing the suitcase carefully on the floor.

"Although I do feel like I'm working out trying to lift it!" he continues, wheezing.

"Alright, I'll carry this one, and one of you can take the other in the haversack. Agreed?"

"Agreed. It'll make me feel much safer!" says Barnaby.

"Okay. It's eleven o'clock now, why don't you all fix yourself some lunch to take with you and I'll get this updated," suggests Uncle Finch.

"Sure. What do we all want?" asks Barnaby, as they begin to climb the stairs to the kitchen.

"Do cheese," answers Polly, nonchalantly, picking at her nails.

"Oh boring, let's do some turkey mayo," interjects Jack.

"Yeah, that is sooo much more exciting," teases Polly, popping herself onto the table.

"Shut up!" squeaks Jack.

"Hey, can we use cling film?" queries Barnaby as Momo trots over with his tail wagging, and places his head on Barnaby's now seated leg.

"No way that existed in the forties. You need to wrap it up in brown paper or something," remarks Marsha.

"What? You think some German soldier is going to stop us and ask 'Vy aff you zis sandwich wrapped in plausteek?'" retorts Jack.

"That is a terrible German accent," adds Barnaby.

"Just make it as authentic as possible," replies Marsha.

Barnaby gets up and sets about making a series of sandwiches, some cheese, some turkey mayo, wrapped in brown baking paper, which is the most authentic-looking thing he could find. Momo's tail continues to wag the whole time in expectation.

"Hey, throw a couple of sodas in there!" insists Jack.

Barnaby gives him a quizzical look.

"Oh! Vy do you aff zeez colas from zi future also?" Jack responds before Barnaby can protest.

"Authentic!" shouts Marsha.

"So what's an authentic forties drink?" asks Jack, wandering over to the fridge and opening it.

"Water? Tea?" answers Barnaby.

"Are you kidding me? Dude, they must have had lemonade or something?" continues Jack waving around a can of coke that he has just extracted from the fridge.

"War rations? Sodas would have been shipped to the UK, so I seriously doubt they would have been willing to use up valuable ship space with bottles of Pepsi and dodge the German U-Boat nets in the Atlantic," replies Barnaby.

"You must not think like a modern boy," Marsha points out.

"Whatever." Jack shrugs and places the can of coke on the table. He leans back on a kitchen chair with his feet up on the table.

The next half an hour is taken up with squabbles about what is acceptable behaviour and accessories for the 1940s. Jack shows the most resistance, while Polly remains indifferent, unless it is to deride her brother in some way, which she enjoys.

"So in that case, why don't we just leave our phones behind? We can't take pictures, we can't phone anybody, so they're pretty pointless right?" declares Jack, finishing off an argument.

"Exactly!" screams Marsha, raising her hands to the ceiling.

"What's all this bickering?" asks Uncle Finch, as he re-enters the room carrying the heavy case containing the back-up time machine.

"Oh nothing," replies Marsha. "We're just trying to teach Jack the basics of time travel protocol."

"Coming from the experts!" Jack quips.

"Never mind about that now," interrupts Uncle Finch. "We need to find a safe place to drop!"

"Golf club?" suggests Barnaby.

"Golf club!" replies Uncle Finch.

"Here we go. La Moye, established in 1902, virtually laid waste by the German Army during the occupation. Ah, but how was it laid waste? Let's dig deeper. La Moye, German Occupation. Ah! Turns out the golf club was Battalion 16's HQ! That's no good!"

"I found another one. Royal Jersey Golf Club," adds Barnaby.

"See if you can find out more," Uncle Finch continues.

"Nope, no good. It was filled with landmines during the occupation."

"So where then?" asks Jack.

"A church maybe?" proposes Marsha.

"Good idea! Look for something old, out of the way."

"How about this one? Saint Clements?" Marsha says, twirling her phone around to show the group.

"This looks perfect! Do some digging, see if it was used as anything other than a church!" requests Uncle Finch excitedly.

Marsha taps away and scans several sites. "Can't see anything about Germans," she finally adds.

"Excellent! Let's set the time for six a.m., just to make sure our arrival goes unnoticed," continues Uncle Finch, tapping away on the lighter of the two time machines, while his foot rests on the other one in the case. "Let's go for, say, 10th July 1942. Nice sunny day hopefully. Now read me the coordinates, girl."

"49°10'25.4"N 2°03'25.0"W" is the response from Marsha.

"Wonderful. Ready?" announces Uncle Finch, his finger poised above the jump button.

"Wait! The sandwiches!" shrieks Barnaby, as he rushes over and sticks them into his haversack. "Would you like some Uncle Finch?"

"No thank you, Barnaby, I have some boiled eggs in here," he says, tapping his haversack. "A great source of protein!"

"Anything else?" enquires Jack, who is clearly dying to see soldiers of the Wehrmacht. "Some bananas? An ice cream? The kitchen sink?"

"Alright, keep your hair on!" replies Barnaby.

"Wait!!" shouts Uncle Finch, reaching into his pocket.

"What now??" screams Jack.

"I don't think I need to be taking my phone with me!" announces Uncle Finch, laying his phone down on the kitchen table.

"Are we done yet?" asks the now highly irritated Jack.

"All good!" answers Uncle Finch, as the group finally links arms. He taps at the iPad, and they are sent zipping off into the past.

Nobody notices Jack reaching for something at the last second.

Chapter 9

Occupational hazards

"Hey! I didn't fall over!!" shrieks a delighted Marsha.

"Lucky you!" groans Barnaby, picking himself up from the wet grass.

The group have found themselves in the cemetery of the St. Clement's Church, an ancient parish church dating back to the year 911 A.D. It's a beautiful little spot, even for a cemetery, with a view over to the church. There's a large tree to it's right that is now allowing the rising sun to push through its foliage onto the group's faces. The sun is also a bit dazzling, so it's difficult to see if anyone has observed their arrival.

Uncle Finch has his hands up over his eyes to better take in his surroundings.

"No sign of life!" remarks Uncle Finch.

"Wait here, I'm going to go and check the street!" Barnaby announces to the group as he trots off across the cemetery.

He joins a path which leads down to the church entrance, and tentatively takes a peek down the road to his left. No sign of life, just a row of cute cottages looking onto a narrow country road. To his right there are more cute cottages, followed by what looks like an open field and another narrow lane leading up the side of the church. He raises his binoculars and focuses on both ends of the street in turn. As far as he can see, the road meanders out of view and appears to be clear. In fact, nothing seems to be stirring anywhere. He turns to the group and gives the thumbs up.

At that, the gang set off towards him, leather shoes quickly dampening in the wet grass.

Polly and Marsha sit themselves down on a bench, having wiped the morning dew from it, as Jack starts to rummage in his haversack.

"See anybody?" asks a breathless Uncle Finch, who has just arrived, carrying both time machines.

"Nope, nothing. Uncle Finch? I'm not sure that carrying two machines around everywhere is going to be entirely practical."

"Oh, I can manage."

"Wouldn't we be better off leaving the big one here? Somewhere safe?"

Uncle Finch contemplates for a moment. Carrying them across the cemetery was bad enough.

111

"Okay, I think perhaps you're right," concedes Uncle Finch. He slips off his haversack, places it on the bench next to the girls and passes Barnaby the smaller of the two machines, while looking around for a suitable hiding place for the other.

"Maybe up there at the back? We could hide it in the woods there," suggests Barnaby, pointing towards the rear of the cemetery.

"Yes, I think that'll…"

Phssst! Crrk.

Uncle Finch is cut mid-sentence by the noise. He and Barnaby are looking at each other, but they know precisely what the sound was. Both slowly turn in disbelief towards Jack, who is drinking from a freshly opened can of coke.

"Do you listen to a word anybody says??" cries Barnaby.

"Rarely, dude, rarely," says Jack, wiping coke from his chin.

"That," continues Barnaby, pointing at the can, "could cause a paradox!"

"Relax! When I'm done, I'll squash it with my foot and pop it in my haversack.

"Correct! And make sure you keep it concealed and don't drop it somewhere," Barnaby adds.

"Yeah, yeah, yeah," mutters Jack, slipping off his haversack and throwing it onto the bench next to Uncle Finch's.

"Unbelievable," exclaims Barnaby, as he turns to face Uncle Finch.

"I think your friend here has a slight rebellious touch," notes Uncle Finch, stating the obvious.

"Come on, let's go hide this thing, give him time to finish it. Then we can make sure he hides it properly and doesn't throw it into somebody's garden or something," adds Uncle Finch, walking back up the path at an angle, against the weight of the case.

Barnaby stuffs the smaller time machine into his haversack and places it on the bench next to Uncle Finch's and Jack's.

"Do not touch that while we're gone," orders Barnaby to Jack, who shrugs as if that was never even a possibility. Barnaby then chases after Uncle Finch.

At the top of the cemetery they come across a broken section of the wall. Barnaby and Uncle Finch clamber over it and observe their surroundings. The woods are quite thick and don't look like they are entered into often, if at all.

"This looks like a good spot," Barnaby points out, as he ducks down under a dense section of bush.

Uncle Finch hauls the case over and swings it in Barnaby's direction, keeping his grip tight as Barnaby grabs at two corners. The pair push their way deeper into the foliage and eventually drop the case down at the bottom of the bush.

"Here, cover it with some of these dead branches," says Uncle Finch, handing Barnaby a handful from the ground. Barnaby takes them, places them over the case and begins to scoop up more from their surroundings. After a minute or so, they are satisfied that it is camouflaged enough to leave.

The pair make their way back to the rest of the group, where Jack is proudly displaying a crushed coke can.

"See! Not a problem," declares Jack, beaming with confidence.

"Put it away then," screeches Barnaby, as his patience is once more tested.

"Alright Adolf," Jack teases, and gives a little Nazi salute.

"And don't give Nazi salutes!! Do you remember where and when we are?"

"What's the worst that can happen?"

"The worst that could happen is that a villager sees you doing that and takes us for Nazi spies!"

Jack pauses a moment and then shrugs and places the squashed can into his haversack.

"Okay geniuses, what's the plan?" asks Polly from the bench.

"I reckon we head south across that field over there," replies Uncle Finch, pointing south. "Then we can follow the coast, keeping out of sight until we can walk undetected into St. Helier. Then, we simply take a look around, under the pretence of just being out for a good old healthy walk."

"What if some sentry or something asks for papers? I've seen them do that in the movies," questions Marsha.

"We'll avoid sentries. If it gets a bit risky, we'll just double back and retrace our steps. If anyone asks, we'll tell them Jack was in charge of bringing them and that he stupidly forgot them," replies Uncle Finch.

"Hey!" protests Jack.

"Sounds perfectly plausible to me," adds Polly.

"Okay, let's go," says Uncle Finch, lifting his haversack and leading the way, glad to not be carrying the big case.

The group grab their bags and turn right onto the little country road and follow it past the row of cottages until they reach the open field they had previously observed on the left. It's got a bit of a trek up to the top of a mild hill, but from there they should have a good vantage point to plan out their route into St. Helier.

About halfway up the hill, Barnaby pauses. Did he just hear something, off in the distance? A sort of splutter?

"Guys!"

The group turns to see Barnaby standing motionless with his finger held in the air.

"What's up BB?" asks Jack, who has just invented a new nickname for Barnaby.

Barnaby strains to listen.

Prrm, beh, prrm.

That's definitely something mechanical. It's coming from off to their right.

Barnaby raises his binoculars and focuses in the direction of the racket. At first he sees nothing and then briefly, between a row of trees, something whizzes by. The sound, at first intermittent, is now constant. It's a motorbike.

There's a clearer section of road on display, just before it enters the little village, so Barnaby trains his binoculars on that spot and awaits the bike's arrival.

A few seconds go by and then the source of the noise comes into Barnaby's line of sight.

"Wow! A sidecar!!"

"Lemme see!" says Jack, grabbing at the binoculars.

"Wowwwww! It totally is! Real live Nazis!!" exclaims Jack.

The bike is now fast approaching the church.

"Guys," Polly interrupts, "shouldn't we be, like, ducking or something?"

"She's right," shrieks Uncle Finch. "We're in full view! Run for the cover of those bushes!"

The group breaks into a sprint, the children covering ground much quicker than Uncle Finch.

"Go, go, go, go, go!" he yells waving his arms.

The children reach the bushes and leap into them. Barnaby instantly turns around and beckons his uncle to run quicker.

"Come on Uncle Finch, faster!"

Barnaby glances sideways and sees the sidecar driving past the bottom of their hill. Suddenly it screeches to a halt. Uncle Finch has been spotted. Barnaby whips up the binoculars from the cover of the bushes and can clearly see the occupant of the sidecar get out, arm his machine gun and start shouting towards Uncle Finch.

"Stop!" screams Barnaby to Uncle Finch, who immediately halts and looks to the bottom of the hill, where two figures are now starting to run towards him.

"Stay down out of sight!" Uncle Finch motions to the children for them to duck down further.

"They've only seen me. I'll try and talk my way out of it."

"But Uncle Finch…"

"Enough Barnaby, we've run out of time. Whatever you do, don't try and jump back a few minutes and warn us. YOU CANNOT occupy the same space and time in parallel."

"What? Why?" shrieks Barnaby.

"Paradox! Very dangerous, now hide!!!!"

Uncle Finch turns to the two soldiers who are now almost upon them.

"Put your hands up!!!!!" screams one of them, to which Uncle Finch willingly obliges.

The children are huddled at the base of the bushes, watching the feet of the three men. Barnaby can feel a trembling sensation against his side. It's Marsha, shivering with fear.

"Where were you going and why are you breaking curfew?" asks one of the soldiers in a loud voice.

"Em, I was out for a morning run, got to try and stay fit at my age, haha. Didn't quite realise the time."

"Show me your papers!!" barks the soldier.

"I'm afraid I don't have my papers with me," replies Uncle Finch, now unable to use Jack as an excuse.

"Then you come with us!!" demands the soldier, as he proceeds to march Uncle Finch off in the direction of the sidecar.

"This is NOT good," whispers Jack.

"What do we do?" asks Marsha, trying to get a better look at the situation.

"I have no idea," replies Barnaby.

"Guy needs rescuing," interrupts Polly. "So all we need to do is find out where they take him."

"Yes!" shrieks an excited Barnaby. "If we go back home, we can check where they take him on the web and then jump in to rescue him!"

"Dude, he has no records here," states an oddly focussed Jack. "They won't be able to register who he is and he's not going to be missed by anyone. And what are we going to do? Say he gets sent back to a POW camp in Germany, are we going to jump into the heart of the Fatherland, unarmed? Us, a bunch of kids?"

"Can't we just jump back a few minutes? Warn ourselves?" asks Marsha.

"Nope, Uncle Finch says that's too dangerous. We cannot meet ourselves."

"Dude sounds screwed," Polly concludes.

"Mega-screwed," adds Jack.

"Oh my God, oh my God, what is my mum going to say?" cries Barnaby.

"What exactly are you going to say to your mum?" queries Jack. "Sorry, I lost your brother? Dude he's the one that invented the time machine, you don't have to say anything. Just play dumb."

"I have to tell her!"

"No, you don't!"

"Do too!"

"Do not!"

"Do too!"

"Do…"

"Shut up!" interrupts Marsha, shoving herself in between the two boys. "Arguing isn't going to help him now. Let's just go back home and see if we can find out any information. Take it from there, yeah?"

Barnaby nods and pokes his head out above the bushes. In the distance he can see Uncle Finch being loaded into the sidecar, while the two soldiers mount the bike. The rear soldier has his gun trained on Uncle Finch. With a roar, the bike's engine bursts into life and they speed off along the country road in the direction of St. Helier and an uncertain future.

"Okay, ideas please!" says Barnaby.

Marsha, having gotten over her fear in the presence of the German soldiers, bursts into life.

"Right, so what could happen here? One, he talks his way out of it somehow and they just let him go, in which case, someone will need to stay here and guard the other time machine until he arrives. Two, they have no idea who he is and why he's here, so they assume he's a spy and lock him up in the local prison until such time they can ship him off to the Fatherland."

"So who wants to wait while we nip back to research his fate?" asks Barnaby.

"I'm pretty good at just hanging around graveyards," announces Polly, the closet Goth.

"I'll stay with you Poll," says Marsha. "What could be less conspicuous than two girls hanging around a church?"

"Okay, that's settled. Jack and I will jump back and find out what happened to my Uncle, devise a plan and come right back."

"Don't be long though!" adds Marsha.

Barnaby looks at her with a quizzical look.

"What?" Marsha continues.

Barnaby continues his look of incredulity.

"Ah, yup, you won't be long, coz, you have a time machine. Okay, okay, I get it, silly me!"

"No, I don't think you're silly, I think…" Barnaby is rudely interrupted by Jack grabbing his arm and leading him away.

"Come on lover boy, we have work to do!"

"No, I just meant…"

"Yeah, yeah, yeah. Shift it!"

"So where are you going now?" shouts Marsha.

"We're going back to the church to… Alright, haha, I get it, point taken. I don't have to walk back to the church to use the time machine!"

Barnaby pulls the device from his haversack as Jack holds on to his shoulder.

"Ready?" says Barnaby, as he hovers his finger over the 'Return' button. Jack nods and with that, they zip away, leaving the girls to walk down the hill to the church, free from the stupidity of boys.

Chapter 10

Getting help

"I did it!" shouts an excited Barnaby.

"Did what?" asks Jack.

"I managed to stay on my feet! Look!"

"Hang on, I'll alert the media," smirks Jack, as he walks over to Uncle Finch's computer.

"I'm getting the hang of it now. Thought I was always going to be falling on my bum!"

Jack sits himself down at the computer and awakens it.

"Right, what's your uncle's first name again?"

"Mathias."

"Okay, Mathias Finch, Jersey, German occupation," recites Jack, typing in the words and hitting return.

The pair scan the search results.

"I'm not seeing anything BB," observes Jack.

"Maybe they just let him go?" adds Barnaby.

"Nope."

"Why nope?" asks Barnaby.

"If he was freed, he'd have gone back to the other time machine, found the girls and jumped back here. He'd be standing right there with the girls."

"Then what in hell's name happened to him?"

"Unknown prisoners, Jersey 1942," Jack's next search produces nothing else in the way of clarity.

"Okay, let's find out where they would likely have taken him," suggests Barnaby.

"Let's see what Wiki has to say," Jack continues, typing away furiously.

"Okay, yadah-yadah-yadah, emergency government, blah, blah, administration, etc, etc. Can't see anything. Okay, let's search for occupation, Jersey, prisons. Right, we've got a nearby prison where POWs were kept before being shipped to the mainland, called… Newgate Street. Also, look here, the HQ of the German Secret Field Police, Silvertide, Havre des Pas. They MUST have taken him to one of those places."

"Okay, but how the heck do we get in there to free him?" asks Barnaby.

"That's not the problem. The problem is, WE can't say with any certainty where he will be at any given time," Jack responds.

"If only he had his phone with him, we could track his whereabouts," remarks Barnaby, grabbing a turkey sandwich from his rucksack.

"Good idea," says Jack, "I'm starved!" He reaches inside his haversack and starts to rummage around in search of his turkey mayo sandwiches.

"What the hell is this?" exclaims a frowning Jack, pulling out a brown paper bag. He peers inside.

"Eggs?"

Barnaby peers inside the bag.

"Those are Uncle Finch's eggs. What are they doing in your rucksack?"

"Oh, oh," announces Jack, pulling out the crushed coke can. "I think I picked up the wrong haversack when I was putting this away."

"So he has yours?" cries Barnaby.

"And my turkey sandwiches! And my phone!!"

"You took your phone!!!???" shrieks Barnaby. "We specifically told you not to take it!"

"I know! But with all the arguing I ended up forgetting!"

"Oh, how can you be so stupid!! If the Germans discover that, we are toying with a paradox on an unprecedented scale!"

"Why?"

"Future tech in the hands of the Nazis?"

"Oh, yeah, that is bad. Anyway, chances are they won't find it."

"And why is that?"

"Somebody created little secret compartments in them. Look." Jack opens the bag and shows Barnaby a hidden studded base at the bottom.

"Woah. I wonder what they used those for? I mean, these are real antiques from the war."

Jack shrugs. "Dunno, maybe they hid messages in them or something."

"Wait! Jack!!! You blooming genius!"

"I am?"

"Your phone!"

"I thought that was a bad thing?" replies Jack.

"It is, but maybe we can locate Uncle Finch using your phone!"

"And how on earth do we do that?"

"We can't. But maybe we can ask for help."

"Who from?" asks Jack.

"It'll mean spilling the beans to my mum, but I bet she knows someone at her work who could get their hands on tech like that. They are arms manufacturers, but they'll do all that triangulation stuff."

"Where is your Mom?"

"Perfect! She's at a work's ball this evening. We'll go there now and tell her the whole story. See if she can get someone to help!"

"Where is it?"

"Ooh, she left the address on the fridge!"

Barnaby and Jack rush upstairs to collect the address.

"Here it is, The Dent Building on Pine Street, forty-fifth floor," reads Barnaby.

"Okay. Wait, forty-fifth floor? How do we select a floor? Do we have any height dimensions on the app?" asks Jack.

"Let's go find out," replies Barnaby.

Back downstairs, and Barnaby checks the app's input fields to see if they can select a floor to jump into.

"Nope nothing, I guess it's too risky. If we get the coordinates wrong, we'd jump into thin air, two hundred feet up above New York."

"So we have to start from the ground then?" queries Jack.

"Yeah, but we'll need to get past their security," explains Barnaby.

"Jeez dude, calm down! A son wanting his mummy is a perfectly valid reason to gain entry, or even for her to come downstairs. This isn't *Mission Impossible* you know!"

"Fair point!" concedes Barnaby.

"Okay, give me the coordinates," says Jack, grabbing the time machine.

"40°42'26.7"N 74°00'32.8"W. Let's set it to 9 pm, so it's less busy for our arrival."

"Done!" shouts Jack as he grabs Barnaby's shoulder and hits 'Jump'.

Barnaby falls forward a little and bumps into the wall of a darkened room, as the rumble from the jump subsides.

"Well thanks for the warning!!" screams Barnaby.

"You're welcome," grins Jack, amused at Barnaby's face-plant into the wall.

Barnaby rubs his nose. "Where the hell are we?"

"Dunno, looks like some sort of conference room."

Jack walks over to the door, opens it and peers along the corridor outside. There are lights at the end of the hallway and muffled voices.

"Let's avoid going that way in case we get thrown out. We'll freak them out if they see us creeping around at this time of night," says Jack.

"Sure, what's up the other way?" asks Barnaby.

"Let's go find out!"

At the end of the corridor is a very dull and ordinary door, suggesting it perhaps leads to a stairwell, rather than an elegant meeting room. Upon opening, their suspicions are confirmed.

"Great! Up we go!" exclaims Jack.

"It's forty-five floors!" complains Barnaby.

"Elevators have security cameras dummy. This is our best bet!" explains Jack.

Barnaby produces a little whimper as the two start their long climb.

***

Upstairs, on the forty-fifth floor, Elizabeth is standing next to her workmate Karen on a raised section of the ballroom. Below them, over two hundred or so colleagues are in various stages of inebriation while either dancing, mingling or flirting with other colleagues. The ball has only been in full swing for two hours, but already inhibitions are being shed through copious amounts of vintage Dom Perignon champagne.

"Would you look at the state Brian Forster has gotten himself into," remarks Karen, who is wearing a full-length black evening gown. Her red hair is up and tied on the top of her head with clasps. One little curl hangs down the left-hand side of her face and is gently toying with her diamante earrings. The dress is Oscar de la Renta, bought for a one-off trip to the Oscars a few years back, but she's still capable of squeezing herself into it, having kept her mid-forties body in reasonable shape.

"Oh my God, he's normally so serious!" declares Elizabeth. She is wearing an equally long evening gown but in red. Her auburn hair is plaited down the back, accentuating her slim, yet long neck. Over her shoulder is a little sparkly clutch bag by Gucci that dangles on a precariously thin gold chain strap.

"He really thinks he's in with a chance at the young girl from HR. What's her name?"

"Bobbi," replies Elizabeth.

"Ah yes, Bobbi boob job," Karen adds. As attractive as she is, she does not respond well to competition from other pretty girls.

"I am not going to join you in any of your cat-fighting Karen Schmidt!" jokes Elizabeth, poking Karen in the ribs and laughing.

"Too bad! Oh look, there's Tom Kennedy, eek! Doesn't he look so handsome in a tux?"

Elizabeth thinks he looks like a complete creep, the kind of smarmy ladies man she's learned to avoid most of her life.

"Not my type!" she utters.

"Oh come on! Look at him, he's a dreamboat!" says an excitable Karen, who's started to do a little dance, as if the dancefloor had come to her. It's only a matter of minutes, thinks Elizabeth, before she's twisting that Oscar de la Renta down the stairs into Tom Kennedy's line of vision. Karen is quite the party girl.

"I'm going in," shrieks Karen, as she, Oscar and Dom Perignon twist their way down the stairs like an overly-ambitious python stalking a wild boar.

Not wishing to join in Karen's fun, Elizabeth opts to stay put. She's Senior Finance Executive here and no matter how much she'd like to join the party, she has to behave herself and retain an air of decorum. Still, it's fun to watch the others make a disgrace of themselves.

"Not joining the party Mrs Brown?"

Elizabeth turns around and comes face-to-face with Darius Dent himself.

At six foot two, she initially comes face-to-face with his chest. Slowly she follows the line of his tuxedo, all the way up to his gaunt but healthily tanned face and rugged chin. His eyes are blue and harsh, almost cold, but he softens it with a 60s style side parting that hangs down at the fringe almost into his right eye. In this light Elizabeth can clearly see the scar he has running from his right eye down to his cheek, a souvenir from a failed arms deal in Afghanistan.

"Oh, Mr Dent, you startled me!" shrieks Elizabeth, putting her hands to her chest.

"I'm terribly sorry, how inconsiderate of me," apologises Mr Dent with a deep New York society accent.

"Not at all, I was just a bit distracted by all of this," she remarks, pointing into the heart of the party.

"It is nice to watch from the sidelines, isn't it?"

"It's safer, I think," says Elizabeth, putting both her hands on the rail over which she is peering.

"So tell me, Elizabeth, oh, may I call you Elizabeth?" asks Dent.

"Oh, certainly, please do," she replies, enjoying the familiarity she is having with the mysterious, wealthy and famous Mr Dent.

"How have you enjoyed your first year with us? I'm sorry I haven't been available to greet you personally and I missed the ball last year."

"Good, yes, great actually! Everyone is very nice and professional, it's a really great organisation you have here!"

"And your earlier qualms about the nature of our business, have they subsided?"

"Oh, I wouldn't call them qualms?" says Elizabeth, trying to be polite.

"Then what would you call them?" probes Dent.

"Initial reservations, Mr Dent, which I put aside very quickly," clarifies Elizabeth.

"Not that quickly Elizabeth. In fact, I tried on three occasions to tempt you over to us before you finally came," Dent points out, while studying her facial responses.

"Third time lucky!" shrieks Elizabeth, before laughing a kind of snorty, piggy laugh and instantly feeling like a goofy fool.

"Well you're here now and that's the important thing," Dent adds, perhaps in an effort to make her feel a little less silly at her animal noises.

"Yes, well, it was a rather difficult period and I only decided to move when the time was right."

"Ah yes, your divorce," announces Dent, bluntly.

"Yes, that," replies Elizabeth, a little bit surprised at his familiarity.

"All done now? Able to move on?" quizzes Dent, perhaps still being a little bit too personal.

"Yes, all done now. All water under the bridge!"

"And your son, is it? How old is he?"

"He's fifteen, although sometimes he seems a lot older. He's a smart little cookie!"

"And who do you have looking after him tonight?"

"My brother, Mathias. They've really started to hit it off! Yes, they were doing a spot of sightseeing today, but now he's safely tucked up… on the dancefloor!" cries Elizabeth, as she sees Barnaby's face coming out of the crowd of revellers.

"You brought your son with you?" asks Dent.

"No, I.. no, he's supposed to be in bed!"

Barnaby and Jack rush up the stairs towards them, completely out of breath, having just ascended forty-five flights of stairs.

"Mum! Mum (pants), Mum (gasps), Uncle (wheezes), Finch…"

"What's the matter, darling? Is something wrong?"

"Your brother's been captured by Nazis," blurts out Jack in his usual heavy-handed fashion.

"What? Look, I'm really struggling to hear you, please come into this office and tell me what's going on," mutters Elizabeth, ushering the boys into the room behind them.

Darius Dent allows curiosity to get the better of him and follows them in, pouring the boys each a glass of water.

The two boys gulp down the water and then wait a few seconds to catch their breath.

"Okay, did you say something about Nazis?"

"Yes, they've got Uncle Finch!" declares Barnaby.

"I didn't think we had neo-nazis in New York," says Elizabeth turning to Dent.

"Not neo-nazis Mum, actual Nazis!"

"You've lost me," replies Elizabeth with a massive frown on her face.

Barnaby realises he's jumped the gun a bit.

"Tell her from the start dude!" Jack pipes up, nudging Barnaby.

"Yes, yes, I'm just coming to that," explains Barnaby, shoving Jack's arm away.

"Mum, remember the rumbling the other night? The smell? When we had words with him at the top of the basement stairs?"

"Yes, I remember darling, carry on," confirms Mum.

"Well, that was Uncle Finch jumping back in time using his time machine. That he invented. In the basement." Barnaby kind of fizzles out as mum looks bemused.

"Honestly, it's true! He invented a time machine and can leap wherever he wants!"

"Darling, I know you think you might have seen something that's made you THINK he has built a time machine, but there will be a perfectly good explanation for this."

"It's true Mrs B, we kinda went to the Moon launch with him," adds Jack.

"Did he put you up to this? Is this a big joke?" Elizabeth demands, as she stands up and puts her hands on her waist.

"No Mum, I'm being deadly serious. It works, he actually made it work. First, he took Momo to Siberia, then we all went to the Moon launch, then we went to England to watch the Spitfires take off and now he's in a prison somewhere in Jersey!"

"Who's we?"

"Myself, Jack, Marsha and Polly. The girls are still in Jersey. In 1942."

"You boys are in serious trouble if you do not tell me what is going…"

"Wait a moment, Elizabeth," interrupts Dent. "I'm Darius Dent, your mother's boss. I read people very well and you boys look VERY convinced by this."

"Look at what we're wearing Mum!"

133

"Hey, those are from the attic. Is this part of the joke?"

"Okay, let's take one thing at a time," Dent continues. "You say you were in Jersey. In 1942?"

"Yes!"

"So if your uncle is in prison, how did you get here?"

"We used the time machine!!" explains Barnaby.

"You have it with you?" asks Dent.

"Dude," Jack buts in, "we should have totally opened with that. Show them!"

Barnaby proceeds to pull the time machine out of his haversack.

"It's an iPad, strapped to a George Foreman grill!" exclaims Elizabeth in utter disbelief.

Barnaby looks to Jack, who nods.

"Show them," says Jack.

Barnaby awakens the iPad. The app is already open.

"Put your hand on my shoulder Mum. You too Mr Dent, we need your help."

Dent stands up and places his hand on Barnaby's shoulder, while shrugging and motioning for Elizabeth to do the same.

"Oh this is ridiculous!" utters Elizabeth, who is starting to wonder just how far they will take this 'prank'.

"Home or Jersey?" Barnaby asks Jack.

"Jersey will be more convincing," replies Jack.

"Come on Mum! Put your hand on my shoulder!"

Dent motions for her to do it.

Finally she reluctantly puts her hand on Barnaby's shoulder. Jack grabs on to Dent's arm, who gives Jack a quizzical look.

"Ready?" shouts Barnaby.

"Ready!" Jack answers.

"Okay, guys, try and stay on your feet!"

"What?" asks Mum.

"You'll see!" grins Barnaby as he locates the previous journey details in the app's history list and taps 'Jump'.

Chapter 11

When I get my hands on him!

"I did it again! Look!"

"You're really getting the hang of this dude. Oh, brother, look at your mom," replies Jack.

Elizabeth is lying face down, flat on the grass, her ball gown revealing a little too much of her legs and her clutch bag splayed out in front of her like a safety rope.

Darius Dent is getting up from his knees and brushing off the grass stains.

"What on earth was that?" shrieks Elizabeth from the ground.

Dent is chuckling away to himself as he starts to take in his surroundings.

Elizabeth is now trying to get to her feet. Dent rushes over to help her up.

"Here, allow me," he says, as she grabs on to his arm.

"Thanks!" accepts Elizabeth steadying herself while hanging on to Dent. She realises she is squinting, having just been in a dark room and now being blinded by what appears to be sunlight.

"It's true!" exclaims Dent with delight.

Elizabeth looks up as her eyes start to focus. She is standing on a hill, looking down towards a church. Two figures, that look like schoolgirls, are waving at her. Tentatively, almost robotically, she waves back. In her confused state, she looks at her arm as if to ask what it's doing.

"Is that Marsha? And Polly?"

"Yup!" replies Jack.

"Where the hell are we?"

"This is Jersey, Mum."

"I don't understand," says Elizabeth, as Dent helps her down the hill. She's very puzzled.

Then the penny drops.

"He did it. Mathias, he did it! He built an actual time machine!!" she cries, grabbing Dent's lapels.

"He sure did Mrs B!" confirms Jack.

"And here we are! In Jersey! In 1942?"

"Right again, Mrs B!"

"Nazi-occupied Jersey!"

"Yup!"

"My brother brought my son to Nazi-occupied Jersey!!!!" she's now screaming.

"Oops!" mumbles Jack, as he walks away from the becoming-more-hysterical-by-the-second woman.

"Mathias Finch when I get a hold of you!!"

"Mum, that's for later, right now we have to find a way to get him out of prison."

"Do you have a plan?" quizzes Dent.

"Yes, we'll explain when we get back to the house," replies Barnaby.

The group start to walk along to the church. As they arrive, Polly and Marsha are there to greet them.

"Hi, Mrs B!" welcomes Polly.

"Miss us?" asks Jack.

"You've only been gone a minute," answers Polly.

"Hehe, this is so messed up," mutters Jack, walking past the girls.

"Girls, this is Darius Dent, mum's boss. He's going to try and help us," shouts Barnaby, as he approaches them.

"Pleasure," Dent utters. He walks past them and follows Jack.

"We're just going back to the house for a bit, formulate the plan!"

"Whatever," Polly responds, eyeing the handsome Darius Dent up and down. She gives him a little wolf-whistle.

"Guys, grab my shoulders!" shouts Barnaby, catching up with the others.

Marsha and Polly watch the group huddle around each other and then disappear in the now familiar fashion, as the ground rumbles beneath their feet.

"Seems kinda normal now," declares Polly.

"Yeah. Totally," replies Marsha. "Anyway, they'll be back in five… four… three… two…"

***

In the basement, Elizabeth is once more picking herself up with assistance from Dent.

"Where are we? I mean, when are we now?"

"Back to the day we left, only it's now 2:30 pm. Uncle Finch set it up so every time we leap back, it's five seconds apart. It's to stop us smashing into ourselves somewhere in space or something like that," Barnaby attempts to explain.

"Well that's good to know!" says a dizzy Elizabeth, holding on to a workbench.

"That was unbelievable!" grins Dent. "Are there any limitations to where you can go with this thing?"

Barnaby shrugs. "We've only visited two time periods so far. I guess you could go anywhere or any... when!"

"Incredible. Imagine what you could do with this! You could transport entire platoons behind enemy lines, you could put mining equipment straight onto new planets! The possibilities are endless. We could rid the world of all tyranny, transport aid to nations instantly! This could make DDent Industries the most powerful corporation on the planet!"

"Only if Uncle Finch wants to sell it to you though, surely?"

"My dear boy, look around this room. Does this look like a well-funded operation to you?"

"Em, no, not really," concedes Barnaby.

"No. I could set up a laboratory that would make your uncle the most subsidised scientist that ever existed. He'd be able to use his creative talents to the absolute maximum!"

"I don't know, he's not big on riches, as you say. Just look around this room. Our family is pretty well off. He doesn't seem to need wealth," explains Barnaby.

"Everybody wants riches, boy. Even your uncle can't refuse the kind of financial support I could offer him. He could create anything he puts his mind to without limitation, even if he does decide to continue living like a reclusive mole."

"Hey, my uncle is not a mole!" states an irritated Barnaby.

Dent slowly rotates around the room, his arms outstretched while all the time watching Barnaby as if to say, 'of course your uncle is a mole'.

Barnaby doesn't entirely trust Dent. There's just something about him. The way he stares, his eyes cold and lifeless, almost looking through him into the distance as if Barnaby were not there.

"So boy! What's your big plan?" quizzes Dent, putting an arm around Barnaby's shoulder.

Barnaby wriggles free, looking bothered.

"We were hoping you'd be able to triangulate Jack's phone, which is in Uncle Finch's haversack."

"And then?" enquires Dent, leaning closer.

"Well, that's really as far as we got. What we can't do is shoot guards and stuff."

"Obviously boy, obviously, that would likely alter our present day. Wait, why does his uncle have your phone?" asks Dent, turning to Jack.

"It's a long story," replies Jack. "Actually, it's not. I mixed the bags up. I do that a lot."

"How fortunate for Mr Finch that his nephew has such a clumsy friend," states Dent, bearing a broad grin.

"Hey! Don't call me…"

"Yup, he IS super clumsy," interrupts Barnaby in agreement.

Jack looks put out.

Dent ponders for a moment.

"Yes, the plan is an obvious one. We'll need some mini transmitters and a locator, plus a small team armed with tranquiliser guns. Once we locate your uncle, we'll leap in, put the guards to sleep and be off with him."

"That simple, huh?" remarks Jack, unconvinced.

"Yes, that simple!"

"So how do you plan to set up your transmitters? Won't you have to place them in a special pattern around the prison? And won't that look odd to any passing Nazis?

141

Remember, all radios were banned on the island," explains Jack.

"Yes, the special 'pattern' you refer to is called a… triangle, and of course we will devise a way of positioning them secretly. My men will have forged identification documents so they will be able to move freely. Trust me, dear boy, I have 'departments' who specialise in this kind of thing."

"And no harm will come to Mathias?" adds Elizabeth. "I need him to be in good health when I wring his scrawny little neck!"

"You have my word, Elizabeth," replies Dent.

"Alright!" declares Barnaby. "When do we start?"

"No time like the present," Dent responds. "Actually, that's not strictly true anymore is it?" He chuckles to himself.

"So what do we do first?" asks Jack.

"Give me the time machine and I'll arrange everything," instructs Dent.

"Oh, no way. This is not leaving my sight!" barks Barnaby.

"Alright then, those that want to tag along, please do. Firstly, we need to return to the time when we started. Can't suddenly appear to be in two places at once, can we Elizabeth?"

"No, not at all," replies Elizabeth, who is now just about able to focus properly.

Barnaby brings up the Pine Street address.

"Right, link up and let's go. Mum, just try and put a steady foot forward as we go and hopefully you can stay upright."

"I'll sure try!" Elizabeth responds with an air of scepticism.

The group grab each other's shoulders and Barnaby sends them back to the conference room on the first floor.

Everyone manages to stay upright, except Elizabeth, who falls forward, face-first into a whiteboard.

"Hahahaha, nice move, Mrs B," laughs Jack.

Elizabeth turns around and, to the gang's delight, finds that her face is now smeared with non-permanent ink that was once a rather crudely drawn flow-chart on the board.

Jack sniggers and heads to the door, which he opens and peers around.

"The coast is clear!"

Dent pushes past and starts to walk up the corridor towards the light. He stops, turns and motions to a surprised Jack.

"Well, what are we waiting for?" asks Dent.

"There are security guys up there!" protests Jack.

Dent sighs.

"I own the building?"

"Oh yeah," mutters a sheepish Jack.

The group trot along behind Dent as he leads them out into the foyer of the building towards the lifts.

"Good evening, Harrison," says Dent to one of the guards at the security gate.

"Good evening, Mr Dent," he replies, as he opens the gate and allows the group to pass through.

"Just glad we don't have to climb those forty-odd floors again," whispers Jack to Barnaby.

Dent pulls out his phone and after a few taps, raises it to his ear.

"Alpha? This is Delta. I have a task for the team. I'll text you the details via the scrambler. Meet me in the boardroom in one hour once you have confirmation that my requirements are being processed." He immediately hangs up, not waiting for a response. He's obviously used to his demands being met instantly.

The lift door opens to the sound of dance music and flashing disco lights.

Dent leads the way and the group set off back to the boardroom.

"Wait!" shouts Barnaby.

The group turn to him, only to find him pushing them all into the nearest office. Sensing something is up, they allow themselves to be corralled.

"What is it Barnaby?" asks Elizabeth.

"You're here!" cries Barnaby.

"I know that Barnaby," comes her surprised response.

"No, look," he says, as he slightly parts the office blinds.

Sure enough, there is Elizabeth standing next to her friend Karen. They are on the mezzanine level overlooking the temporary dance floor.

"Oh my God! That's me!! Hey, this dress DOES look good on me!"

Jack rushes over, shoving Elizabeth out of the way for a better look.

"Crikes!" exclaims Jack. "How did that happen?"

"Of course!" shrieks Barnaby. "We've arrived shortly after we did the last time. That means you and I are still climbing the stairs!"

"Even more interesting is that this hasn't caused some sort of catastrophic event!" adds Dent.

"This could have gone sooooo wrong. We need to be more careful in future. But yes, it appears we can inhabit the same space after all!" remarks Barnaby, still peering through the blinds.

"We're going to have to wait it out here until we know for sure that we've all jumped back to 1942," Dent points out. "Then everything can carry on as normal."

"So, how do we know for sure when we've gone?" asks Elizabeth.

"You'll feel it," continues Barnaby.

Sure enough, after an agonising twelve-minute wait, the room shakes as a rumble passes through it, knocking the office owner's family picture off of the desk onto the floor.

"That's it!" declares Barnaby, as he pulls open the door. Outside the revellers have paused, wondering what just happened. A massive rumble in a New York office tower could have sinister origins, post 9/11.

Dent takes the lead and makes his way onto the dancefloor, just as the music stops. The crowd are looking at each other in bewilderment. On one part of the floor, Elizabeth spots Karen, who is hanging around the neck of Tom Kennedy like a damsel in distress, overplaying her need to be held.

"You three head up to the boardroom, I'll handle this," instructs Dent. He outstretches his arms and pushes his way into the middle of the crowd.

"Ladies and gentlemen, I hope the work being carried out on the floor above hasn't startled you, but now that I have your attention, I'd like to thank you all for coming tonight, to celebrate our twentieth anniversary…"

"God he's good," remarks Jack, ushering Barnaby and Elizabeth up the stairs to the boardroom.

From there they can hear cheers, as Dent continues to rally his loyal office troops into an excited frenzy. A different kind of troop will be assembled soon!

Five minutes later and Dent rejoins the group.

"Sorry about that," Dent apologises, as he sits down at the head of the table. "Now, what can you tell me about this machine? How does it work?"

Barnaby shrugs. "We're not entirely sure. Uncle Finch was trying to build a teleport machine. Somehow, he discovered it can also move through time."

"It must take tremendous energy to do what it does. What does he use to power it?"

"Dude, it's an alien crystal!" Jack exclaims, his eyes lighting up.

"An alien crystal?" enquires Elizabeth disbelievingly.

"Really? That bit surprises you?" says Jack.

"Where did he get it?" Dent continues.

"We're not sure of that either. All we know is that some of it is made from stuff that's not on the periodic table," explains Barnaby.

"Interesting." Dent, rubs his chin. He is interrupted as his phone rings in his pocket.

"Alpha, is everything moving?" asks Dent.

He listens for a moment.

"Excellent. No, no, just assemble. On second thoughts, don't bother meeting us here, we'll come to you. What's the ETA? 11:30, good." Dent hangs up.

"I assume we're not going to bother hanging around here?" enquires Barnaby.

"Precisely," confirms Dent. "Set your machine to this address. 85 St Nicholas Terrace, New York, NY 10031, USA. Time, 11:25pm."

Barnaby pulls out the time machine and punches in the address.

"What is this place?" quizzes Barnaby.

"My state-of-the-art research facility."

"Sweet," adds Jack. "Is it full of laser guns and poisonous satellites and stuff?"

"No. I'm not a Bond villain," comes the stark reply from Dent.

"Ah nuts!" grumbles Jack. Dent finds this odd little boy very amusing.

"Before we go," Dent continues, "how do we avoid being sent into a concrete overpass or something?"

"Uncle Finch has added an intelligent scan into the software. It looks at our surroundings and pops you in the safest possible place."

"I say, he really has thought of everything, hasn't he?"

"Thankfully!" adds Elizabeth. "That still won't save him when I get my hands on him!"

Jack gives a little chuckle.

"Okay everyone, link up! You know the drill," instructs Barnaby.

The group grab arms and Barnaby hits the 'Jump' button.

Chapter 12
The facility

"Did it again!" Barnaby announces, delighted to be on his feet once more. It's a short-lived triumph though, as Elizabeth stumbles into him and knocks him to the ground.

"Sorry darling!" Elizabeth apologises as she helps Barnaby to his feet.

The group have jumped into the heart of Dent's research facility, a sprawling village of futuristic glass structures, connected by a network of paths and highly manicured lawns and trees that are now tastefully lit in a variety of colours.

"Wow!" exclaims Jack. "Are you sure this is the right year? This is amazing!"

"This is where all of my technology is born," explains Dent. "The ideal place to create and, hopefully, somewhere your uncle would like to continue his work."

Barnaby is doubtful.

The group saunter up the path leading to the main research facility. A large metal sign, headed with Dent's corporate logo of two interlocking 'D's', sits to the right of the entrance, below which are the words 'Group Military Research Centre'.

Two armed security guards instantly open the door for Dent, and the group move towards the reception. This is also manned by two stern-looking gentlemen, one of whom stands up as they approach.

"Three passes with Level One clearance," requests Dent. The man immediately punches some data into his computer, which is hidden by the large desk.

"Name," says the guard to Elizabeth.

"Elizabeth Brown."

"Look into the camera please." He motions to a black ball on a metal arm that rises from the desk.

Elizabeth stares forward, fluffing her hair slightly and pouting as the guard fiddles below the desk. She is then handed a plastic card with a security strip on it and the Dent logo. She looks at it and is dismayed to find it neither contains her name or her picture. This is obviously stored on the system and somehow linked to the reusable card she has been handed.

The process continues for the two boys before the party is ushered to the security turnstile.

"You are required to swipe your card upon entering each room within the facility. Failure to do so will result in you being removed from the entire complex," explains the guard, sternly.

"We obviously take our security very seriously," adds Dent. "So no wandering off. Clear?"

"Crystal!" replies Jack.

"Right, let's go." Dent swipes himself through and awaits the others on the opposite side. As each one enters there is a beep and a green light appears on a display next to them. Barnaby is last to pass through and as he does the light flashes red.

"It's all right," says Dent, waving away the guards. "I can vouch for the contents of his bag."

The guards allow the group to proceed.

"How did I set off the alarm?" asks Barnaby.

"The time machine in your bag, dear boy. The scanner checks for weapons and foreign objects," explains Dent.

The party makes their way to a group of four lifts. Dent approaches number three and presses the call button. It opens immediately, having been used recently by exiting staff.

As the doors close, Dent swipes his card on a panel before motioning to the others to do the same. Their destination is the eighth floor, but Barnaby can see there are sixteen buttons. Eight of them are BELOW level one. How intriguing. He wonders what goes on down there.

"Why do we all have to swipe?" enquires Jack.

"It's a smart lift. It won't proceed until we've all presented our passes."

"That must be annoying if there are twenty people in the lift!" chuckles Elizabeth.

"It only takes one person to infiltrate this complex," replies a stern-faced Dent. "We have some clients who require the utmost security. The US Government in particular."

Jack is now getting quite excited about what may lie within these walls. Perhaps not laser guns and poisonous satellites, but there HAS to be cool stuff somewhere.

On the eighth floor they are met by one of Dent's personnel, a huge well-built man dressed in black army fatigues, armed with a sidearm holster containing an equally black pistol.

"Is everything ready?"

"Yes, sir," replies the man, who Dent does not introduce.

The group walk down a long corridor before entering a room that contains three other personnel, one dressed in black like the first man, and two dressed in 1940's attire of grey suits, ties and trilby hats. Behind them sits a stack of metallic flight cases. It's a very boring room with grey walls, the odd workstation and a large table with a matte glass surface that is backlit by white lights.

"Do you have the papers?" Dent enquires.

"Right here," says one of the other men. From a folder, he produces eight brown card documents and hands them to Dent.

"These are very good!" The man bows slightly in return. "And you're positive these are a match for the historical documents?"

"One hundred per cent, sir."

"Right, let's get our photos taken," announces Dent, as he passes the cards back. At the side of the room there is a grey curtain running the full length. One of the men ushers the group towards it.

"This will make the ideal backdrop," states Dent. He removes his tuxedo jacket and bow tie and straightens himself.

Man number three raises what looks like a futuristic polaroid camera and snaps Dent's photo. A small square of card pops from the bottom, which Dent takes and proceeds to wave in the air.

"This camera is calibrated to replicate the original one used to produce these identity documents. We've used it many times to gain us access to under-developed countries." Dent continues to wave the card.

After a minute he hands the card to Elizabeth.

"That's amazing! It looks like it was taken in the 1940's!" she responds, "But fresh!"

"You'd be surprised just how outdated the equipment is in some African nations," adds Dent with a smile. He takes the card back from her and hands it to man number two, who takes it over to the light-table to trim down and stick onto one of the forged documents. Five minutes later, the same man is handing them their Jersey ID documents.

"How on earth did you turn these around so quick?" asks Jack, examining his card.

"We have some very skilled personnel in this building. This authentic look can only be achieved by a few people in this city and fortunately they all work for me!"

"Incredible," remarks Elizabeth, admiring Dent's minion's work.

Dent turns to his four operatives, who are awaiting his next command.

"Some of you may have been wondering why these documents are dated 1942. Well, believe it or not, that is when our extraction is taking place." The four men briefly look at each other, confused, before refocusing on Dent's words.

"Gentlemen, we're going back in time. Please leave all of your side-arms here. Tranquilisers only, we CANNOT encounter losses on either side here, do you understand?"

After some more glancing, the lead man responds with an "Affirmative!"

"Barnaby?"

"What?"

"Your turn. Tell these men all they need to know to ensure we and our equipment arrive intact."

"Well," begins Barnaby. He pulls the time machine from his haversack, embarrassed at being shoved into the limelight. "My uncle, the man we're going to rescue, says that the device knows what to bring and what to leave behind. Just sitting on one of these cases won't bring it with us, we have to be actually holding it. Other than that,

154

like Mr Dent says, we cannot interfere with past events. When we jump back, you'll experience a sort of dizziness and you'll feel like you're falling over, so make sure you have a strong foot forward. It's sort of like being pushed from behind."

"Well done Barnaby!" Dent now resumes the lead of the conversation. "We'll be setting up a command centre in a wooded area at the back of a local church. From there, we will require Davis and Sheppard here to enter St. Helier and scan two buildings for a mobile phone signal, which is concealed near our main target." Davis and Sheppard are the ones in the 40's attire.

"Once we have located Mr Finch, we will send in Crowe and Vasquez to make the extraction, along with young Barnaby here," continues Dent, patting Barnaby on the head.

"Wait!" shrieks Elizabeth. "You're not seriously considering sending my son into a Nazi prison!!"

"Mrs Brown, your son has had multiple experiences with this machine. He knows its quirks and the inner workings of the software. We'll need to react at speed, and Barnaby is our best bet for success. I assure you, these two gentlemen will keep him completely secure. He'll also be able to correctly identify your brother, should the need arise."

"No, I absolutely forbid it!!" screams Elizabeth.

"Mum!" shouts Barnaby, pushing her against a wall, "I can do this! I have a time machine for goodness sake!! If it looks ropey, I can jump away at any point."

Elizabeth is clearly not happy.

"Well, I'm coming too!" Elizabeth exclaims.

"You'll need to stay at the command centre I'm afraid Ma'am," adds Crowe, the team lead.

"No, I need to be with my son!"

"Ma'am, the fewer people we send in the better, you'd just be one more person to protect. Relax, we have this all in hand."

"You guys don't seem phased by time travel at all!" observes Jack.

Crowe smirks.

"Elizabeth, this is the only way we can bring your brother back alive. As long as he remains there, our presence in this time zone is precarious. They are the best extraction team in the U.S. and your son is the most experienced handler of this time machine. There is no better option for us, believe me," adds Dent.

Elizabeth sighs. Her shoulders slump in submission.

"Alright, let's move," commands Dent. Vasquez hands him a forties style sports jacket. He links arms with Elizabeth, Jack and Barnaby. The four other men throw their tranquiliser guns onto their shoulders and pick up one of the four flight-cases. They place their left hands on the person's shoulder to their left and Barnaby completes the circle by grabbing Crowe's sleeve.

"Ready?"

Ater a collective nod from the group, Barnaby once more hits 'Jump'.

Chapter 13
Locating an Uncle

"...one," counts Marsha.

One second later eight people appear followed by a loud rumble and the smell of electrical discharge. To Polly and Marsha, it seems louder and more intense than usual. Perhaps this is due to the size of the group.

"Five seconds exactly," confirms Polly, nodding.

The four members of the extraction team stumble forward but remain standing. Jack is impressed.

"Quite something, isn't it gentlemen?" announces Dent.

"Yes, sir!" replies Crowe as he squints into the sun.

"Right then, let's set up base," insists Dent, motioning to the rear of the cemetery.

"Look alive people," shouts Crowe. He picks up one of the flight cases and starts running in the direction that Dent has indicated. The other three grab a case each and join in pursuit.

"Come on Poll," says Jack.

Polly bursts a gum bubble and nonchalantly follows her brother, with Marsha joining the rear.

At the top of the cemetery, Barnaby steers the group over the tumbledown wall and into the heart of the wooded area. He takes care to direct them away from the place where the backup time machine is hidden, having decided to keep its existence a secret for the time being.

The four soldiers lay the cases flat on the ground and open them up. Inside each are a series of electrical devices and wooden poles, all encapsulated in moulded protective foam. They immediately begin to assemble and calibrate the equipment.

"Everything checks out fine, sir," Crowe announces with a thumbs up.

Dent pulls out a map of St. Helier and lays it flat on top of one of the now-closed cases.

"Right, we have two potential spots, Newgate Street and Silvertide. We're going to have to hike there as we can't risk jumping into the area," explains Dent as he points out the various places on the map. "Silvertide is a forty-minute walk from here by road, but we're going to have to use the fields until the curfew lifts at seven. If he is not at that location, we'll move on to Newgate Street prison."

"Can't we just jump a bit closer and save ourselves a walk?" enquires Jack.

"No," replies Dent. "We have no reconnaissance data from this period. We could leap straight into a minefield or worse. I'm afraid you'll just have to burn off a few calories," says Dent as he walks past Jack and taps his tummy.

"Hey! I'm not fat!"

"Yet!" teases Dent over his shoulder.

Davis and Sheppard slip their devices into canvas fishing rod holders, leaving a section of wooden pole protruding. It gives the impression of two fishermen on their morning trip to the harbour. Their tranquiliser guns are now strapped across their backs, covered by their forties-style suit jackets.

Polly, Marsha, Elizabeth, Crowe and Vasquez stay behind out of sight.

"Be careful, darling!" shouts Elizabeth, as the rest of the males head off down the cemetery towards the road.

Their route to Silvertide takes them across the field where Uncle Finch was captured, down onto the back streets, safe in the knowledge that the curfew period has now ended. They then head towards the main A4 road into St. Helier.

As they reach the bottom of the Rue du Hocq, the coast unfurls in front of them, along with the Le Hocq round tower, where they get their first glimpse of German troops. There is an armoured vehicle sat at the base of the tower and the group can clearly see two soldiers on top of it, dressed in the standard M40 Wehrmacht infantry uniform.

"Look!" shrieks a delighted Jack, "More Nazis!"

"Calm down boy," whispers Dent. "Try not to draw attention us."

As they start to wander along the main coastal road an odd thing happens. One of the German soldiers on the tower gives them a friendly wave. Dent replies with an equally friendly morning wave and the two boys eagerly copy him.

"They don't seem that bad!" remarks Barnaby.

"They'd seem bad enough if they looked in your haversack," replies Dent.

As their walk continues along the coast, it becomes painfully apparent that avoiding German soldiers will be utterly impossible. The entire shoreline has troops stationed every two or three hundred metres with occasional camouflaged gun placements. Dent, however, feels quite safe hiding in plain sight. What kind of lunatic on a mission would march through these troops, other than one with a death wish!

After half an hour of nail-biting walking, with the occasional wave to local wives hanging out washing or men off to work, they reach the Hotel De Normandie and the junction onto Havre des Pas.

"Okay, our target is close-by. Davis, Sheppard, split up and find somewhere secure to start searching for the boy's phone. We'll meet back here in ten minutes," instructs Dent.

"Right away, sir," replies Davis, as he crosses the street and disappears around the back of the White Horse Inn. Sheppard goes in the opposite direction, across another road to a lane which runs parallel with the main street.

Dent, Jack and Barnaby continue on along the Havre des Pas, past Silvertide itself, where two armed soldiers stand to attention outside what is actually a very nondescript and narrow three-storey seaside townhouse. Parked in the street is a black *Morris 8* automobile, the only car visible, most likely requisitioned from a local owner and gifted to the German Secret Police who occupy the Silvertide address.

"Is this it?" asks Barnaby in a hushed tone, trying not to look at the two guards as they walk past.

"Not very ostentatious, is it?" Dent responds, as quietly as he can, his heart thumping in his chest.

"Huh?" replies Jack, whose vocabulary is devoid of the word 'ostentatious'.

"He means," explains Barnaby, "you'd have thought it would be a lot grander for an organisation of such power."

"Well," Jack continues, "they are, after all, the 'Secret Police'!" Dent turns to Jack and grins, enjoying his logic. At the end of the row of tightly-packed buildings, they make their way down onto the beach. Jack and Barnaby spend five minutes picking up and admiring seashells and skimming pebbles on the water to kill some time, as Dent looks on, occasionally checking his watch.

"Boys! Come on, time to go!" shouts Dent after ten minutes of boredom, having given his team enough time to have completed their task. The boys run back towards him tossing away their collection of fairly dull-looking shells. There was a time when this treasure would have come home with them.

"I wonder if they've found Uncle Finch," ponders Barnaby.

"Fingers crossed! The old guy has sure dropped us slap bang in the middle of a big adventure!" replies Jack, as the two boys catch up with Dent, who is now striding across the beach to the main road.

"Yes, who would have thought the day I met you on the bus that all this would happen?" Barnaby grins.

"Hehe, certainly beats a farting competition!" Jack adds.

Back at the meeting point, both Davis and Sheppard are waiting for them.

"Well?" enquires Dent.

"Positive signal sir, the target is in the building," reports Davis.

"Excellent." Dent ushers the group back along the way they have just come. "Let's return to base and prep for the extraction."

"Are we going to leap back, Mr Dent?" asks Jack.

"Boy, do you have something against exercise?"

"No, it's just that I think we might be pushing our luck walking past all of these Nazis again!"

"Wehrmacht!" replies Dent, growing tired of pointing out Jack's mistake. "But you're right, it's a risk I think we don't need to take."

Dent moves alongside Davis.

"Is it secluded at the back of that inn?"

"Yes, sir," Davis answers.

"Okay, this way," instructs Dent, diverting the group towards the lane at the back. It is indeed secluded, hemmed in by the sea wall, a garage and a high garden wall behind the houses on Havre des Pas.

"Do you mind if I give the machine a try?" Dent asks Barnaby.

"Um. Okay." Barnaby reaches into his rucksack.

He allows Dent to take the time machine and walks him through the process.

"These are our recent destinations," Barnaby continues, pointing at the menus on the screen, "and this is the time setting. If you want to adjust the time, just tap in here."

"This is incredibly simple," Dent remarks. "Maybe you don't need to join us in the extraction!"

"My mum would love that!" replies Barnaby.

"And I just hit here?"

"Yes, the 'Jump' button."

"Right. I'll set the time to now. No point tempting fate and running into ourselves from earlier. Okay, let's go!" commands Dent and the group all link arms.

The cemetery reappears before them and the party heads back up towards the others at the base. Elizabeth is delighted to see them all return.

"Well?"

"Success Mrs Brown, we've located your brother!" Dent joyfully announces.

"Wonderful!" she replies.

"Crowe, Vasquez, it's a narrow building, six main rooms in total. Obviously we have no idea where he's

163

being held, so we'll go in on the ground floor, tranquilise all targets in succession and secure the location," plans Dent.

The four soldiers take out their tranquiliser guns and arm them.

"Right, form a circle," orders Crowe, "we need eyes on all areas of the room. Get ready to shoot on sight. We'll have the element of surprise on our side."

"Good luck!" says Elizabeth, longing for this all to be over.

"Don't wait up!" Dent smirks, as he readies the time machine.

"You're not going Barnaby?" asks Elizabeth.

"No, I gave Mr Dent a crash course. He's going to drive," replies Barnaby.

"Ready in three, two, one," Crowe declares, at which point Dent hits the 'Jump' button and the five men disappear from sight.

"Get ready for Uncle Finch!" cries Barnaby, excitedly grabbing Elizabeth's arm.

Polly starts the countdown.

"Five, four, three, two, one…"

Nothing.

There is a moment as the group, half smiling, stand awaiting the return of the six men.

Still nothing.

"Give it a moment," says Barnaby.

A moment is given.

Elizabeth is the first to look confused.

"Shouldn't they, like, be here by now?" asks Polly.

"Yes," replies Barnaby. He walks around the jump space, afraid of being landed on by the group, and surveys the length of the cemetery to the original jump spot.

"They're not there either," frowns Barnaby.

"Something's not right," adds Marsha.

"This can only mean one thing," announces Barnaby, as he grabs at tufts of his hair with both hands.

"They've failed," nods Jack.

"They can't have failed, they're a crack unit apparently!" exclaims Elizabeth.

"Well they're clearly not here!" screams Barnaby, waving his arms. "They would have come right back! There's no reason for them not to have come right back! The quickest way for them to return, without rekeying, is to jump straight back to the starting point!"

"Oh God!" exclaims Elizabeth. "Have I just killed my boss?"

"It's not your fault, Mum!" responds a dejected Barnaby. "We thought we were dealing with the best. Apparently not!"

"Barnaby?" asks Elizabeth.

"What?"

"How on Earth do we get back home?"

"Oh we're fine, we have another time machine," Barnaby answers.

"You do?" squeaks Elizabeth in a high-pitched voice, and then clears her throat.

"Yeah, we were worried things might go wrong, so we brought the prototype with us as a backup plan. It's hidden under a bush over there." He points to the other side of the small area of woods.

"So what do we do now?" enquires Marsha.

"I don't know!" shrieks Barnaby, who is clearly very frustrated at the turns of events.

"Maybe we just head back home and see if we can work out what happened?" suggests Marsha.

"I vote for that!" says Jack.

"Me too!" seconds Polly.

Barnaby continues to stare down to the bottom of the cemetery.

"I was sure these guys would succeed," mutters Barnaby quietly, now quite dejected.

Jack places his hand on Barnaby's shoulder.

"Hey, there's nothing more we can do here. We're not soldiers, we don't have tranquiliser guns. Let's just go back and think about how we're going to fix this, huh?"

"Yeah, I guess you're right." Barnaby turns around, his shoulders now hunched forward.

Dismayed, the remaining group slowly wander over to the other time machine and drag the case out from under the bushes. Barnaby opens the case and powers up the iPad.

"Oh thank God!" Barnaby heaves a sigh of relief as he views the Leaper app.

"What?" asks Jack.

"Our home coordinates are stored. There's no way we could have recovered those without the internet," replies a very relieved Barnaby.

"Oh yeah, I never thought of that," adds Jack, realising that would have been VERY bad.

"Let's set it to 10 pm, I think we could all do with going to bed," suggests Elizabeth.

"But we've got to come up with a plan!" insists Barnaby.

"We can do that in the morning, Barnaby. Let's just go home, get some sleep and tackle this fresh tomorrow," continues Elizabeth.

"Yes Mum," he mutters, conceding to the request.

He taps away at the app and then motions for the group to link up, which they do.

Barnaby takes one last look down the cemetery before finally, and very unwillingly, hitting the 'Jump' button.

"What the?" cries Barnaby, as the rumbling subsides.

The group survey the scene.

"Dude, it's all gone!" shouts Jack.

They are standing in an almost empty basement. The workbenches are still there, as are the bookcases and filing cabinets, but all of Uncle Finch's equipment, his books and notes, the alien crystal, everything else is gone.

"I don't understand!" says a bewildered Barnaby.

"Someone's been here!" Marsha declares, as she wanders over to the main workbench.

"But that's not possible!" adds Barnaby. "We're the only people who know about this stuff!"

167

Jack grabs Barnaby's arm.

"Dude, no we're not."

"Yes, but they're in…" Barnaby halts. The penny drops.

"What?" asks an impatient Elizabeth.

"He didn't. He couldn't have!" yells Barnaby in a borderline rage.

Jack nods.

"Oh, what a complete scumbag!!" shouts Barnaby, kicking a filing cabinet.

"Will someone please tell me what you're talking about?" Elizabeth screams. "Who else knew about this?"

"Mum, this is Dent and his cronies. They've been back and taken all of the equipment."

"No, that can't be right. He wouldn't leave us there! That's ridiculous!" says Elizabeth with a half-laugh.

"Mum, I think he did just that!"

"No, no that's not right. He knew we would use the other time machine to come back. Maybe one of his men was hurt or…"

"Mum, Dent didn't know about the other time machine. We didn't tell him."

Elizabeth stands for a moment, her mouth hanging open.

"What is it with bloody men!!!!!?" she shrieks.

"Calm down, Mum," replies Barnaby.

"First your dad walks out, then your stupid uncle drags you into a war zone and now this! My own bloody boss left me stranded in World War Two with a bunch of kids!!"

"He's a billionaire warmonger, it's not that surprising," Polly remarks.

"When I get my hands on him, I'll…"

"Mum, please, calm down. He's an incredibly powerful man who now has a time machine. God knows what havoc he can reap. We'll come up with a plan, but as far as he knows we've probably all died of old age or are in a concentration camp, so we have the upper hand now."

"What a devious snake!" screams Elizabeth, pacing around the room.

"Guys," says Barnaby to his friends, "you better head home and get some sleep and we'll reconvene in the morning. Mum, let's get you a glass of whisky."

"Suits me, I'm exhausted," sighs Jack, who has been up a lot longer than the girls. For them it's only really 12:30 in the afternoon.

"I'm still wide awake," Marsha exclaims. "I can't believe it's 10 pm".

"Jet-lag, or rather, time-lag," replies Barnaby.

"Okay, off you go upstairs kids and get changed back into your normal clothes and we'll see you tomorrow," orders Elizabeth, ushering Jack, Polly and Marsha towards the stairs.

The three trot off to get changed.

"Come on, Mum, let's get you that whisky!"

Moments later, Barnaby's three chums slam the front door behind them. Not on purpose, it's just a loose heavy door.

In the living room, Elizabeth sits on the couch, her head resting on the glass of whisky in her hands.

"I can't believe he did that. I knew he was a bit crooked but still," groans Elizabeth, taking a sip of whisky and wincing.

"We'll make it right, Mum, you'll see." Barnaby reassuringly places his hand on her shoulder.

Elizabeth holds his hand.

"You're a good boy. The only good one in my life, it seems."

Maybe Elizabeth still partially blames her father for the car crash. It certainly would explain her attitude towards men, perhaps what finally drove her husband away, and could even be the reason her relationship with Uncle Finch is so prickly.

Barnaby lifts his hand away and pops it and the other in his pockets.

"It's not going to be easy Mum, sorting all of this, but I think the good guys always win. All we need is a little bit of luck."

In Barnaby's right pocket, he feels something rectangular and plastic.

"Mum!"

Chapter 14

Rescuing an Uncle

"What?" Mum is confused by Barnaby's exclamation.

"Look!" Barnaby pulls out the security pass from Dent's research facility and holds it to her face.

"Oh my! I must still have mine also!" remembers Mum, and reaching for her purse, pulls out her version.

"This is it! This is how we get in!" Barnaby cries, as he starts to pace the room. "We've got level one clearance still. Dent won't delete these because as far as he knows they're stuck in 1942 with us!"

"Yes, but surely their security will notice them missing and delete them from their system?"

"Eventually! But we have all the time we need! We can jump in, find Uncle Finch and the time machine and jump out!"

"Barnaby, Barnaby," interrupts Mum, shaking her head. "If only it were that easy. They'll have the time machine in a vault if they're not using it, and they'll probably not keep Uncle Finch at the facility. I think we may have to face the fact that they've won."

"No!" yells Barnaby. "We can go in, hide somewhere until we can reach Uncle Finch and then devise a plan with him. We can ask him to signal when he's alone with the time machine and then we'll just grab him and go."

"Actually, that does sound feasible," admits Elizabeth, defeated by Barnaby's protestations. "Alright, you head up to bed and we'll see where we are in the morning."

"Alright Mum, see you in the morning," replies Barnaby. He kisses the top of Elizabeth's head on the way past.

"Love you, darling."

"Love you too, Mum!"

***

The next morning sees an overcast day, perhaps mirroring the mood of Polly and Marsha as they approach Barnaby's front door with Jack.

"It took me AGES to get to sleep last night," yawns Polly, looking very tired.

"It's all that jumping around. We need to make sure in future that we follow our watches for the time we should be in. Make sure they are in alignment with our internal clocks," Marsha adds, looking equally exhausted.

"I feel great!" announces Jack, as he skips up the steps to Barnaby's front door and rings the doorbell.

Barnaby answers quickly and is equally as chirpy.

"Morning guys! Come on in!"

The group enter and wander into the kitchen, where bagels are being eaten.

An excited Momo trots over to welcome them with licks on the hand and random jumps up for cuddles. Marsha, who has a real soft spot for Momo, falls to her knees and runs her hands through his big floppy ears.

"We have a plan!" announces Barnaby and he stuffs the last bit of his bagel into his mouth.

"Wicked!" replies Jack. "Does it involve sending Dent and the time machine into the cold vacuum of space?"

"No, not quite," Barnaby frowns. "We're going to use our security passes to find Uncle Finch at the research facility and then rescue him!"

"That's it?" queries Marsha, as she stands up, much to Momo's dismay. "Doesn't sound like you've given it much thought!"

"Well, what would your plan be?" asks Jack.

"Well, it wouldn't involve kids roaming the corridors of Dent's research facility, trying doors until they locate your Uncle!"

"She's right," interrupts Elizabeth, as she joins them in the kitchen. "I'm the only one that won't raise suspicion."

"Mum, he kinda knows what you look like!"

"Then I'll go in disguise, darling!"

"Mum!" whispers Barnaby, annoyed at being called 'Darling'.

"Listen, some strategic make-up, one of Marge's wigs and a pair of scientist overalls from the medical supplies department and he'll never recognise me."

"So how do you get near him? Dent's not stupid enough to leave the time machine with your brother," adds an annoyingly accurate Polly.

"Maybe it's enough just to get Uncle Finch back? Once he's free, he can surely come up with a plan to retrieve it somehow," Barnaby points out.

"Good point," agrees Elizabeth. "But finding him will be the difficult bit."

"Wait!" yells Jack. I wonder if they still have my phone in the bag? We could use the 'Find My Phone' app thingy."

"Possibly, but the bag might have been discarded," replies Elizabeth.

"Jack! You genius! You've done it again!!!" shrieks Barnaby.

"I have?"

Barnaby reaches into the centre of the dining table and picks up Uncle Finch's mobile phone, which he placed there before the jump to Jersey.

"Let's see if he has it!" Barnaby announces, as he tries the iPad's unlock code on the phone. Sure enough, it works.

"Now, let's have a look. Extras, Find iPhone, locating… Got it! Look!! Right there, 'Mathias iPad 2,' and sure enough, there it is at 85 St Nicholas Terrace."

"How accurate is it?" enquires Elizabeth.

"Pretty darned accurate. Probably to the nearest ten metres or so."

"So how do you get him out once you've found him? You can't carry that big thing around with you," Polly adds. She points to the basement where the prototype time machine sits in its suitcase.

"We'll use Barnaby's card. We'll literally just walk out the front door!" states Elizabeth. "Then, we just meet up with the rest of you and leap back here."

"It's so simple, yet so cunning," quips Jack in a menacing voice. He has his chin resting on two index fingers.

"Alright, it's settled," confirms Elizabeth. "I'll go pick up what I need and come back here. In the meantime, you guys stay out of trouble. Go watch a movie or something."

"Haha!" yells Barnaby, "Darius Dent, you are TOAST!" As Barnaby shouts his favourite word in the world, he punches the air. Then, an odd thing happens. One of the cups on the table flies off and smashes on the floor.

"Barnaby!" shrieks Elizabeth.

"What? I didn't do anything!"

'You threw a cup!"

"Did not!!"

"Oh it just jumped there by itself did it?"

"I, uh, I don't know what happened," pleads Barnaby, looking oddly at his hand.

"Well you can clean that up while I'm out!" demands Elizabeth. She flings her bag onto her shoulder and marches out of the room.

"Dude, how did you do that?" quizzes Jack.

"I swear, I never touched it!"

"Did you throw something at it?"

"No! I was just pretending to be *Iron Man*, shoving Dent into the next universe."

"Well, you must've nudged the table or something. Maybe you had something up your sleeve?" adds Marsha.

"No! None of those. It can only be a coincidence!"

"Coincidence? The exact moment you shove your hand forward? Dude, the odds of that are into the billions," states Jack.

"Well, it could happen," responds Barnaby, at which Jack laughs. "No, seriously, remember on that Discovery programme about infinity? A room full of monkeys could type out Shakespeare on typewriters. Not on purpose, but by accident. One in a trillion, trillion chances of it happening, but there is still that one possibility!"

"Do you admit there's a higher chance you had something up your sleeve you weren't aware of?" enquires Jack.

"Well, I guess, compared to the monkeys…"

"See! I win. Right, what do we want to watch?"

Barnaby admits defeat and reluctantly starts to pick up the broken fragments of the cup. The rest of the gang head to the living room to find a film to watch. Each piece of cup gets carefully placed into a small plastic bag until he has the last part in his hand. He stares at it and thinks deep.

"I felt something." He rolls the remaining remnant around in his fingers. "When I shouted 'Toast', I felt something within me. Like I did want to throw the cup straight into Dent's face. But it was on the other side of the table. I MADE it move. I'm sure of it."

"Barn?" shouts Jack from the living room.

"Yeah?"

"*Back to the Future*?"

"A little bit too close to home right now Jack!"

"*The Goonies*?"

"Sure, why not!"

For a moment, Barnaby stares at his hand then walks over and lifts an orange from the fruit bowl before placing it carefully on the table. He steps back and raises his hand. Suddenly, he punches his hand forward and shouts "Toast!"

"What's that Barn?"

"Nothing," replies Barnaby, as he walks across to the table and places the unmoved orange back in the bowl.

"What am I doing?" he mutters to himself, before wandering through to the living room.

***

The kids have gotten through *The Goonies* and *Raiders Of The Lost Ark* before Elizabeth finally returns.

"Wow! What a pigsty!" moans Elizabeth, as she looks around at the four kids sprawled across couches, chairs and the floor. Around them lie soda cans, chip bags and candy wrappers. "Had a little feast did you?"

"Um, you've been gone for over four hours! Besides, we're kids, we don't know how to cook!" grins Barnaby.

Elizabeth realises it's probably not a great argument, chastising the kids for not cooking up lobster thermidor while she was out shopping.

"Okay, I'll let you off just this once. Anyway, want to see my 'disguise'?"

"Sure Mrs B," Jack replies on everybody's behalf.

Elizabeth removes a handful of items from her shopping bag and lays them on the coffee table.

"Stick them on then!" requests Barnaby.

"Hold your horses!" Elizabeth tears open a plastic bag and pulls out a short, bobbed, black wig. "Ta-dah!"

"Verrrry sexy!" coos a nodding Jack. Incensed, Barnaby gives him a dig in the ribs.

Elizabeth tucks her natural hair inside the wig and pulls it tight onto her head, allowing the bob to flop down naturally. From her bag, she lifts out a pair of black-rimmed glasses and puts them on.

Next comes a paper-wrapped package. She rips it open to reveal a starch-white doctor's coat, which she continues to slip over her clothes. It's at this point that Momo trots into the room looking for leftover chips. Upon seeing this 'stranger' standing in HIS living room, he goes berserk.

"Woowoowoowoowoo!"

"Cool! Even Momo doesn't recognise you, Mum. Or should I say, 'complete stranger'?"

"Let me see." Elizabeth trots over to the mirror that hangs over their ornate fireplace.

She makes a few adjustments to the hair and then stops to inspect the results. Popping her hands on her hips and leaning forward, she produces a large pout and is clearly starting to revel in her new look.

"Mum!"

"Yes, darling?"

"Composure! Practice looking all scientific," Barnaby commands, bringing his mum back down to Earth with a bump.

"Gotcha!" replies Elizabeth, who straightens up but can't quite get rid of her pout.

"Mum! Look serious! You've got to practice NOT drawing attention to yourself."

"Sure, sure, I can do this," she responds, dropping the pout and frowning.

Barnaby stands up from the couch and grabs a pen from the coffee table where it had sat on a half-finished crossword in the *New York Times*. He walks across the room and pops it in the breast pocket of the doctor's coat.

"There! The finishing touch," Barnaby chuckles.

"Right, you go grab the time machine and I'll make myself a quick cup of coffee," announces Elizabeth, as she leads Barnaby to the hall. "I'm going to need my wits about me!"

"Sure Mum, I'll go break my fifteen-year-old-back, while you lounge around drinking coffee!"

"Complaints get you nowhere young man!" retorts Elizabeth, strolling off to the kitchen.

Moments later and Barnaby wheezes his way into the kitchen, dragging the suitcase by his side. He lets it flop onto its side on the floor as he collapses into one of the kitchen chairs. Polly, Marsha and Jack are already sitting around the table with more glasses of soda. Jack shoves one in Barnaby's direction.

"Thanks, buddy!" gasps Barnaby, almost adopting a little American twang. This makes Jack smile.

"Okay, so what now?" asks Polly. She picks up a pepper pot and shakes it near her ear.

"What do we need?" adds Elizabeth, looking around the table.

"Uncle Finch's phone for starters," states Barnaby. He slides the device across the table in between two glasses of soda. "You'll not find him without that!"

"Great," Elizabeth responds, slipping it into one of her coat pockets. "What else?"

"A plan?" says Polly, sarcastically.

"We have a plan, dear girl. I just go in, find my brother and leave!"

"As easy as that?" questions Polly.

"As easy as that!" Elizabeth replies. "Jack, what's your mobile number?"

"Here, Mum, I'll send it to you."

Barnaby brings out his mobile phone and pulls up Jack's number.

"494-4771."

"Got it! I'll need that to get in touch with Mathias. Hopefully, he's alone when I call."

"Okay, let's go do this!" announces Jack, slapping his hands together.

At that, the group stands up and Barnaby opens the suitcase. Kneeling down next to it, he taps in the coordinates for Dent's research facility.

"What time?" quizzes Elizabeth.

"Let's aim for 8:30 pm. It should be pretty much deserted, but it won't be unusual for people to still be coming and going. Sun should also be down by then," explains Elizabeth. "Oh! Barnaby, I'll need your pass." Barnaby hands his mother the security pass and she tucks it into one of the jacket pockets.

"Okay, link up everyone, we're going in!"

Seconds later the group find themselves back in the grounds of the research facility. Looking around, they can see that they've once more arrived unnoticed.

"Okay kids, go hide somewhere over there next to the bushes," instructs Elizabeth pointing back towards the main street. "I'm going to try Jack's phone."

"Good luck, Mum!"

Barnaby and Jack carry the suitcase between them, flanked on either side by Marsha and Polly.

Elizabeth gives them a thumbs up and retrieves her phone from her pocket. As the group look back towards her, Elizabeth has it up to her ear, having already called Jack's number. It rings for about thirty seconds and then stops. "Come on Mathias! Hear the damn phone!!"

She redials the number. This time it rings for about five seconds before someone answers it. There is silence at the other end.

"Hello?" whispers Elizabeth.

"Hello?" comes a soft response.

"Is that you, Mathias?"

"Elizabeth?"

"Yes, it's me! Where are you?"

"I'm in some sort of research facility."

"Good. I'm right outside and coming to get you."

"Good God, how on Earth did you find me?"

"It's a long story, I'll explain later. Do you know which floor you're on?"

"It's sub-level four, I seem to recall," confirms Uncle Finch.

"And where are you once you come out of the lift? Left or right and how far?"

"Let me think. We turned right and walked about twenty metres. The door is on the left."

"Is there anyone with you?"

"No, but they'll be back here soon. They check on me every now and then. I'm in a locked room and there's no way for me to get out."

"Don't worry about that, I'll get you out. Listen, stay on the line so I can hear if anyone comes in before I get there. If they do, just talk loudly so I can hear."

"Ok, will do!"

"Holy moly, your mom's really brave!" yelps Marsha, who is watching her every move.

"Yeah, she's very determined. Once she puts her mind to something, there's no looking back!"

Indeed Elizabeth is not looking back. She's marching at a steady pace up to the entrance of the facility. The two armed guards from the previous visit aren't there. They must come on later. Swinging the door open, she strides across the foyer with great purpose, looking every bit the part of a research scientist with work to do.

She doesn't look towards the security guards at the gate, but simply approaches the turnstile and confidently swipes the access card across the panel. The light flashes green and the gate swings open. Internally, she breathes a HUGE sigh of relief.

She then makes her way to the lifts and presses the call button. Anxious seconds tick away as she struggles not to look back toward the guards. "Stay focused! You're supposed to be here, it's perfectly normal," she thinks to herself.

She watches the numbers count down to Level One, then the lift pings, announcing its arrival. As the doors glide open, she steps in.

Lifting the phone to her ear, she listens for sounds at the other end. Nothing, except the odd bit of background noise. Certainly no talk coming from Uncle Finch.

She presses sub-level four and quickly hits the 'close door' button, avoiding the chance of someone jumping in at the last second. She listens on the phone again, it still sounds quiet. All good so far.

Approaching sub-level four, her heart starts to pound. What on earth could be waiting down here when she steps out of the lift? An army of Dent's soldiers? Just one of them would cause her to crumble and jump back in. "Stay calm Elizabeth, just stay calm."

The lift doors open and even though her stomach is turning into jelly, she confidently marches out, turning right into a well-lit but very dull concrete corridor. Not a soul to be seen, thank goodness.

"Mathias?" Elizabeth whispers into her phone.

"Yes, Elizabeth, I'm here."

"Get your stuff together, I'm in the hallway outside."

"Will do!"

The corridor is about a hundred metres long and has roughly twenty doors on each side. Elizabeth doesn't dare to knock on each one trying to find her brother. That could give away her presence.

"Mathias, can you gently tap on your door so I can get your location?"

"Sure," replies Uncle Finch, as he starts to softly knock.

There are security cameras at twenty-metre intervals for the full length of the passageway. Each is trained on different areas to ensure there are no blind spots. All have a little red light signifying they are active. Certainly, under scrutiny, Dent will be able to identify her once they are far from here, but right now it's not a problem. She hopes.

Finally Elizabeth pinpoints a faint tapping. Pressing her ear to one of the doors, she realises it's not the correct one and moves on to the next. Yes, this is the one, a white painted door with no signs or any indication of what lies within, just a number. Room S410.

On the left of it is another security card reader. She swipes her pass and hears the familiar 'click' of a lock releasing. The door is pulled open from the inside and there in front of her is a battered and bruised Uncle Finch.

"Oh my God, what did they do to you?" she cries and gives him a big hug.

"I'll explain later, but let's just say I met some people who don't seem to like me very much!"

"Come on, let's get you out of here," orders Elizabeth, grabbing him by the arm.

"How did you find me?" Uncle Finch enquires, as they tiptoe towards the elevator.

"The boys. We were able to track Jack's phone."

"Did the boys tell you what happened?"

"Yes! Everything! We'll discuss this later, Mathias, but really? Taking my son into Nazi-occupied Jersey?"

"Ah, so you know about the time machine?"

"Know about it? I'm a seasoned time traveller now!"

185

"Ah. Oooh! My time machine! We need to find it!"

"Later, we just need to get you out of here first! Far away from Darius Dent!"

They reach the lift and press the call button. The door opens instantly having never been requested to another floor.

"Here, take this," insists Elizabeth, handing Barnaby's security pass to Uncle Finch.

Upon entering, Elizabeth presses level one and then swipes her card. She motions for Uncle Finch to do the same, which he does. She then calls Barnaby.

"Hi darling, success! I have your uncle. Make sure the time machine is ready for us all to jump when we arrive."

"Okay, Mum. How is he?"

"Not bad, considering. We'll be with you in a couple of minutes!"

"Okay, see you soon."

The lift arrives on level one and they exit, making their way immediately to the security gate.

"Stay calm and look normal," Elizabeth advises Uncle Finch.

At the gate she swipes her pass and then walks through. Uncle Finch, inhales deeply and does the same with Barnaby's card. Success, his works also.

"Just smile and don't rush," Elizabeth mutters under her breath.

As the pair start to walk away, the security guard calls on them.

"Excuse me!"

Elizabeth spins round.

"Yes, is there a problem?"

"Your card ma'am, you're supposed to hand it back in."

"Ah, how silly of us. Here," responds Elizabeth as she hands the pass to the guard. Uncle Finch hands his over too.

"Thank you, have a good evening," acknowledges the guard.

"You too," replies Elizabeth, who is now beginning to sweat. She takes Uncle Finch by the arm and marches him away. They're not running, but they are certainly moving at speed.

"Aren't we moving suspiciously fast?" asks Uncle Finch.

"I just want to get out of here as soon as possible!"

"I'm with you on that one!" laughs Uncle Finch, as he pulls ahead of Elizabeth.

The security guard sits back at the desk and starts to process the cards so they can be used by someone else. Scanning them, he sees something odd.

"Hey, Ed, look at this."

"What you got, Frank?"

"That woman. She entered last night but she didn't leave. Then she entered again five minutes ago."

"Must be a system error. What about the other one?"

"It's fine, swiped in last night and again to leave now. Hey, what the hell? Look at this!"

Ed leans closer.

On the screen is a picture of Barnaby.

"Barnaby Brown. Arrived with an Elizabeth Brown and a Jack Warner."

"They must have gotten the cards mixed up or something?" replies Ed.

"I don't like it. Hey, Miss!"

Elizabeth and Uncle Finch ignore the call.

"Excuse me, Miss!!" Frank shouts louder.

By now, they are at the door, pulling it open.

"Run!" yells Elizabeth and the two tear out onto the ground's pathway.

Frank pulls out and activates his walkie-talkie, which was neatly clipped to his shirt.

"Mr Dent, we have a situation here!"

Elizabeth and Uncle Finch are now running down the path towards the spot where Barnaby and friends have readied the time machine for departure.

"Barnaby, get ready!" she cries, as they approach.

"We're ready, Mum!" yells Barnaby.

As she reaches the group, there is a rumble from behind them and the ground shakes. Turning around, she comes face-to-face with Darius Dent and his four mercenaries.

"Going somewhere Elizabeth?" he quizzes, raising a gun to her chest.

Chapter 15

A new ally

"You scumbag! You left us there to rot!!" Elizabeth shrieks back at Dent.

"That's a very good point. How did you get back?" asks Dent, as his eyes are slowly drawn to Barnaby on the ground with the time machine. "Ah! How clever of you to bring a back-up. I assume that's the original prototype?"

"Just as well we did!" exclaims Barnaby.

"Indeed!" Dent replies. "Although we now find ourselves in a rather precarious situation. You see, I need your brother here in order to produce smaller versions of the machine. My quandary is that I don't need the rest of you."

"What are you going to do with us?" yelps Elizabeth starting to pace.

"I'm afraid by interfering in my business, you have left me no other choice."

Elizabeth realises where Dent is going with this and starts to tremble. "Please, shoot me, but let the kids go, they won't talk."

"Oh, I'm afraid we're long past that point. Goodbye Elizabeth," grins Dent, as he readies himself to fire. Marsha begins to whimper, Jack's bottom lip is quivering, while Polly is getting ready to run. It's all too much for Barnaby.

"No!" screams Barnaby. He raises his hand up and rushes forward to protect the group and his mother. As he does, he feels all of his emotions surge forward. Dent is sent reeling backwards, as if by some invisible force, the gun knocked from his hand. Staggering, he finally falls over, confused and dazed.

Barnaby stops and once more stares in disbelief at his hands. What the hell just happened?

"Shoot them!" roars a surprised Darius Dent, as he crawls over to retrieve his pistol.

His men raise their weapons to fire, but as they do there is a sudden burst of light and once more the ground rumbles. The group are temporarily blinded and rub their eyes in an attempt to refocus.

Barnaby's eyesight returns first and he is aware that a large figure now stands between his group and Dent's.

"What's going on?" shouts Jack.

The figure walks forward, raising its hands, upon which the men's weapons ascend rapidly into the sky, disappearing in another large flash of light. Dent sits upright and stares in disbelief at the character before him.

It is a huge armoured being, clad entirely in a reflective metallic suit, humanoid in nature but clearly not of this world. The head is covered by a helmet, made of the same material as the suit. It wraps around to the front, meeting in a t-shaped visor, not unlike something from ancient Greece. The area where the eyes should be is dark and opaque, down to just below the chin. It's a powerful look and all Dent's men can do is stand and stare, ready to run.

"Who are you?" shouts Dent. No sooner are the words out of his mouth, than the figure raises its hand and pins him to the ground, his head staring up to the stars.

The colossus turns and walks towards Barnaby, who trembles slightly, but somehow does not feel any fear. Behind him the rest of his party are huddled together and whimpering.

The being crouches down to Barnaby's eye level. As it does the helmet retracts, revealing an almost human face. The eyes are further apart, the face longer and the chin shorter but there is no facial hair to be seen. Otherwise, everything else is the same, the colour, the lips, teeth, nose, all where they should be, although perhaps the nose is flatter. One thing is for sure, Barnaby senses this is a kind, relaxed face, not the type that is about to implant eggs into his brain.

"Thank you," mutters Barnaby, remembering his manners. Not that his mother ever sat him down and told him to thank any aliens that may ever rescue him from a potential gunshot wound to the face.

The creature pauses for a second before responding.

"Whooakyo."

Barnaby blinks, shakes his head and then shrugs.

The creature motions to Barnaby's mouth and then rotates two of his fingers around each other. He seems to want Barnaby to keep talking.

"You want me to talk some more?" The figure nods and repeats the gesture.

"Uh, okay. I'm Barnaby," he states, tapping his chest. "This is my mother, Elizabeth, my uncle, Mathias Finch and my friends Jack, Polly and Marsha."

The creature regards them each in turn, their terrified faces nodding as they are announced.

"Shokawa," bellows the creature, patting its breastplate.

"Your name is Shokawa?" Barnaby repeats. The creature nods.

"Can you speak our language?" quizzes Jack, as he slowly stands up.

Shokawa looks at Jack and then puts its hands together before slowly pulling them apart until they are fully extended on either side of its shoulders.

"I think it's saying it needs time," says Marsha, also getting up. "He looks like he's processing what you're saying. Do you want to learn?" Marsha asks, raising her hand to her forehead.

Shokawa nods. "Learn." The voice is deep but soft and clear.

Barnaby stands up. He points to the ground. "Earth!" Shokawa looks down and nods. Then Barnaby points up. "Space." Again Shokawa nods.

192

"Bad man," says Polly, motioning in the direction of Dent who is still pinned to the ground.

"You'll all pay for this!" screams Dent, unable to move. "You'll wish you'd never been born!! In fact, I'll make sure you were never born! You've crossed me for...mumph." Dent is cut short as his mouth is clamped together by the same invisible force that is holding him down. Shokawa has obviously grown tired of his cursing. He then reaches to a control on his arm. There he locates a dark strip which he swipes. Suddenly the area above it becomes active with sparks of matter that hover and dance. After a minute or so, the prancing particles stop and Shokawa spends the next moment deep in concentration.

Upon completion of whatever he was concentrating on, he stands up to full height.

"Please, my apologies to you to accept. I have had time to process your language and your customs. My computer devices neural connectivity I have."

"He sounds like he's using Google Translate," sniggers Jack.

"I think that's closer to the truth than you know Jack," replies Barnaby, turning to his friend.

"I am Shokawa, Group Chief of Moderation. I am here to moderate and teach."

"Teach what?" enquires Barnaby.

Shokawa reaches over and points to Barnaby's hand.

"Power have in you now. Crystals you have experienced. You have travelled and strength now have. You learn control and to teach more."

Barnaby looks down at his hands.

"The power comes from the crystals in the time machine?"

Shokawa nods.

Unfortunately, Dent is listening and is already planning deadly ways to use this power.

"Old I am. Many etoiles travelled, teaching of balance. Security of universe I and my moderators are trusted with."

"Many what?" asks Jack.

"I think he said 'etoiles'. It's French for stars. He's not just translating to English. It's like he's scanned all speech he can access and is replying as best he can."

"Coooool!" grins Jack in awe of Shokawa.

"Shokawa," interrupts Uncle Finch, wandering over. "This bad man has my time machine. He will do evil things. Can you help?"

Shokawa nods. Dent's muffled protestations grunt out in staccato packets.

"Can you locate it for us?"

Shokawa nods and lowers his head to concentrate. A few seconds later he raises his hand and instantly the time machine appears in front of them along with the crystal from the laboratory.

Dent's stifled curses fill the air and can probably be heard from the Statue of Liberty.

Barnaby reaches down and picks up the crystal, rotating it around in his hand, before slipping it into his pocket. Uncle Finch, delighted to be reunited with his time machine, slips it back into Jack's haversack and slings it over his shoulder.

"Is that okay for him to just stick that rock his pocket?" Elizabeth asks Shokawa.

"Good for boy. No harm come," he replies.

"It's not gonna give him cancer or something? Make his leg fall off?"

"Perfectly safe. Will allow cure of cancer."

"Wow! That's gonna be a handy thing to have around!" nods Elizabeth, slightly stunned.

"Bad man," says Shokawa, addressing Dent. "Learn now of the power of the crystal and what the future owns for you. Crystal make strong, but weakness stays. Will destroy you. I guarantee."

There are muted protests once more from Dent.

"Be not concerned with supreme power. It will downfall you."

Then Shokawa shoos away Dent's men. "Go, no need of you to remain."

"We're not leaving him here," Crowe declares.

With that, Shokawa waves his hand and Crowe and the other three men vanish, likely teleported somewhere far away.

"Sit all," commands Shokawa, and he motions for them to gather around him. Shokawa sits down on the ground next to Dent and then releases his hold over him.

"Listen, or compressed you will be once more."

Dent nods and gets into a sitting position, all the while staring at Elizabeth with venom.

"The story of my worlds I will tell you now."

"Awesome!" yells a star-struck Jack.

"It is awesome," replies Shokawa in all seriousness, which makes Jack smile.

"I will rewind time to say history. All the way back to the start of this phase of universe."

"Phase of universe?" enquires Uncle Finch, who is feeling excited and giddy about the potential depth of the information he is about to hear.

"Universe has been born many times. Crystals are part of birth, the heart of singularity, the compressed source of all life. With bang, crystals spread throughout universe, millions of them, being powerful, bestowing onto beings great gifts and giving life. Crystals give great energy with waves to brain. Brain become so powerful, makes manipulation of matter, of atoms possible."

"That's why I was able to throw Dent to the ground! That's why the cup broke in the kitchen!" Barnaby shrieks, delighted to have an explanation at last.

Shokawa continues.

"When crystal being used for first time, all Moderators in universe will know, because signal unique and great. This is new region place, so I come to teach and you to learn. Save you from crystals in wrong hands."

The group all listen, enthralled. Even Dent has dropped his evil stare at Elizabeth to concentrate on Shokawa's words.

"Crystals make enhance in mind. Good person becomes better," Shokawa motions to Barnaby. "Bad person becomes worse," he points to Dent, who looks around the group a little sheepishly.

"When power used correctly, like time machine, it change matter. Warp space, warp time."

Uncle Finch simply cannot get enough of these words. He stares like a child at Santa's grotto.

"Moderators also job to make bad being to see errors in behaviour. Users of crystal must not be evil or Moderators seek and destroy." This information is directed to Dent, who ponders briefly, wondering what form 'seek and destroy' could take.

"Without balance in favour of good, universes tip, darkness descends and end of days begin. Everything falls to singularity. Already the crystals and souls are reuniting. When all once more, universe is reborn in big bang. Same happen over and over."

"Universes?" asks Uncle Finch.

"Many universes. Hidden from view, but crystals allow to see."

"Incredible." Uncle Finch grins and rubs his forehead.

"How are you able to time travel without a machine?" queries Marsha.

"No more machines in my world. Not required. All computation, all travel, all manipulation exists in mind, only small interface to read data and make change air," explains Shokawa, pointing to the dark strip on his forearm.

"Are all civilisations you encounter advanced?" interrupts Uncle Finch.

"We most advanced. Others are not so. Very like yours, still killing, still greed, much darkness. Some have war of galaxies, many weaponised, much slaughter and suffering."

"Galaxy wars?" sighs a delirious Jack. "With real spaceships and stuff?"

"Wars in space, yes."

"Do they shoot lasers?" Jack exclaims, jumping up and down.

"Burst of light and heat make destruction of other craft. Continues until one winner. Yes, you call lasers."

"Oh my God, oh my God! Can we see some?"

"Important you see. I will arrange."

"Wait a minute," interrupts Elizabeth, stepping forward. "I've only just managed to bring my son back from Nazi Jersey. I'm not very keen for him and his friends to step into the middle of a galactic space battle! Besides, they have school on Monday!"

"I ensure safety. View only. School important."

"First thing we need to do is lock this criminal up," announces Barnaby, pointing to Dent. "Do you have some sort of intergalactic judicial system? I can't see any court on Earth believing what's happened here."

"No, local courts for local problems," replies Shokawa, as he leans over the subdued businessman. Dent backs away.

"But believe me, bad man, you cause trouble, any harm come to Shokawa new friends, Shokawa find you and make pain of eternity. You hear?"

Dent nods.

"Then go," roars Shokawa, swiping his hand in the air and throwing Dent off through a wormhole.

"Where did you send him?" asks Elizabeth.

"To desert. Time to think."

Elizabeth laughs.

"Has cold heart. Will always be trouble. I see darkness in his future."

"That'll perfectly match his past. I can't believe he was genuinely going to shoot us!"

"He's too dangerous Shokawa. Couldn't you just throw him into space or something?" Jack enquires.

"All life deserves one more chance. Has happened before. Ambitious man change and become good man. It occurred here, on your Earth. Ashoka, warrior emperor, killed many with lust for power and land. Learned his errors and became kind man, religious man. Taught many, changed world."

"Well, right now I can't see Darius Dent ever becoming a kind man," quips Elizabeth.

"Is our rule. He is warned. No more chances for him after today."

"So what now?" Barnaby asks.

"Shokawa hungry."

"Ah, okay, Why don't we take you to our home?" Elizabeth offers. "We can make you some food there, if you like?"

"Thank you," replies Shokawa, bowing.

"Can we PLEASE go back to the time we left? I don't fancy another day of time-lag," requests Marsha.

"I still have all of the settings ready to go on the prototype," Barnaby states, at which point Shokawa walks over and lifts up the prototype time machine.

"Very crude. I teach good way, not this child toy."

"Oh," sighs Uncle Finch, a little hurt.

"I make joke," grins Shokawa, showing the group he has a lighter side.

"I like this guy!" announces Jack.

"So how do you leap?" asks Uncle Finch.

"I see travellers, objects, I can see destination, inside home, then I command manipulation of space."

"So you just think about all the details and voila?" queries Elizabeth.

"Yes, voila!" Shokawa responds.

Everybody readies themselves as Barnaby walks over to Uncle Finch.

"Uncle Finch, I'm so sorry we got Mr Dent involved, I fear we've gone and messed everything up!"

"Don't you worry about it Barnaby, you did what you thought was right. Clearly Mr Dent is not at the top of our Xmas card list, but if it wasn't for him, I'd be on my way to Buchenwald right now, so he was the lesser of two evils."

"But still…"

"But still nothing," interrupts Uncle Finch. "I was the one stupid enough to get caught in the first place. The fault is all mine!"

"Is everyone ready?" asks Shokawa.

The group all collectively nod.

They are now standing in Uncle Finch's kitchen.

Chapter 16

Pizza and Brukash

"Wow! How did you do that?" asks Jack. "Look, nobody fell over! It was mega-smooth!"

"Shokawa been warping space/time for 487 years."

"487 years!?" shrieks Marsha.

"Wow, I need to get my hands on your moisturiser!" adds Elizabeth.

"Would you mind telling me exactly how you are able to live so long?" Uncle Finch enquires.

"Power of crystals, alter body with mind. When organ fails, grow another one, swap over. Always rejuvenating."

"You're going to have to teach us that one, for sure!" smiles Elizabeth.

"Shokawa teach all. First food," replies Shokawa, sitting down at the table and making it look ridiculously small. His knees have to point sideways, as they simply cannot fit under the table.

Elizabeth wanders over to the fridge and opens it.

"Oh good God, what on earth do I feed an alien?" she mutters to herself.

"Do you eat meat?" she asks, after rummaging for a moment.

"Shokawa will not eat meat."

"Okay, what do I feed a vegetarian alien?" she mumbles. "What should be his first taste of planet Earth? If indeed, it is a 'him'."

"Mum! Pizza!" shouts Barnaby.

"Well, it is New York. I guess pizza is as earthy as it gets!"

Elizabeth closes the fridge door and opens the freezer. After more searching, she pulls out three twelve-inch Margherita pizzas and carries them over to the oven.

"A little taste of planet earth for you Shokawa."

"Thank you," he replies.

"Hey, Shokawa, do you have a family?" Marsha pipes up.

"All moderators vow to love all. No time for one family."

"Sorry, does that mean you have no family or many?" Marsha probes further.

"Universe is my family. Moderator is parent to whole universe."

He hasn't truly answered Marsha's question, but she opts to let this one go, as it perhaps isn't translating well.

"Do you guys fart?" Jack grins.

"Really?" exclaims Barnaby. "Of all the questions to ask an alien, do you guys fart?"

There is a moment's silence as Shokawa watches the pair.

"Well do you?" Jack asks again.

"Expulsion of gases from the body is necessary. It amuses you?"

"Hehe, it sure does."

"What about gases from mouth?"

"Nah, that's not funny at all."

"Hmm," frowns Shokawa, intrigued by this odd little boy.

At that moment Momo wanders into the room and promptly trots over to Shokawa. He sits at his feet, as if to say 'Hello'.

"What about pets? Do you keep animals in your homes?" quizzes Marsha.

"All beings on my world are free to come and go. If against its will, it should not be."

Momo then licks at Shokawa's hand, which has been offered to him.

"What about music? What's your favourite band?" Polly joins in, still chewing on the same bit of gum from yesterday that she has recently picked off the table.

"Music is part of life. Shokawa embraces all music from all worlds."

"Cool," she remarks, and proceeds to connect her iPhone to the Bluetooth speaker next to the toaster.

"What's your favourite kind of music? Do you like it loud?" continues Polly.

"No favourite, always what suits the mood."

"It's amazing!" adds Uncle Finch. "You can be raised on entirely different sides of the universe, yet the same principles of intelligent behaviour are identical in so many…"

Uncle Finch is interrupted by the sound of Nirvana's *Smells Like Teen Spirit* blasting out of the Bluetooth speaker. The all too familiar opening guitar riff and Dave Grohl's mighty drum intro fill the room, making Shokawa sit up with a start.

"Polly, turn it down!!" shouts Elizabeth.

"No way, this is the first Earth song he's gonna hear and he's gonna hear it properly!" hollers Polly, even though the song has slipped into the quiet section of the verse.

"Shokawa likes," he informs the group.

"See!" says Polly, and holds up a hand for a high five to Shokawa. He stares at it, so Polly picks up his opposing hand and slaps it into hers for him. "Such a dude," she continues.

While the song carries on its angsty and merry way, Elizabeth proceeds to put the pizzas in the oven.

Meanwhile, Polly is now dancing around the kitchen. Jack has his head in his hands, cringing with embarrassment, but Barnaby watches on with glee. At this precise moment he is finding her very cute, yet strong.

Shokawa nods his head in time to the music and by the end of the song is tapping away on the table.

"Song is very good. More songs please," says Shokawa, revelling in the planet's musical awesomeness.

Polly picks up her iPhone and points to the speaker.

"This is going to blow your mind!"

For a second or two, there is silence, then…

"*Is this the real life, is this just fantasy…*"

For the next five minutes and fifty-five seconds, Shokawa is thoroughly entertained by the collective antics of the group. All of them, even Uncle Finch, join in with the singing, the operatic mid-section, the head-banging and the softer outro segment. By the time *Bohemian Rhapsody* comes to a close, the Freddie Mercury classic has won over yet another race, nay, species.

"Is this Earth's anthem?"

"It should be. It would certainly make Dr. Brian May's day!"

"More, more!" insists Shokawa.

"Okay, one more song, then it's pizza time," says Elizabeth to the group.

"Could I have a little look?" asks Uncle Finch, holding out his hand to Polly.

"Sure, but no rubbish, okay?"

Uncle Finch taps away at the iPhone until he finds what he's looking for. The Dave Brubeck Quartet *Take Five*. The familiar saxophone of Paul Desmond rings out and Shokawa smiles.

"This is how the people of Earth relax after a hard day at the office," explains Uncle Finch.

Polly huffs in disgust. Not a big jazz fan.

"Pizza time!" shouts Elizabeth, who has recently carved up the three pizzas with a Vespa shaped pizza cutter. The group watches as the mighty Shokawa raises a slice of pizza to his mouth and takes a large bite. He chews it for a while, his face full of curiosity, before swallowing and addressing them.

"Shokawa likes this taste. It has good sensation in mouth. This is good food!"

"It certainly has been an odd twenty-four hours", thinks Barnaby to himself. "Yesterday morning I was waving to Nazis in a watchtower and today I'm in my uncle's house watching an alien eat pizza."

The group continue to watch Shokawa shovelling more than his fair share of pizza into his mouth. Satisfying his appetite looks like it may be difficult, and it's only lunchtime.

When he's finished, he licks his fingers, sucking at the ends of them with a gratifying smack of the lips.

"Shokawa enjoyed this food very much. Thank you, Elizabeth! I will have pizza again in the future."

"Is it just me or is his English getting better?" whispers Polly in Barnaby's ear.

"Yes, it does seem to be. He learns very quickly."

"Can we take him in for a show-and-tell tomorrow?"

Barnaby laughs and notices that Polly is giving him a broad smile. Quite an endearing one, with her eyes looking equally as attentive. Barnaby shifts uncomfortably in his chair as it dawns on him that the smile might just mean 'I'm attracted to you!' It's a feature of Polly he's not noticed before, her usual tough exterior giving way to her softer side. As he continues to stare into her eyes, she raises an eyebrow, smirks and punches him on the shoulder.

"In your dreams!" she teases.

Barnaby regains his composure and gives a little nervous cough, a clearing of the throat before standing up.

"Right, what next?" he says, backing away from Polly who continues to grin at him.

"Shokawa would like to show you his home."

"Where is your home?" asks Elizabeth, nervously.

"My home planet is called Koyakashi, it means 'Motherland'."

"How far away is it?" enquires Uncle Finch.

"You measure distance by light travel?" is Shokawa's response.

"Yes, how do you measure?" replies Uncle Finch.

"My people no longer need to measure such distance. All measuring is relative to travel. Our travel is instant. By your calculations, we are forty-four light-years away."

"Incredible," exclaims Uncle Finch, "and we can go there instantly?"

"Yes."

"And can we breathe your atmosphere?" Uncle Finch continues.

"Our atmosphere is very similar. Much vegetation, much oxygen. Slightly more carbon dioxide, slightly less nitrogen. You may feel much more energy, more alive, but only for a short time, then fatigue. When that happens, Shokawa will help."

"I have no problem with feeling more alive!" Elizabeth pipes up. "Considering, if it wasn't for you, we wouldn't be!"

"You are welcome," replies Shokawa.

"Will we need to bring my time machine?" asks Uncle Finch.

"Yes and the crystals." Shokawa motions to the haversack on the kitchen table, which Uncle Finch promptly picks up.

"Come now. See Shokawa's home!"

Shokawa stands up, inadvertently shoving his chair away in the process with his enormous frame and stretches out his arms over the group.

In an instant they are standing in a wide-open room, with highly polished marble floors, dimly lit by natural sunlight. At the end of the room it's much brighter with huge panoramic, glassless windows that look out to what appears to be jungle. The ceiling is quite high and contains no visible form of lighting. The walls are featureless and it's not evident what they are made from. It appears to be some sort of stone, but matte on the surface, not displaying much reflection. Other than that, the vast room is entirely empty, devoid of furniture and featureless.

"Um, where are we?" asks Elizabeth.

"This is my home," replies Shokawa.

"You live here? This is where you eat and sleep?"

"Yes," he says looking around.

Jack is giggling.

"Are we seriously on Koya-what's-it-called?"

"Koyakashi. Yes, this is home."

"Like, Earth is now forty-four light years away!!?"

"Yes. You are very far from home."

"Holy moly this is unbelievable!" declares Jack, wandering around the room. "This makes us, like, bigger than Neil Armstrong!"

"Oh no, you need a speech! A 'one giant step' kinda thing!" Barnaby shouts over to Jack.

"Who spoke first, it was you, Mum, wasn't it?" he continues.

"Yeah, I said, um, 'where are we'?" replies Elizabeth.

"Meh, that's not one for the history books," Jack comments, squirming. "How about, 'Hey dudes, how's it hanging?'"

"Something a bit more poetic perhaps?" suggests Elizabeth.

"Let's pick that up later. I'm too fired up to see this place," is Jack's response.

"So, Shokawa, do you just sit or sleep on the floor?" quizzes Elizabeth.

"Shokawa sits on a chair. Sleeps on a bed."

"Do you have someone who puts them all away for you? You know, a maid who sticks them in a cupboard or something?"

"My house reacts to your needs. Please be seated," replies Shokawa, beckoning Elizabeth to sit down.

She looks around her, confused by the request. So assuming he means for her to sit on the beautiful marble floor, she begins to crouch down. As she does the floor rises up in tiny segments to meet her, moulding around her buttocks and arms, allowing her to gently sink into the shape created.

"Oh my God! Oh this is incredible," shrieks Elizabeth. "This is the comfiest thing I have ever sat on!!" and at that she starts to laugh out loud, doing her crazy pig snort again.

The rest of the group tentatively follow suit, each one being offered up a similar experience and all reacting with the same amount of shrieks and giggles.

"Ah this is amazing!" shouts Barnaby. "Uncle Finch, you gotta try this!" He looks about but can't see his uncle. "Hey, Uncle Finch?"

Swinging around in his seat he sees Uncle Finch standing over at the far window, motionless.

"Come and see Barnaby," he beckons, his voice echoing across the room.

Barnaby leaps from his chair, which instantly disappears back into the ground, and runs over to the window to join his uncle. Shokawa follows on behind him.

"Oh my God! Guys, come and look at this!"

Shokawa reaches Uncle Finch and Barnaby, towering behind them.

"This is my home. This is Brukash."

A palatial, yet subtle metropolis unfolds before them. It is a panorama of mountains off to the right, moving down through jungle and spotless marble streets, past vast neoclassical structures, to a beach, shaded pink instead of the usual golden or white sands. Beyond that, a sea stretches out to the horizon. Here it meets a beautiful blue sky, with light touches of cloud that try, but fail, to obscure two moons; one large with traces of its own seas and landmasses, the other further away and not unlike Earth's moon.

On the streets, they can see beings of Shokawa's race intermingling with other mammalian looking creatures. They all seem to be happily sharing the space in harmony.

A waterfall cascades down one of the mountains, carving its way through the city and out to sea. Its spray forms a partial rainbow that frames the whole scene perfectly.

The trio is soon joined by the rest of the group, who stand with them, their jaws hanging open.

"Oh my God, it's so beautiful!" cries Elizabeth, who starts to sob at the sheer beauty of this magnificent vista.

Then, almost to interrupt the mood, a beautiful bright blue bird lands on the stone balcony over which they have been peering. It is a bulbous creature with a long slender neck and yellow throngs running from its beak to the back of its head. As it lands, it tucks its wings in, but due to their length, they protrude up over its body. It looks awkward, something akin to an enraged headmistress with her arms folded.

Elizabeth holds her hands to her mouth in awe of the bird as it begins to flick and tilt its head from side to side and stare at her curiously. Just as she is falling in love with its magnificence, it turns around and aims its bottom over the shiny marble floor. This elegant creature then proceeds to poo an enormous yellow waterfall of excrement that splashes over everybody's shoes.

"Oh, yuuuuuuuuk!" shrieks Marsha, her hand over her mouth as she reels back in horror and gags.

"Oh that is soooo gross!" screams Jack, also covering his mouth. "That's the worst stink I've ever smelled!"

Shokawa steps forward.

"This is the Bunjika bird. It feeds on the universe's most pungent insect, the Kakwaka."

As Shokawa continues to move forward he raises his hand and the blob of stinky excrement lifts into the air, collating in one large mass that hovers above the group.

"What are you going to do with that?" asks Jack.

"It makes good food for trees," replies Shokawa, forcing his arm towards the jungle area outside his home. The large globule of poo shoots away from the group and into the trees.

"Jeez," says Jack squinting. "I sure hope there weren't any botanists in there, studying plant life!"

"Come, I will show you Brukash and tell its history," continues Shokawa. He waves his hand in front of the balcony and it silently folds apart and remoulds itself into a flight of super-thin stairs that lead down to a shiny marble pathway. The only sound it makes is when the steps touch the plants that grow beneath it.

"How do you do that?" exclaims Barnaby, tentatively putting his foot on the first step down.

"The mind arranges matter. My mind is in unity with the atoms. They are happy to move, so I guide them."

"What about the buildings?" asks Uncle Finch. "Are they built using this same method?"

213

"Yes," Shokawa answers. "All you see is changed for the needs of the populace. Only a small amount remains untouched from before the awakening. We leave them out of respect, to remind us of the past."

"The awakening?" quizzes Elizabeth.

"The time when our great warrior Solsha discovered our crystal in this river. He was the first to use its power, first to create for good. His heart was pure and strong, not destroyed by hate. He banished the Gundari warriors to Arkavia, instead of destroying them. He had much compassion."

"Okay Shokawa," interrupts Polly. "You're going to have to slow down and explain. The Gundari? Arkavia?"

"The Gundari were a warrior people from the north of Koyakashi. They lived in a colder, harsher climate and hunted and killed. They were uncivilised, like wild beasts. Eventually, they came to Brukash and killed many Brukashi. They took precious metals from the ground. There were many wars, but no winners, only losers. We learn the pointlessness of war and try to explain to Gundari prisoners. We set them free to spread the word, but again, they return with weapons and try to wipe out the Brukashi. They failed, and Solsha lifted them into the stars, to a new home Arkavia, the next planet to Koyakashi."

Shokawa is staring up to the stars as he recites his story.

"What became of the Gundari?" asks Polly.

Shokawa sighs a little.

214

"They did not learn their lesson. Four thousand of your years in anger, mining metals, creating their own technology, own Empire, until one day, their army leader, Lord Kallick discover his own crystal. Its power increased his hatred, his desire for control. Now he commands armies, stretching out through the universe under the new flag of Arkavia and its Emperor, waiting for the day when he reigns supreme and returns to destroy the Brukashi. Come, I will show you."

The group trot off down the marble path behind Shokawa, intrigued by his stories and wondering what he will bestow upon them next.

For five minutes they walk by other Brukashi, who stop to regard their new guests. They pass glorious structures of marble, mixing many styles, some smooth and rounded, almost Art Deco. Others have harsh, sharp edges, but are all constructed harmoniously so that they work together without clashing.

At the bottom of the marble pathway, they reach a large circular plaza, with one enormous neo-classical looking building in front of them. Towering columns rise some fifty feet into the air, supporting a huge marble roof, not far removed from the Parthenon in Athens.

"These buildings," enquires Uncle Finch. "They look very similar to ones we have on Earth. Why is that?"

"All architecture evolves in same way. Houses are made from wood and leaves, then mud, then stone, then more stone. Then they fall down, then we discover geometry, then make pillars. When they fall down, we learn of stress on materials, we evolve arches, buildings become stronger and style changes, but we don't forget the old styles and keep them, to enjoy them."

"I guess simple mathematics will drive the same laws, the same inventions, the same push to make things better, to expand knowledge. As long as you have a viable atmosphere and gravity, you will all likely evolve in the same way once intellect is born," adds Uncle Finch.

"It is the same over and over, across universe. Only the odd exception, such as life in zero-gravity, but mostly the same as here, same as on Earth."

"Incredible!" replies Uncle Finch.

"I'm not really following this. Can we go to the beach?" asks Jack, his arms folded.

"Soon," Shokawa answers. "First I will show you the prophecy."

"The prophecy?" asks Marsha.

"Yes, come." Shokawa leads them down another pathway, away from the enormous structure they were standing outside.

"What was that building?" questions Barnaby.

"The Council of the Brukahsi. Twelve members reside within the halls. The lead of the council of twelve is Shokawa. I am the Moderator for this world. All council is elected by the populace, the ones who show the best values of the Brukashi, with elevated minds. No one Brukashi asks to be elected. They are recommended. It is a great honour to be put forward. All decisions for the Brukashi happen after intellectual debate. There are no hidden agendas and all Brukashi can watch. Here, there is no crime, no hate, only that which benefits the Brukashi. Not living like this is stupid and destructive."

The group continue to wander down the path, approaching the river that runs through the heart of the small city. As they approach the bridge, two pig-like creatures, dark brown and hairy, trot past them, clearly on their way somewhere. Barnaby pats one of them as it passes. It stops, sniffs his hand, smiles and then continues on its way.

"Hey, that pig just smiled at me!"

"That is not a pig. It is a Grukan. There is a very clever mind inside that head."

Marsha turns to watch the little Grukan trot off into the distance.

"Come on, Marsh!" hollers Polly.

"Coming," she shouts back, as she runs toward the group, still turning to look at the Grukan as they get further away.

"So what is your society like? Do you have a religion?" asks Uncle Finch.

"There is no religion in Brukash now, only a community of combined thought. I believe Gods were made for those who needed answers to life and death but could not find one, which is why there are so many different Gods as there are so many different answers. But I respect the religion of others when used for good, provided it does not interfere with our ways. Now, the Brukashi could not return to this way. The old Brukash

217

religion died and only pure intellect remains. We live only for facts, no need for faith. One less thing to argue about. All Brukashi work together as one. There is no confusion, no ownership. Harmony exists for us here."

"No hell below us…" sings Elizabeth with a huge smile on her face, "above us only sky!"

"Muuuuuuuuum!" groans Barnaby.

"What?" replies Elizabeth, shrugging. "This place is like the lyrics to *Imagine*! He has no possessions, no religion."

Shokawa nods but obviously does not get the reference. He turns and directs the group to a white-domed building that stands about twenty feet high. Inside the walls are lined with what looks like gold, making it look like a very posh egg.

"This is the chamber of the Prophecy," announces Shokawa, as he enters through the large circular aperture that is the doorway.

Inside there is only one object. A huge stone, very rough in nature, but standing on perfectly smooth sand-coloured marble. It is evident that the structure has been built around the object to protect it, having once probably stood in a jungle for goodness knows how long.

Shokawa walks around to the far side of the stone and beckons for the group to gather around him.

"This is the prophecy," Shokawa declares, pointing to the stone. As the group look closer, they can see carvings. A group of figures with two central characters in the middle, their arms outstretched with a series of lines between them.

"What is the prophecy?" asks Barnaby.

"The prophecy was told to the ancient Brukashi by the bearer of a sacred stone. The prophet came from the sky. We now believe that the story told to the Brukashi came from one who carried one of the crystals. Someone who came to this world with a warning about the future. The story of good and evil fighting the final battle of this universe. It is said the pure-in-heart will be victorious."

"The pure in heart? Like some super good guy?" enquires Barnaby.

"What makes you think it's a guy?" sneers Polly, folding her arms.

"By 'guy', I didn't mean, necessarily a man. Could be a woman I suppose!"

"You suppose?" retorts Polly, giving Barnaby a very stern look.

"So who is the bad 'guy'?" says Barnaby, fingering quotation marks in the air as he says 'Guy' for Polly's benefit.

"Head of the Arkavian Empire, we think. Unless in the future, somebody more evil than Lord Kallick comes to power."

"And who is Lord Kallick?" asks Polly.

"As I say before, he is most powerful Arkavian. He built an army for Emperor, made many starships. Powerful weapons. He is the reason I watch new worlds such as Earth. As the technology becomes noticeable, Kallick adds it to his list of world's to conquer. He has his eye on your Mr. Dent."

"Why Dent?" Elizabeth interrupts.

"He is powerful. He created all of his wealth from nothing. He is very ambitious but has a bad heart. Kallick loves these beings. He will use him to organise infestation of Earth."

"Wait, an infestation of Earth?" cries Barnaby.

"It is the Arkavian protocol. First, infest the planet with a virus, then arrive to rule. Set up legions, use people as slaves, mine planet, steal water, build more resource to destroy the Moderators of the universe. The ultimate goal of Kallick is to rule the universe without moderation."

"Well he sounds like a barrel of laughs!" announces Jack.

"Lord Kallick is…" continues Shokawa, but he is cut short by a sensation and once more lifts his head to the sky.

"Lord Kallick is on Earth!"

Chapter 17

Revelations in the sand

Darius Dent squints into the sun. He holds his hand up to try and get a bearing on his surroundings. It's a desert as far as he can see in all directions.

"Son of a bitch!" he screams at the top of his voice, but no one is around to hear, just the wind whipping at his fringe and ears.

It has to be somewhere in the region of forty degrees, so he removes his jacket and throws it down. It lands in the sand and rolls over a couple of times as the wind whips it away on a journey of its own.

"Think, dammit," he mutters to himself, as he paces around his landing spot, rolling up his sleeves.

Raising his arm, he taps away at his smartwatch.

"Where the hell am I?" he ponders as he launches his maps app. "Bilma?"

Zooming out, he can see he's a long way from home.

"Niger!?" he shrieks, flapping his arms and looking around. "It's the damn Sahara!" He kicks at the ground and a billow of sand lifts into the air.

Bringing out his phone, he calls Crowe. There is no answer.

Reverting back to his watch he can see he is two kilometers south-west of the nearest road and another six kilometers from the town of Bilma itself. It's 9 am, which means that Shokawa has thrown him ahead in time. It was 9 pm when he left New York. It would be four o'clock the following morning now.

Nothing for it but to head to the road and hope he gets picked up by a car, although a camel is probably more likely!

The wind is really starting to blast sand into his eyes now, seemingly getting stronger. Then there is a rumble creating an even greater sandstorm.

'Oh for God's sake!" he screams and covers his eyes with his hand.

The sand slowly starts to subside and Dent lowers his arm back down. Looking up, he sees a dark figure standing five metres in front of him.

"Ah Jesus!" he roars at this sudden apparition.

The figure raises its hand and swipes at a control panel on its forearm. A series of dancing lights flutter for a minute or so and then disappear from sight.

"Who are you?" asks Dent.

"Are you Dent?" comes the reply with an intense and throaty voice.

Dent seems a little stunned by the question. Squinting he tries to focus better.

"Yeah, I'm Dent!"

"You have met the Moderator Shokawa?"

"Yeah, I met him alright. He doesn't play fair!!" says Dent, still screwing up his eyes.

Kallick steps forward. It's only now that Dent can see the figure is covered entirely in a dark hooded cloak, which is being whipped by the wind, shadows completely covering the face.

"Then common wish for us Dent."

"And what's that?" Dent enquires.

"We want to see him torn apart by wild animals."

"So are you going to tell me who you are?" probes Dent, becoming impatient.

"I am Kallick, Overlord of Arkavia," he replies. He draws back the hood to reveal a terribly scarred face, not unlike Shokawa's. It has the same feature placement, but with a full head of hair pulled back tight across the top of his head, descending down into a ponytail that is now stretched out some two metres in the wind. He's tall, standing at what must be about eight feet and his shoulders are equally as wide. Dent guesses there must be a fair amount of muscle under there.

"Wow, a worthy addition to any basketball team," sneers Dent, unphased by Kallick's appearance.

Kallick has no idea what he's talking about but can tell from the look on Dent's face that he may have a valuable pupil in his presence. He comes right up to Dent's face and stares deep into his eyes. It's a stand-off! Dent doesn't even blink and glares back with equal severity, looking for some sign of submission or even a nervous blink.

"Hmm," mutters Kallick, rubbing his chin.

Dent moves closer still until their noses are almost touching.

"Get me out of here," Dent utters, continuing to stare.

Kallick raises himself to full height, towering above Dent, all the while not losing eye contact. He smirks and waves his hand and all that is left behind is swirling sand as Dent and Kallick disappear.

"Is this more to your liking?" asks Kallick.

Dent looks around. They are on a beach. It stretches for miles and the sun is beating down from blue skies. Out on the sea, a medium-sized pleasure boat bobs merrily, while children jump from its upper level into the sea. Behind them is a dune covered in grass that stretches up into high hills, at the end of which is a tall peak that extends into the distance.

"Better," replies Dent, wiping the sand from his eyes.

"You enjoy these quiet places?" enquires Kallick.

"I only enjoy peace when I need to talk or think. Relaxing is a waste of time and is the pursuit of the ignorant and weak."

Dent looks at his watch, which still has the map app open. A yellow strip and a little green camera that says

224

'Tai Wan'. Zooming out, he sees he's in an area North East of Hong Kong.

"Not getting any closer to home, am I?" announces Dent.

"Not yet. We must discuss your future first."

"Well, I'm all ears!"

Kallick looks at Dent oddly and leans to either side of his head, examining him.

"It's an expression! I only have these two ears. They're ready to hear what you came to tell me!"

Kallick smirks again and places his hand on Dent's shoulder.

"How would you like to rule your world?" suggests Kallick, nonchalantly, before again staring into Dent's eyes, which have now completely lit up.

"Let's just say it's something I have very much considered," replies Dent, his eyes narrow and full of meaningful intent.

"What has stopped you doing this?" enquires Kallick.

"Too many laws that I cannot circumvent yet. I have many connections though. I intend to rule from behind the scenes. Power is everything."

"Yes," continues Kallick, "but you will never know power until you can execute one of your enemies in front of many people and ask 'Who's next?'."

Dent is obviously curious about what this enormous figure can offer him. As Kallick turns away and walks a little, Dent marches after him, his footsteps appearing small in comparison to the mighty ones that Kallick produces.

"So you think you can help me achieve this?" Dent shouts after him.

"Of course. I can make you more powerful than you could ever imagine."

"Has this got something to do with the crystals?" quizzes Dent.

"Partly. Once you have it, it will consume you and make you strong, give you abilities you can only dream of."

"And you will show me how to achieve this?"

"Of course. I have done this many times and in many worlds. Once your powers are ready, my armies will unleash a virus upon this planet, from which you will be their redeemer. You will control the medication and allow vast swathes of your population to die. You will control the armies and topple all who show you resistance. Your subjects will grow up bowing before you and will follow you across the universe to fight when the time comes to destroy Shokawa and his band of Moderators!"

Dent nods and smiles.

"I get it. You're recruiting me for your own army?" asks Dent.

"As I say, when the time comes, you will repay your debt to me."

Dent reflects a while.

"Okay, you got yourself a deal," he says, moving forward to shake Kallick's hand. Kallick stares at it for a moment and then, almost reluctantly, shakes. All the while Dent has his eyes firmly on Kallick's.

"You are aware of the location of the crystal you have encountered?" questions Kallick.

"Not exactly where it is, but I know who has it. I'm sure I can gently persuade them to hand it over."

"Gently, Mr Dent?"

"Well, perhaps not as gently as they would prefer, Mr. Kallick," grins Dent.

Kallick smiles broadly and produces a deep, slow, menacing laugh, to which Dent responds with his own evil smirk.

***

"Oh wow, the water is so warm!" shouts Jack, who has rolled up his trouser legs and is now paddling around in the sea. The others stand watching him, perhaps waiting to see if he will be eaten alive by some enormous Koyakashan sea beast.

Barnaby shakes his head at his friend and returns his attention to Shokawa.

"So you think this Lord Kallick will try to help Dent?"

"I am sure of it. Many times I see this same pattern, over and over."

"Can't you go and stop him?" cries Barnaby, almost pleading.

"Kallick will not allow the arrival of the Moderator Shokawa in his space. In the same way, I will not allow his arrival here. This I do in your defence. I have a veil of protection in place for you."

"So you can influence things from very far away?"

"Yes. The universe is connected like one giant fabric."

"Can you move planets with your mind?" asks Barnaby.

"No, our powers cannot manipulate items with such large gravitational force surrounding it. Gravity is like putting a rock into sand. When you drive it deep into the sand, the force pushes back against it, pressing from all sides, trying to return to the space it once occupied. Always pushing against the object. When the object is large, there is more force and we are unable to alter that pressure. But, if the object is small, then it has a weak force and it becomes malleable."

Uncle Finch has been eavesdropping and is taking everything in.

"I have so many questions I want to ask you Shokawa," he states.

"In time, my knowledge will be your knowledge Mathias, but first there is a great need to make you understand the power of the crystals. In the wrong hands or untrained hands, they become a great danger."

"So, you will teach us all how to use them?"

"Sorry, not all. Barnaby has the strongest will. I sense a will stronger than most I have encountered. He made the crystals work after such short exposure to them. I have never seen this before."

"I was wondering why I can't move stuff," remarks Jack, walking out of the sea.

"One day perhaps. Now, I focus on Barnaby. He is what you call a 'quick win'."

"And then the rest of us?" enquires Polly.

Shokawa looks to Polly, deep into her eyes and lowers his head.

"What's he doing?" asks Polly to the group. They shrug.

After a few seconds, Shokawa raises his head back up and looks tenderly into Polly's eyes.

"Much confusion in your future Polly. It is for Barnaby to decide on your training when the time comes."

"Wait, I decide?" exclaims a startled Barnaby.

"Yes, when you become a Moderator."

Barnaby's mouth is hanging open.

"Wait, he gets to be a Moderator?" continues Polly, a little put out.

"He shows all the signs I have seen many times, on many worlds. But the strongest yet."

Barnaby's face lights up and he turns to Jack and gives him a big wink.

Shokawa rests his hand on Barnaby's shoulder.

"And the first thing you must control is ego. Great responsibility is this, not a toy to yield, not to show off. Control is the first thing you learn, how not to abuse power for your own gain. A Moderator is the father of the universe and the people of the universe are your children.

You will grow up very quickly and put aside childish pursuits."

Jack winks back at Barnaby, whose face has now dropped its smile.

"Sounds like you get to miss out on all the fun, Barn!" Jack teases.

Elizabeth now steps in.

"Wait, Barnaby is still my son, I still get to decide whether this is the right thing for him. I must protect him from danger. I don't think it's a good idea for him to lose out on all of the things that will make him grow up to be a healthy young man!"

"Barnaby is fifteen. For him, playtime is over. For all children of his age, the great learning years have started. He will continue his Earth studies, but he will learn much more with Shokawa."

"Well that's just not fair!" screams Polly. "He gets to hold a rock and consume the knowledge of the universe! What do we get?"

Shokawa once more looks to Polly.

"Polly, your time will come, but these crystals are dangerous until you can control these thoughts. You must reason with your inner self and cast aside thoughts of jealousy."

"Jealous? Of him?" shouts Polly, pointing at Barnaby and hurting his feelings a little.

Shokawa crouches down, his eyes once more probing deep into her soul.

"Shokawa has much experience. I have trained many Moderators. I had some failures in the beginning and pupils failed to control these demons within them. They are now allied to Lord Kallick. You have a special place in the heart of Barnaby and you must be protected."

This last disclosure leaves both Barnaby and Polly blushing.

"No, you've got it all wrong, he has the hots for Marsha!" blurts out Jack.

"Jack!" shrieks Barnaby and Marsha in unison.

Jack shrugs as if to say 'Am I wrong?'

Polly has found herself staring at Marsha, with the tiniest little shred of jealousy. She catches herself before anyone can spot it and quickly looks away.

"So, shall we get started with the training then?" suggests Barnaby, quickly moving the subject along and hoping to make his cheeks stop burning.

"Yes, we will train now. All sit please, except Barnaby."

The group follow Shokawas' orders and plop themselves down in the sand. Barnaby is left standing, looking at them and feeling a little self-conscious.

"Take the crystal from your pocket," Shokawa instructs.

Barnaby obeys.

"Hold to your head, like this," continues Shokawa, bringing his thumb and forefinger to his forehead.

"You have already made a connection to this crystal, but now it must connect with you. Your link is like wisps of smoke from a fire, but now you must touch the flames."

"I hope you mean metaphorically!" replies Barnaby.

'Yes, no flames." answers Shokawa. "Now, you will feel the connection, like a door opening."

Barnaby is focussing, unsure what this sensation will be like. At first, his concentration gets in the way. His thoughts are contrived, almost blocking a distant light he can see off in the distance.

"Relax your mind, Barnaby. Get rid of all thoughts, clear your mind of expectations and the door will open." Shokawa's voice is now softer, more soothing.

Barnaby takes a deep breath and then exhales slowly. As he does, he relaxes his chest and shoulders. Now unaware of the group around him, his thoughts are drifting away.

"Good, the mist in your mind is clearing."

As Barnaby continues to release his tension, the light in his mind grows stronger. Even though his eyes are closed, the brightness increases and fills his inner vision.

"Now, step through," says Shokawa. His voice much firmer.

Barnaby imagines himself walking into the light. As he does, faint images start to appear. At first, they are just blurred, dancing ghosts in the mist, but then they begin to form more defined shapes. A mountain, peering through misty clouds, trees and rooftops. The haze is rapidly clearing and streets become visible, indistinct initially and then razor-sharp. Barnaby realises he is seeing an aerial view of Brukash.

"You see the city?"

"Yes, I see it," replies Barnaby.

"Always your own true surroundings you will see first. This is orientation. Right now, you see two-dimensions?"

Barnaby views the city, sprawling before him, all the way to the sea, to the pink beach where the group are gathered.

"I see everything, it's blurry but becoming clearer!"

Then, the city seems to come to life. People appear and as they do the whole scene takes on a more realistic aspect. Suddenly the objects fade from two-dimensions to three.

"Oh my God! This is like wearing virtual reality goggles! Or 3D glasses!"

"Why not try moving?" suggests Shokawa.

"No way! Wow, I'm flying!!" shrieks Barnaby. Momentarily he feels like he is the centre of the image and that it has been swapped from inner vision to reality.

He tentatively moves forward and the landscape below starts to slide past him. Following the main street, he has the sensation he is about one hundred feet from the ground.

"This is incredible! If you've ever had a dream and had the feeling you're flying, it's exactly like this! No, wait, this is even better! I'm in control!"

"Good," says Shokawa. "You have connected quickly. Explore your space, come and visit the beach."

Barnaby pushes his arms out in front of him and thinks himself toward the beach. As he does, he zooms quickly forward until the beach is twenty or so feet below him. Looking around, Barnaby sees the group in the distance.

"Hey! There's us!"

"Take care, Barnaby. All is not as it seems. This is your view on the universe of knowledge. The things you can see here are from all time. Some things will be clear and others not so."

As Barnaby zooms towards the group, he's aware there are differences. At first, it isn't apparent what they are, he can see himself standing facing Shokawa and there's Mum and Uncle Finch. There are three others but at first, Barnaby does not recognise them. Then, as he lowers down further, he sees that one of them is perhaps Jack's father. That's odd, what's he doing here? Standing either side of him are two women. One is in a black suit of some kind with bobbed purple hair, the other is wearing an army uniform. Clearly it has seen a lot of action. The woman with the purple hair is crying and falls to her knees. What on earth is going on here?

"What do you see Barnaby?"

"I see you, Mum! Hello!"

Real Elizabeth waves to him.

Barnaby does not see this. Mum in the vision is standing completely still.

"I can see you, Uncle Finch, except you look MUCH older! Jesus, you're an old man!"

"Let's hope that's a vision of the future Barnaby!" shouts Uncle Finch with a massive smile on his face.

"There are other people here too. There's a lady crying. Jack your dad's here!"

"What? What's my dad doing there?"

"No wait." Barnaby takes a closer look at the face. It suddenly dawns on him that this isn't Jack's dad. "Jack! It's you!! You're, like, all grown up!"

"What? Really?? Am I still devastatingly handsome?"

"Yeah! You don't look bad at all!"

So, if that's Jack, that must mean…

"Marsha! You're all grown up too! You're dressed like a soldier!"

"A soldier? I grow up to be a soldier??" Marsha is slightly shocked as she has always intended to go into law like her mother.

"Do not read these signs literally," Shokawa explains. "They are snapshots of times to come."

"Thank God!" replies Marsha. "What do I look like?"

Barnaby falls silent and blushes again.

"OMG! Look at him!" teases Jack. "By the looks of those rosy cheeks, you're still super-hot!"

Marsha turns to Jack.

"Still super-hot?" she asks with her eyebrows raised.

Jack realises he's made a boo-boo.

"I mean…"

"That means you think I'm super-hot now!" Marsha grins.

"No, what I meant was…"

"Well, Jack Warner, there's a turn up for the books!"
Now it is Jack's turn to blush.

"What about me?" interrupts Polly, changing the subject.

"You're dressed in black. You have purple hair."

"Cool," she responds approvingly.

In his vision, Barnaby stands before Polly and then kneels down to where she is now sitting cross-legged in the sand, her head buried in her hands as she sobs uncontrollably.

As he crouches down to her level, she removes her hands from her face and looks directly at him. Her eyes are a blurred mess of black eyeliner that now runs down her face. She's older, perhaps very early twenties and is incredibly beautiful, despite her state of despair. He looks deep into her eyes. They are hurt and broken, full of tragedy.

"I'm so sorry, my love," she wails reaching her cupped hands out to his face. "Forgive me, please!" With that, she breaks down once more. Her hands fall into the sand to support herself, as tears stream onto the beach causing wet marbles of sand to clump together.

"What's up Barn?" asks the real Polly. "Why are you crouching?"

Barnaby opens his eyes and looks up at the real Polly who is staring down at him with a curious look on her face. He quickly stands up.

"Nothing, I was just, em, checking out your boots! Yeah, you're wearing future boots, very cool," remarks a quick-thinking Barnaby, giving Polly the thumbs up.

"Oh yeah? Sweet," she replies, with a puzzled look on her face.

"Now, you have the connection," announces Shokawa, "we can do all teaching remotely. Shokawa does not need to be by your side. Every day, after your Earth school, we will have one hour."

"Okay, I look forward to it!"

"You all see how training starts. You have heard of our values, of being in a state of readiness to accept training. Easier for a child, nothing to undo, so Elizabeth and Mathias, some power may come to you but I must limit it. Marsha, you also have a strong heart and maturity. You will become a pupil of Barnaby in time. Jack, you will mature before training, the power of the crystals requires much responsibility. Polly, be patient, your time will come. Think hard about control."

"So you think I'm immature?" exclaims Jack.

"Yes."

"Meh, you're probably right," he grins.

"Barnaby, your next lesson is the early control of matter. Do not attempt to move anything until this lesson. For now, practice the projection of today. With this, you can see places all over the universe. Enjoy this."

"I sure will!" replies an excited Barnaby.

"Now, let's get off the beach for your return home. Kick the sand from your shoes!" smiles Shokawa, as he walks away from the beach with the rest of the group in tow. Barnaby and Polly bring up the rear.

"Barn?"

"Yes, Polly?"

"Why was I crying?"

"What do you…"

"Don't kid me around. You said a lady was crying and you were kneeling at my feet. I'm not stupid, Barn, why was I crying?"

Barnaby pauses for a second, looking solemn.

"I don't know Poll. I honestly don't. You were very upset and you apologised to me." Barnaby chooses to omit the part where she calls him 'My love'.

"Ok," replies Polly, and she stops walking for a bit. Barnaby hangs back and stands with her.

"Are you okay, Polly?" he asks.

Polly takes a deep breath.

"Obviously, I like to be the tough girl, okay?"

"Yes. But why is that?"

Barnaby is looking at her with his big honest eyes. Damn it, this boy is getting to her. She bites her lip and Barnaby can see she is clearly wanting to discuss something.

"Poll, you can tell me anything, you..."

"I was bullied." she blurts out, not looking Barnaby in the eyes.

"Really?" says Barnaby in genuine surprise.

"Yeah. It was tough. If it wasn't for Marsha, I dunno, I couldn't take much more. All the other girls instantly liked her because she's so cute. She took pity on me. After that, everyone pretty much left me alone."

"I'm really sorry to hear that, that's awful," Barnaby consoles her. "You know, I was also picked on at my old school in England, so if you want to talk about it, you can. Any time."

"Thanks." Polly regains her composure but is still staring at her feet.

"Listen, you don't have to be on your guard around me, Poll. If you want to pop over when everyone else is away, you're more than welcome. I'm a good listener, you know?"

Polly nods and then looks up into Barnaby's eyes. "Thanks. It's just that, if I'm apologising to you in the future and crying, it means I must have hurt you somehow and I just want you to know, that's not something I would ever want to do."

"And why is that?" asks Barnaby softly, fishing for some sign that Polly likes him as more than just a friend.

"Because you're not like all the other stupid boys, Barnaby," replies Polly with her rebellious tone kicking back in a bit.

"In what way?"

"None of them have saved my life." She leans over and kisses Barnaby on the cheek, before walking off to join the rest of the group. Barnaby stands for a moment, almost frozen, in a dreamy daze. That's the first girl to kiss him that wasn't his mother!

"Come on, Barn door!" shouts Jack.

"Huh, yeah, sure, coming!"

Barnaby begins to run. The group have stopped to empty sand from their shoes, oblivious to the moment of fondness that has just occurred.

"Can we come and visit again?" enquires Elizabeth.

"My new friends are always welcome here. I will teach you how to travel without a machine."

"Excellent, it would be great to see more of your world," she responds.

"Now, if you are ready, I will return you to your home.

"Shokawa, can we make sure it's Sunday afternoon, please? That's the time it would be for us," asks Marsha.

"Of course." Shokawa raises his hands above the group and they are gone.

Chapter 18
School frenz

The school bus is a weird place to be after the events of the past three days. Barnaby sits at the back with Marsha, awaiting the arrival of Jack and Polly. Barnaby is particularly looking forward to seeing Polly.

When they parted ways yesterday he stood and watched the three friends leave from the front porch of his house. Down the path they went and he longed for Polly to look around and smile. As they turned left out of the gate at the bottom of the drive, he concluded it was perhaps just a spur of the moment thing. Then just as the group reached the opposite side of the garden wall, Polly briefly glanced back at Barnaby. It was only a fleeting glimpse and she didn't smile or wave, but she looked back and that was the important thing.

Barnaby's heart is thumping in his chest in anticipation. What on earth is going on? Only yesterday he was swooning over Marsha, having never really looked at girls in that way before. However, sitting here with her now, he's still quite taken with her beauty.

"Did you get a good night's sleep?" asks Barnaby.

"Yes, finally! I tell you, it took me a while though, all this bouncing around time has left me out of sync with the real world."

"Yeah," laughs Barnaby, "I know what you mean. But at least we are back to reality."

Barnaby is straining his neck, looking up the long straight road on which they are travelling to get a sight of Polly at the next stop.

"Hey, you seem a bit distracted, Barnaby. Is everything okay?" Marsha enquires, having sensed a cooling in his mannerisms around her. From the start, she had guessed that Barnaby was attracted to her, which she liked. Now he doesn't seem interested in the slightest. Tsk, boys!

"Oh, nothing, just a bit agitated with the whole 'Become a father to the universe' thing."

"I know, it's so weird. That must be freaking you out."

"It is a bit. I am looking forward to the training though."

"Yes, me too. I can't believe you're going to be my tutor," says Marsha, patting Barnaby's arm and laughing. Actually, it's a blatant flirt, but he is not taking the bait.

"Yes, it's strange," Barnaby remarks, still straining to see up the road.

Marsha's smile drops and she takes a mini-huff, folding her arms and staring out of the window with a face like thunder.

Barnaby can now see Jack and Polly standing at their stop further down the road. He sits back in his seat, trying to act calm.

"Okay, Barnaby, be cool," he mumbles.

"What?" asks Marsha.

Barnaby had not intended to speak out loud. That was supposed to be an inner thought.

"Um…" is all that comes out of him.

For Marsha though, the penny has already dropped.

"Oh my God!"

"What?" asks a startled Barnaby.

"You're in love with Polly!"

"That's ridiculous!" Barnaby exclaims. He is now as red as a UK mailbox.

"Oh, this explains everything!" announces Marsha proudly.

"What do you mean, this explains everything??"

"Barnaby, I'm not blind. Until yesterday you turned into mush every time you had to speak to me." At which, Barnaby's face turns the red blush dial up to eleven. "Now I see why that has changed. Look, I don't blame you, Polly is lovely once you get to know her. She's just got a bit of a hard shell that takes a while to crack. Awwwwww, two of my best chums getting it on!"

243

"We're not getting it on!" whispers Barnaby aggressively. "She doesn't know that I like her, but I think she likes me. It's all so confusing."

"It's only confusing for you guys. For the rest of us, everything is sooooooo obvious."

The bus comes to a halt and the hydraulic door once more hisses in protest at being opened.

Jack gets on first and the anticipation has Barnaby nearly having a panic attack. His heart is doing a Neil Peart drum solo in his chest as he fidgets and twists in his seat.

Then he sees Polly board. Her hair is in pigtails which hang down to her shoulders. She's clearly spent a bit longer on her make-up this morning and for once she's wearing a school uniform. However, it has skulls pinned to the lapels and the tie is half its proper length. As she walks down the bus aisle, she struts nonchalantly.

"Oh my goodness, she is definitely into you Barnaby," whispers Marsha with a big grin on her face.

"Shoosh, she'll hear!" Barnaby is seething.

"Morning, Barn Door, Morning, Marshland!" bawls Jack as he slips into the seat in front of Barnaby and Marsha.

"Morning, Jackboots," says Marsha on behalf of Barnaby and herself. Barnaby cannot speak at this point.

"What's wrong with you, loser?" Jack enquires. "Finally got to sit next to Marsha and freaking out, eh?" He punches Barnaby on the shoulder just as Polly approaches to hear the last comment.

Polly stops for a second, looks at Barnaby and Marsha, scowls and then plops down into the seat next to Jack, facing forward.

"Jack, why don't you and I swap seats?" suggests Marsha, noticing the sudden tension.

"Sure." Marsha gets up and Jack shoves past Polly and dives into the seat next to Barnaby.

"Well, oh father of the universe, moved any good rocks lately?"

"Don't be silly. I'm not allowed to move rocks yet," replies Barnaby, distracted by Polly whose face has not been visible since she sat down.

"What is it, man? You seem so distracted. Why do you keep looking at my sis..., oh man, are you kidding me?" mocks Jack, for whom the penny has also instantly dropped.

"What? I don't know what you mean," utters Barnaby, in what has to be one of the least convincing performances of all time.

"You've got the hots for my sister!" announces Jack, loud enough for the whole bus to hear. Marsha turns around, looks at Barnaby with raised eyebrows and smiles, as if to say 'see, it's obvious to everyone!'

Barnaby almost slides under the seat in front in embarrassment.

"Please, Lord, teleport me back to Koyakashi!" he groans.

"You don't need the Lord to teleport you! You can do it yourself."

"Not yet I can't. All I can do is this remote viewing thing. Last night, I picked a spot on Google maps and focussed. Before I knew it I was there, circling above people's heads."

"Where were you?"

"Em," comes Barnaby's stunted response.

"Oh no!" Jack looks at Polly, "You weren't spying on my sister, were you? Tell me you weren't circling above our house?"

"I might have drifted by at one point," comes the defeated response, at which Jack bursts out laughing.

"Oh man, this is gold," continues Jack, as he wheezes with laughter.

Polly has still not looked back, but Barnaby can see that she and Marsha are now deep in conversation. He strains to hear what they're saying, but their words are drowned out by Jack's laughter.

The rest of the bus journey is excruciating for Barnaby. Having half a conversation with Jack about nonsense, and all the while praying for eye contact with Polly. It does not materialise. Even when they arrive at school and Polly and Marsha get off the bus, Marsha is the only one to glance back as they walk up the main drive towards the school steps.

Barnaby trails his school bag along the ground, lovesick, with the weight of the world on his shoulders and all the while being taunted by Jack.

Lunchtime comes around and Barnaby finds himself a spot under one of the oak trees that grow on the school

246

grounds. He has no desire to be around Jack with his constant teasing, or Marsha the distraction. All he wants is for Polly to walk by, notice him in his lonely state and take pity on him with, perhaps, a kiss on the lips this time. Alas, just as Barnaby spots Polly walking down the school path in the direction of the main gate, Jack appears directly in front of him.

"Leave me alone Jack!" growls Barnaby, swaying from side-to-side.

"Hey, that could really hurt a guy's feelings, you know?" Jack frowns.

"I'm just not in a sociable mood right now," answers Barnaby, his eyes following Polly down to the main gate.

Jack looks around and spots his sister turning right out of the school gate.

"You are such a loser."

"Jack!"

"I mean, she's right there! Go after her you fool!"

Barnaby looks up at Jack, shaking his head.

"She's not interested."

Jack plops himself down next to Barnaby. The grass is a little bit wet, which makes Jack sit up and squat.

"If you don't try, you lose. When I call you a loser, it's not a term of endearment, you really are a complete loser," states Jack in all seriousness.

"Thanks!" groans Barnaby sarcastically.

"Look, I love you man, but you are kinda pathetic. It's maybe just an English thing, like self-harm or something.

You seem to torture yourself instead of allowing yourself to try."

"What's the point? She hates me, I can tell," cries Barnaby.

"Look, I've spent my whole life with that girl. We shared a womb together. I know her better than she knows herself and I can tell you, she REALLY likes you."

"Really?" exclaims a surprised Barnaby.

"Sure. All that effort this morning? She was in the bathroom for an hour. She was making an effort for you!"

"And then you ruined it with your Marsha quip," announces Barnaby, staring at Jack.

"Hey, I didn't know then that this was a thing! But now we all know the facts, can you PLEASE just do something about it? I hate seeing you two moping around the place. I mean Poll is a grungy, goth type, so it's normal for her, but you! You make me wanna jump off something high!"

Barnaby giggles a little.

"See, there you go! Life's not so bad if you stay positive and have a laugh." Jack punches Barnaby's shoulder once more.

"Ah, you're a good man, Jack Warner."

"I know, I know, now go after her!"

"Ach, she'll be miles away by now. I'll wait until after class and grab her," replies Barnaby. As he does he gives a sudden shudder. Frowning, he looks down at his body as a cold wave sweeps through it.

"Oh, ugh, what was that?" he cries, standing up.

"What is it dude?" asks a concerned Jack.

"I dunno, it was weird. Like a really cold shudder going through my body. It's left me feeling quite anxious."

"Is it love?" smirks Jack.

"No, this is, I dunno, I feel like something is wrong."

"Well, what?"

"I can't put my finger on it. It's like an instinct or something. Like something bad has happened."

"Like Alderaan blowing up?" Jack grins.

"Actually, yeah, something like that," replies Barnaby. Jack's smile suddenly drops.

For a moment, Barnaby and Jack stand beneath the oak tree looking around. Neither knows what they're looking for and perhaps Jack is just following his lead, but Barnaby is genuinely concerned.

"Hey, you're freaking me out," shrieks Jack.

"That's because you know what's out there now," Barnaby responds.

"Yeah and I kinda wish I didn't anymore." Jack chuckles nervously.

"Let's get inside anyway and find Marsha," continues Barnaby walking toward the main entrance. Jack follows behind and the pair head into the school. After a minute of meandering through bland corridors, filled with lockers and notice boards, they come to the canteen. Inside, they find Marsha, her face buried in a romantic novel for teenagers.

"Hey, Marsha," says Barnaby sitting opposite her, with Jack sliding in next to her.

Marsha looks up from her novel to find herself surrounded by boys.

"Hey, guys, what's up?"

"Barn has the jitters," announces Jack.

"Is this because of Polly?" enquires Marsha.

"No, I'll sort that, that's not a concern. No, I felt something, a cold wave pass through me, like something strange happened. Did you feel anything?"

"Nope," replies Marsha. "But it is cold in here, so maybe I couldn't feel it."

"Cold? It's roasting in here!" Jack cries.

"Oh, I get like that when I skip lunch," Marsha points out.

"Why are you skipping lunch?" asks Jack.

"I don't want these getting any bigger." Marsha pats her hips.

"Your hips aren't big!" adds Barnaby.

"I dunno, let me have a good look at them," grins Jack, leaning back and admiring Marsha's waistline.

"Hoi!" Marsha yells, punching Jack's leg as he gives out a hearty laugh.

Marsha smiles at Jack and it's at that point that it dawns on Barnaby he might not be the only one with an infatuation. Two supremely attractive people like Jack and Marsha cannot remain platonic friends forever.

"Hey, do you know where Polly was going?" quizzes Barnaby.

"Yeah, she was nipping to the Seven-Eleven for a pack of gum," replies Marsha.

"Really? The bell's about to go, she'll be late!" remarks Barnaby, surprised.

"Have you even met Polly? When has she ever been early for class?" Marsha points out.

"Well that's true," says Barnaby, just as the bell rings for the end of lunch break. At its sound, about a hundred chairs screech across the canteen floor in unison, as the kids start to make their way back to their respective classes.

In their classroom, Barnaby stares at the empty chair that will soon be occupied by Polly. Marsha sits at the rear left of the class next to the window, whereas Jack has a desk right in front of the teacher, one would assume to keep an eye on his cheeky behaviour.

Barnaby's desk is central in the layout of the class and Polly is two in front and to the left. This means Barnaby will be able to gaze at her dreamily without her noticing, praying that she turns around and rewards him with a big smile.

On the blackboard in front of them is written the words 'Of Mice and Men - Steinbeck'.

"Great," thinks Barnaby. "We already did this in my old school."

Their teacher, Mrs Albright, is around fifty years old and sports a Farah Fawcett hairdo as if to cling to a youth she never quite lived. Nostalgic somehow, but considering she was about ten years old when the late Ms. Fawcett was a thing, she lives by the motto: 'Once a classic, always a classic'.

Mrs Albright is starting her dialogue on the great American novel when the door opens. Barnaby, who had been staring out of the window, leaps in his seat. He spins around expecting to see the source of his anxiety walk through the door. Instead, it's one of the school's secretaries who is now whispering into the teacher's ear.

"Barnaby Brown!" she announces.

Barnaby looks a little confused.

"There is a call for you. Please follow Miss Atkins."

"Yes Miss, um Mrs, um," stutters Barnaby, as the rest of the class start to giggle. In his old school all the female teachers seemed to be called Miss, even if they were married. Here, in the US, he's still not quite sure what the protocol is.

Barnaby manoeuvres himself between the rows of desks until he reaches Miss Atkins. He follows her out of the classroom and down the corridor towards the admin section.

In the office, Barnaby is seated in a comfy Swedish style couch, neatly placed behind a cheap-looking coffee table. He nervously looks around. It's smallish, would sit about five staff members and, rather nondescript. His nerves are rising as students are only allowed calls for emergencies. Has something happened to mum? Maybe Uncle Finch has burned the house down.

Miss Atkins trails a phone on a long cable over the office reception desks to where Barnaby is sitting.

"Sorry, we don't get many calls for students," remarks Miss Atkins, placing the phone in front of him.

"That's quite alright, thank you," responds Barnaby, politely.

"Just pick it up when it rings," she explains.

"Okay, thank you."

About 30 seconds later, the phone rings and Barnaby picks it up, shaking a little.

"Go ahead please," instructs Miss Atkins on the other end of the line.

"Hello?" says Barnaby.

"Barnaby, my dear boy," is the reply. It's Darius Dent!

There is a pause as Barnaby is rendered speechless.
'How did he know which school I go to?'

"Hello, are you there, Master Brown?"

"Mister Dent?" replies Barnaby.

"Ah good, you are there. How is school today?"

Barnaby is very wary.

"It's em, good, thank you. How was the desert?" enquires Barnaby, becoming a bit braver.

"Hot, windy, sandy, deserty, but then I wasn't there that long you see," continues Dent.

"Ah yes, I believe you had a visit from Kallick?"

"Lord Kallick, correct. He was kind enough to bring me back home and is currently assisting with some plans I have in motion."

"How kind of him," adds Barnaby, playing along, hoping Dent gets to the punchline soon.

"And that's where you come in dear boy. You see, part of our plans requires access to the crystal you have in your possession. So I need you to pop over to our labs, where you previously visited, and give me the crystal AND the time machines, plural."

"And why would I go out of my way to bring them to an animal like you?" Barnaby announces.

"Because if you don't, then your little friend here will find herself with some new piercings. Some rather large bullet-shaped piercings."

Barnaby freezes as the cold wave passes through him again. In the background, he can hear muffled noises and then one voice very loud and clear.

"Barnaby!" It's Polly.

"Poll??!!!" screams Barnaby standing up, as the office admin staff look up from their desks.

"They grabbed me outside the school, give them nothing!!" she cries, before letting out a loud blood-curdling squeal.

"So you see Master Brown, I hold all of the cards. Bring the crystal to me tonight and your little friend will walk away. Fail to bring them and you know what will happen, the same thing that will happen if you alert the police or anybody else for that matter, do you follow?"

There is silence as Barnaby desperately thinks.

"Do you follow?" screams Dent.

"Yes! I follow, just don't harm her," pleads Barnaby.

"Oh, I'm afraid it's too late, you see one of my men has just accidentally cut off the end of one of her little fingers."

Tears now stream down Barnaby's face as he hears the screaming and crying in the background, coming from a clearly distraught Polly.

"You'll pay for that, Dent!" yells Barnaby through his tears, as his concern for Polly is mirrored by his desire to punish Dent.

"8 pm, don't be late," barks Dent and he hangs up.

Barnaby is left standing in a state of shock, crying relentlessly, the hate rising in him.

"Are you okay, Barnaby?" asks Miss Atkins, who has rushed over.

Ignoring her, Barnaby turns and rushes from the office, leaving behind a very concerned secretary.

He sprints down the corridor until he reaches his classroom. As he bursts in, the door crashes against the wall, and a stunned Mrs Albright turns to face him.

"Jack, Marsha, we've got to go!"

"Are you alright, Barnaby?" exclaims Mrs Albright.

"Guys, now!" screams Barnaby observing the lack of movement from Jack and Marsha.

"What's wrong Barnaby," says Marsha, rising from the back of the classroom.

"It's Polly," Barnaby shrieks, the tears still streaming down his face. At this, Jack rushes forward and grabs him by the shoulders.

"What's wrong, what's happened to her?" yells Jack, trembling.

Marsha is now running through the desks, shoving them out of the way to reach Barnaby.

"Dent has her! He has her," exclaims Barnaby sobbing.

"I told you he should've been blasted into space!!" Jack hollers angrily.

"What is all this, what's going on?" quizzes Mrs Albright.

"This is going to take too long to explain Mrs Albright, sorry, but we've got to go!" Marsha blurts out, as she rushes past the teacher and pushes both Barnaby and Jack into the corridor.

"What happened?" cries Marsha. Barnaby recounts the call and Dent's request.

"That miserable snake!!" screams Jack, kicking one of the corridor walls.

Inside the classroom, all of the other kids are straining to see what's going on. Mrs Albright closes the door to allow the trio some privacy.

"So what the hell do we do?"

"We need Shokawa," announces Barnaby.

"Well, do you just call him or what?"

"Let's just get outside and think," suggests Marsha, shoving them further down the corridor towards the main entrance.

Outside Jack is pacing around in circles. Barnaby is sitting on the ground being comforted by Marsha.

"Barn, she'll be fine, she's a tough girl. We'll get Shokawa and he will sort everything," Marsha explains while rubbing his back.

"He has this Lord Kallick with him. I don't know how this will go. Is Kallick stronger? Could we lose Polly trying to save her?"

"Let's just speak to Shokawa. Can you reach him?" asks Marsha.

"I shouldn't have to. He should have sensed this and appeared by now. I think, somehow, Kallick is blocking us out. Let's just get home and speak to Mum and Uncle Finch. See if we can work out a plan."

"Jack!" shouts Marsha.

"What?" Jack stops pacing for a second.

"We can't get the police involved. You'll have to phone your dad and say you and Polly are going to Barnaby's for dinner."

"Come on, I need to let my dad know what's happened, it's only right!"

"I don't think we should be piling this on him right now. Let's not put him in harm's way as well," adds Barnaby.

"Alright, we'll go to your house and work out a plan. Again."

Barnaby pulls his phone from his pocket and calls his mum.

"Mum, are you at home?"

Chapter 19

Learning to fly

Half an hour later, Elizabeth and Uncle Finch are sitting with the three kids in their living room, having driven them home from school.

"So you think this Kallick is blocking Shokawa's access?" she enquires.

"He must be. He'd be here by now," replies Barnaby.

"Have you tried reaching out to him yourself?"

"No, but I don't know how to!" barks Barnaby, losing his patience.

Elizabeth sighs and then sits down next to Barnaby on the floor where he plopped himself when they walked into the room.

"Listen my darling," she says, putting her arm around him, "I know this is a lot for someone of your age to handle, no one is expecting you to fix this alone. We have limited resources to play with so we really need to explore all of the avenues open to us. How about maybe sitting on your bed upstairs and seeing if you can reach out to Shokawa? See if you can picture Brukash again and locate him. Maybe you will be able to see Polly in the same way? That could all work to our advantage. Hmmm?"

Barnaby nods solemnly.

"There's a reason why Shokawa singled you out. Why he believes you are so strong and have a good heart. Because it's true! You just need some time to think it through and realise it for yourself. I think that once you open up your mind to the possibilities, and you can see the answer, you will give us the opportunity to save your friend and defeat that monster."

Again, Barnaby nods.

"Come on love, let's get you upstairs," continues Elizabeth, taking Barnaby's arm. He slowly gets to his feet and the sombre group watch as he makes his way up to his bedroom.

In his room, Barnaby kicks off his shoes and sits in the middle of his bed.

"Are you sure you don't want to lie down darling?" asks Elizabeth.

"No, I don't want to fall asleep. I need to be focused."

"Okay, darling."

Momo trots into the room just as Elizabeth is leaving Barnaby to his meditation.

"Come on Momo, out you come!" she calls.

"It's fine, Mum, let him stay," interjects Barnaby.

"Okay, darling."

Momo jumps up onto the bed as Elizabeth gently closes the door, a task she has performed so many times before after laying a little boy down to sleep.

"Hi, good boy." Barnaby takes a chunk of blonde fur and neck skin and wobbles it around, one of Momo's favourite interactions.

"I need to get in touch with your big new friend, Momo," Barnaby continues. "But I have to see her first. I have to know where she is."

Barnaby closes his eyes and attempts to clear his head. It's not easy when all his thoughts are of Polly screaming in terror.

He tries to focus on just one thing. After a minute or so, he settles on a water lily floating in a pond. He lets the lily sink into the water, where it is promptly replaced by an emerging white glow. The light increases until it fills his mind and then dim objects start to poke their way through. As the haze clears, the sun begins to creep across the lawn until the whole scene is transformed into a beautiful summer's day. Eventually it becomes a real-life three-dimensional view. At this point Barnaby can start to move around.

He gently lifts himself up to a height of a thousand feet and then points himself due west towards Manhattan. He can still feel the bed beneath him, giving the sensation of sitting on a cloud. That doesn't help his fear of heights though. He takes a deep breath and then looks down.

"Oh dear God!" he screams, scanning the network of streets far below him. "Okay, just take a while to get used to this!"

He stares down, stroking a dog that is no longer visible for comfort and tries to become accustomed to the view. After around five minutes of trembling, he finally feels confident enough to move forward but, as he does, his progress is halted by a sudden rush of wind. This hadn't happened when he was motionless. It's as if the final piece of the experience has been opened up to him. The breeze is now whipping at his hair and it takes him another few seconds to embrace it and slowly start to proceed.

Inching his way forward, Barnaby holds his hands out in front of him as a steering mechanism. It seems like an obvious option to take, and it worked pretty well last night. Presumably different people with this ability move in various ways, but it's the one that makes the most sense to him. Okay, it's not the classic Superman pose, but that would involve lying on the bed, which he could still feel and would restrict the motion.

"Okay, let's try going a little faster," says Barnaby as he gently pulls his clenched fists towards him. Each millimetre he shifts his hands seems to increase the speed, precisely as he'd imagined. For sure, it's his brain that's driving the experience. If Barnaby wants he can bring his hands towards him without moving quicker, it just helps him to solidify the action.

Glancing ahead, the sheer size of New York is overwhelming. There are no tall structures out here on Long Island, just miles and miles of residential areas and parks, but off in the distance, he can see Manhattan and the tall structures of Midtown and Lower Manhattan. His destination is north of that in Harlem.

As he zooms forward he finds himself approaching La Guardia, one of New York's airports. Using the runways as a guide, he sweeps across the East River. At the end of M.L.K. Jr Boulevard he catches his first glimpse of the leafy area where Dent's research facility stands.

He circles around it looking for signs of life. Suddenly, he feels a warm, tingling sensation. Below him, he sees a black SUV with tinted windows pull through the front gates. Instantly he drops to the ground and follows it, finally catching up as it waits for entry to the lower car park. He floats into the vehicle and sits amongst its passengers, who are obviously unaware that Barnaby is viewing them remotely.

There, clutching one of her fingers and crying is Polly. To her right is Crowe, who has a gun loosely pointed into her side. Barnaby doesn't recognise any of the other occupants other than Dent, who is riding up front. Barnaby glides through and comes face-to-face with him.

"I am going to kick your butt into the fires of hell, Darius Dent!"

This gives Barnaby a certain amount of pleasure, but it would be preferable saying it to his actual face.

The car continues into a lower parking level and the group all exit, shoving Polly along with them. She looks terrified, which enrages Barnaby.

"Come on Barnaby, don't go all *Vader* on us, you've got to keep calm. What would Shokawa say now? He'd want me to do this logically. He's all about intellectual solutions. That's how we'll beat these animals."

Barnaby follows the party down through many levels, to sub-level eight. There they march Polly to the far end of the corridor into a vast, circular room, full of monitors and banks of desks.

"What the hell is this?" Barnaby wonders.

Dent then grabs Polly by the shoulder and marches her to a chair, forcibly shoving her down.

"Why are you doing this?" she cries.

"That's no real concern of yours, girl, all you need to know is that when your precious Barnaby turns up, I'll be taking the crystal and then the future of the world will be very much up for debate. You can decide whether or not you want it all to end then, or whether you want to stick around and witness it all fall to bits under my direction."

"But why would you want to do that?"

"Oh, most of the world will become a mine or work camps, but I will keep some bits nice to holiday in. Paris, the Bahamas etc." at which Dent gives a little chuckle to himself.

"You're insane!" shrieks Polly.

"Insane is working twelve hours for a minimum wage, dear girl. Hehe, under my jurisdiction they'll be doing it for scraps of food and to spare their miserable lives. It's amazing how hard people can work with a little motivation."

"It's a fool's dream, Darius, like all of the megalomaniacs before you."

"No, my dear, do not compare me to the likes of Hitler or Stalin. They failed because all they had was words. That was their only power, the power to convince. I will have a little bit more than just promises up my sleeve. In time, I will have a fully mechanised global army to do my bidding for me and the backup of an elite force of alien warriors."

"Evil has never won, Dent!" roars Polly as Dent strides away towards the exit.

"Yet!" he replies. He marches out the door, which slams behind him.

Polly is left in the room with two guards.

Barnaby draws nearer as she sits in the chair nursing her wounded finger. Looking around, she sees that there's no way out other than the door that Dent just left through.

Barnaby is now directly in front of her, gazing into her face as she scans the room. He raises his hand, wishing he could touch her and give her comfort. As he does, Polly stops looking around the room and stares straight ahead, right into his eyes. Obviously, she can't see him, this is just a coincidence.

He places his hand on her cheek, but it merely passes through her. At the same time, Polly raises her hand to his and holds it there. A single teardrop runs from her left eye down her cheek and reaches the tip of Barnaby's finger.

Polly's mouth drops open and her eyes quickly dart from side to side, as if trying to see something that's not visible. Somehow, she feels his presence.

"Barnaby?" she whispers, looking around the space directly in front of her.

"I'm right here, Polly," replies a startled Barnaby, but she cannot hear him. She does seem to sense his hand though. Maybe it's her exposure to the crystal also that is causing this connection.

Barnaby leans forward and gently kisses her on the lips, at which point Polly's hand moves from her cheek and her fingers softly touch her mouth.

"I can feel you, Barnaby, I can feel you!" she laughs through her sobs.

"We'll be together again, Polly, I promise." Barnaby puts his arms around her. Polly bursts into tears, her shoulders jerking with each fresh waterfall. She looks up at him, her eyes streaming, the eyeliner starting to run down her cheeks.

Barnaby lifts his head a little and kisses her forehead.

"We're coming for you, Poll, we're coming."

Polly starts to cry again, but then quickly shuts the tears down. Composing herself, she looks straight ahead.

"I know, Barnaby. I know you're coming to rescue me. I know I will get out of this. You've seen the older me, I know I survive. Just make sure that YOU stay safe. I need you safe, Barnaby. I can't lose you."

Barnaby stares deep into her blue eyes a little bit longer.

"I promise, Polly, I promise."

"Go, go now," she mutters and she lowers her head as if to dismiss him.

Barnaby hovers a few seconds more and then opens his eyes. He's still on his bed with Momo curled up beside him. But now, Barnaby is super-charged. Before visiting Polly he was at a low, feeling very pessimistic about the whole situation. Now seeing her, knowing her pain and realising he can save her, he has turned his outlook to one of optimism.

"Shokawa, you must hear me!" he cries through gritted determined teeth.

Closing his eyes, he once more imagines the lily on the pond, but this time it slips immediately into the light and the vision of Brukash instantly unfolds before him. It takes about five seconds to focus and appear as real as actually being there.

He's about fifty feet in the air, looking down over the beach where he last experienced dream-state Brukash.

"Shokawa!" he shouts out.

There is no response. Barnaby motions over the plaza and up the marble street to the outside of Shokawa's house. He enters to find it as empty as ever.

"The Council Chamber!" he roars as he spins around heading back down the street to the plaza and into the enormous neoclassical structure.

There, in the centre of the building, is a circular room, flanked by marble seating steps and columns. In the middle sits Shokawa, surrounded by the other eleven council members.

"Shokawa!" Barnaby yells into the centre of the room, unaware of whether or not he can be heard.

"Barnaby! Are you not supposed to be in school?"

"Dent took Polly! He's hurt her! He wants to trade her for the crystal."

"Hmmm," says Shokawa, as he closes his eyes for a moment. "Kallick has placed a veil of deceit over your Earth. I cannot see him. Your world is a black hole of information at this time."

"We must do something. We must rescue Polly and keep the crystal safe," insists Barnaby.

Shokawa motions for Barnaby to stand by him, which he promptly does.

"Of course. Not the first time Kallick has done this. I will bring forward your training for today. You need to learn to control matter. It will help to defeat Dent and Kallick."

"When can we get started?" replies Barnaby.

"We start immediately!"

Chapter 20
Something's not right!

By the time Barnaby opens his eyes again, three hours have passed. It has been an incredible afternoon. He achieved skills that have even surprised Shokawa.

"Wow, it's time to get off of this bed!" he says, leaning over. His legs have gone to sleep and he finds it difficult to stir them into action. Momo appears to be having the same issue. He lies on his back and stretches out all four legs, before falling back onto his side to continue his extended rest period.

Barnaby rushes downstairs into the living room where Jack and Marsha are asleep on the couch and Elizabeth is sitting watching some daytime T.V. trash.

"Where's Uncle Finch?" he enquires.

"Oh, he's in the basement twiddling with the time machine. How did you get on?"

"I saw Polly, Mum. She's in a terrible state," murmurs Barnaby, feeling emotional again.

"Oh poor Polly." Elizabeth rushes to give him a hug.

"Dent was there, Mum. He's planning to rule the Earth and make everyone slaves. Apparently, he is going to have Kallick's help with an Arkavian army!!"

"Well he won't be doing it without our crystal, so we need to stop him. How did you get on with Shokawa, did you reach him? Every time I popped into the room you were in a trance."

"Yes, Mum, I found him and we did our next training session. I learnt loads of cool stuff. He also taught me some of Kallick's weaknesses."

At that moment Marsha stirs and has a long stretch.

"What time is it?" she asks, deliriously.

"Nearly five o'clock," replies Barnaby.

"Oh crumbs, I better be going home for dinner!" Marsha jumps up from the couch and rubs her eyes.

"I don't think that's such a good idea," answers Barnaby.

"It's not safe until Dent is out of action. We need to teach him a lesson that we can't be attacked or kidnapped ever again!" he continues. "Isn't that right, Mum?"

"Look, Marsha, I agree with Barnaby, it's not safe right now, for you or your family. I'll call your mum and say we're having dinner with Jack and Polly and that you're welcome to join us."

"God, I wish this was all over! I just want life to go back to normal!" Marsha grumbles, plopping back down on the couch. She narrowly misses Jack's head, who has just started to wake up.

"Woah!" he shrieks, sitting upright. "Watch what you're doing with that butt!"

"I didn't think you'd mind," says Marsha, sniggering.

"Well, gimme a moment to wake up at least," smirks Jack, as cocky as ever.

"How's Polly?" asks Marsha. At the mention of her name, Jack suddenly becomes alert, eagerly awaiting the update from Barnaby.

"She's pretty terrified. I don't think any more harm will come to her though. He's using her as a lure. The weird thing is, when I went up to her, she could sense I was there. She called my name and said she knew we were coming to help!"

"Well, that's good! Hopefully, that'll keep her spirits up until we can rescue her," replies Marsha.

"What about the big guy?" Jack enquires. "Did you reach him? Can he help?"

"Yes, he's coming. We did heaps of studying and he taught me some really cool stuff."

"Like what?" An enthusiastic Jack leaps up from the couch.

"You'll see," grins Barnaby, giving nothing away.

"Wait, he won't see!" interrupts Elizabeth, shaking her head. "These guys are staying right here with me until Shokawa returns with Polly. I'm not letting any harm come to anyone who isn't capable of protecting themselves from lunatics with guns. It's bad enough you're going to be there!"

"Oh, Mrs B!!" shrieks Jack. "He's got MY sister!!"

"I'm sorry Jack, we'll be in the basement standing next to the time machine until all of this has been cleared up," orders Elizabeth with her arms folded. Jack plops back onto the couch with a huff.

"You know what's strange?" remarks Marsha with a frown. "Why hasn't Dent just come here, shot us all and taken the crystal?"

"That is odd. Maybe he's worried Shokawa has placed a safety net around the house or something," replies Elizabeth.

"But Kallick has already placed a net around the planet to stop Shokawa detecting trouble. It doesn't make any sense!" adds Barnaby.

"Unless he wants us to be here for some reason?" suggests Jack, shrugging.

Barnaby paces the room and then pauses.

"What is Dent expecting us to do when we leave to bring him the crystal?"

"Um, jump into the research lab to grab Polly?"

"Yes," cries Barnaby. "He expects us to use the time machine! Either to go back and rescue Polly before she is kidnapped, or use it to teleport ourselves into sub-level eight. Also, if Shokawa is with us, he can manipulate outside of the time machine. Whatever happens, it will start from this house!"

Elizabeth stares at Barnaby.

"Could they have booby-trapped the house perhaps?"

"I wouldn't put it past him!" Barnaby announces.

"Oh God," Elizabeth suddenly shrieks as she runs towards the basement door, "Mathias!" It instantly clicks with Barnaby what his mum is thinking and rushes after her.

***

Downstairs in the basement, Uncle Finch is adding some more features to the time machine. He thinks he can now track other time displacement signatures that will allow him to locate people or things moving around the Earthly space. All he needs to do now is test it. A quick jump somewhere to track his own recent movement should do the trick.

"So, where should I go?" he wonders. "How about Paris, 1944 for the liberation? 25.08.1944." He taps in the date and searches through his maps for a suitable jump site. "How about the Tuileries Gardens at 10 pm. Most people in Paris should be suitably drunk by then."

Bang, bang, bang.

"Oh bother, what's all that noise?" grumbles Mathias, as he finishes adding in the coordinates. "Don't they know I'm trying to work?"

"Mathias!!"

"Hang on, I'll be back in a minute! I've just got one quick test to do," he shouts up the stairs.

"No, no Uncle Finch, don't use the time machine!! It's a trap!"

Elizabeth and Barnaby stand at the basement door which is locked as usual.

Bang, bang, bang!!

"Mathias!"

"Uncle Finch!?"

Silence.

"Oh no, has he just blasted himself across the universe?" cries Barnaby.

Suddenly, the bolt slides across and the door opens.

"Oh, thank God!" Elizabeth rushes forward and hugs Uncle Finch.

"What's all this fuss about?" he asks.

"We think Dent and Kallick may have set a trap."

"What kind of a trap?"

"One that involves us all being killed if we use the time machine!!"

"Oh my, I was a finger stroke away from using it!"

"How do you know for sure he has?" queries Uncle Finch.

"Just a gut feeling. The fact he hasn't come here for the crystal. It didn't add up for me," explains Barnaby.

"So what will our next move be? If we are on to him, he will likely have a backup plan," Elizabeth adds.

"He'll be watching us." Barnaby glances at the front door.

"I reckon you're right," agrees Elizabeth, pulling everyone back towards the living room. Marsha and Jack have been listening in the doorway.

"Okay, I'm going to take a look outside," announces Barnaby, closing his eyes. He thinks of the lily. The light comes quickly and he is in the street floating towards the opposite side. Most of the houses have driveways, but there are several cars parked on the road. Three are bunched together so Barnaby decides to try them to begin with.

The first and second are empty, but as suspected the third one contains two men, dressed in black. It's Vasquez and Sheppard from the Jersey extraction team.

Barnaby opens his eyes.

"Yup, we're being watched," confirms Barnaby. The group collectively grumble.

"Right, we've gotta get out of here without being seen and then we need to get as far away as possible to summon Shokawa," orders Elizabeth.

"Fancy dress?" suggests Jack, pointing up towards the attic.

"I was thinking we just climb the fence at the bottom of the garden?" replies Elizabeth frowning.

"Yup, that works too," Jack nods.

"What about Momo?" asks Barnaby with great concern.

"Momo? I'm sure he'll be fine here alone," points out Elizabeth.

"No, he's coming with us," insists Barnaby.

"And how are we supposed to get him over the fence? It's ten feet high!"

"Same way you'll get me over the fence - with great difficulty," adds Uncle Finch.

"Right Mathias, go grab your time machine and we'll get moving! Don't forget the crystal section from the prototype. We don't want to leave that lying around, do we?"

"Indeed," confirms Barnaby.

"Tally ho!" cries Uncle Finch, and he wanders back down the stairs.

"Tally ho? Indeed? It's terribly English in here," Jack smirks.

***

At the bottom of the garden, the group are gathered around the fence behind Uncle Finch's toolshed. Fortunately it is wooden, which will work in their favour.

"Okay, stand back everyone," declares Uncle Finch as he prepares to hit it with a hammer. "I've got this!"

"Um, all that will do is break your elbows, Uncle Finch. Use it to pull the plank out by the nails," suggests Barnaby, watching his uncle pull the hammer back.

"What? Oh, yes, I was never much of a carpenter!"

He jams the claw end of the hammer behind the section that contains two rusty nails. He tugs at it and the nails begin to squeal in protest, along with the sound of creaking wood. After about three minutes, he has managed to remove them.

"Just four more to go!" he remarks, moving the hammer up to the next section.

"No rush, Uncle Finch." Barnaby impatiently grabs a hold of the bottom section of the wooden plank. "Come on, Jack!" he motions for his friend to join in.

With the combined effort of the boys, the middle section squeaks and creaks until it also releases with a jerk, quickly followed by the last nails at the top. Finally the whole plank comes away.

"Bravo boys!" exclaims Uncle Finch. "Exactly what I was going to do next!"

The group waste no time in squeezing through the gap into their neighbours garden. Even Uncle Finch, who's clearly been snacking in the basement of late, is able to make it.

On the other side of the fence is a row of conifers, obviously there to give their neighbour some privacy. As they push their way through, they walk out into a lawned area where a family of three children and their parents are at a table having dinner. After spotting the group appear from the bushes, the father freezes in astonishment, his fork halfway to his mouth.

"Hi Bill!" waves Elizabeth. "Sorry, just having to pass through, there's, um, a rubbish truck parked across our drive!"

The group are now gently trotting past the dumbfounded family.

"No problemo," stutters Bill, still dumb-struck. His wife and family are silent, all sporting the same jaw-dropped expression. The only exception is their youngest daughter, aged about five, who is giggling at the silly family stomping through their garden.

As they pass Bill's SUV parked in his drive, they break into a sprint towards the busy intersection at the end. Jack is at the head of the pack, followed by Marsha, Barnaby (plus Momo), then Elizabeth with Uncle Finch bringing up the rear.

"See if you can grab a cab!" shouts Elizabeth to the front of the pack.

"Okay!" Jack replies over his shoulder. At the end of the street, he instantly spots a familiar yellow cab with its light on and continues to run, chasing it down the road. Fortunately the driver has seen him and is looking for a safe place to pull over.

The back door pops open and Jack jumps in as the rest of the group arrive in dribs and drabs.

"Where to fella?" asks the cabbie, who is a big round-faced guy in a New York Jets t-shirt. His hair, likely once thick and red, is now thinning and almost white.

"That's a good question. Can you give us a minute?" requests Jack.

"As long as you don't take all day!"

"Oh, there's five of us and a dog, is that okay?" Jack adds.

"Five is my limit buddy!"

"Five humans right?"

"Mmmm, if we're gonna be pedantic, yeah," replies the cabbie.

"He can lie across us, he's really tame and, um, we need to get him to a vet!" explains Jack, lying through his teeth.

"As long as he doesn't take a dump in my cab, I guess it'll be okay!"

"Thanks, buddy!"

"Where are we going?" queries Elizabeth, squeezing herself into the cab.

"Harlem, MLK, we'll work out where's best when we get there," shouts Barnaby.

"No problem," confirms the driver.

"Come on, Momo, hup, hup!"

Momo leaps into the car and puts his right paw into Barnaby's groin.

"Ahhhhhhh! Momo!" squeals Barnaby, as he attempts to get Momo into a comfier position.

"Hehe, first injury of the day," smirks Jack.

The front door opens and an out-of-breath Uncle Finch jumps in.

"Is that us?" enquires the cabbie, "No cats? No goldfish?"

"No, we can go now, thanks!" Elizabeth hollers from the back as she pulls the seatbelt across her chest.

The driver pulls away into the stream of traffic and starts the journey west across Long Island towards Harlem.

"So what's the plan when we get there?" asks Marsha.

"Well, again, you guys are not going to get involved, it's too dangerous," remarks Elizabeth. "We'll find a nice quiet spot where you-know-who can't find us and then we'll give Shokawa a call. He and Barnaby can rescue Polly and then we'll deal with the bad guys in whatever form Shokawa thinks is most appropriate."

The cabbie's ears have pricked up at the plan.

"Hey, sounds like you guys might be heading into some trouble?"

"Could you just pay attention to the road please?" snaps Elizabeth.

"Sure, sure. It's just my brother's a cop in Harlem, in case, you know, you run into any trouble."

"That's very kind, but we'll be fine. The presence of the police would be a very BAD thing for us right now, so we need to totally avoid that avenue."

"Okay, okay, just letting you know," replies the cabbie.

"Like I was saying, we need to find a nice quiet spot to call Shokawa. Barnaby, do you think you can reach him?"

"Sure, Mum, he's expecting me anyway," Barnaby answers.

"So who's this Shokawa? Some kind of Indian? Navajo maybe?" the nosey cabbie butts in.

"Please, Native American or First Nation! Anyway, he's an alien from the planet Koyakashi," Elizabeth announces.

"Haha, good one!" laughs the driver, nodding and blissfully unaware that Elizabeth is being serious.

It is another hour before they finally pull onto Martin Luther King Jr. Boulevard due to the heavy traffic.

"Okay, can you take us to St. Nicholas Park please?"

"Sure lady, no problem."

"Okay, it's 6:15 pm, Dent isn't expecting us until 8 pm, so we have enough time to come up with a plan."

"Mum, we're not working to Dent's timetable. We'll just grab Polly and then we'll see to Dent."

"Fair point!" nods Elizabeth. "What do you think Shokawa will do to him?"

"I don't honestly know, Mum," Barnaby shrugs. "He can manipulate anything on Earth, so in the future we are safeguarded. Right now we have all of this mess to fix before Shokawa can do anything."

"Why didn't he just safeguard you in the first place?"

"They have this crazy rule. You know, everyone gets a second chance. Shokawa gave Dent the option to be a good man. He chose wrong."

"I think Shokawa can be too much of an idealist. It's obvious you couldn't trust Dent."

"Is it? We did at first," Barnaby remarks. Elizabeth makes a 'You have a point' face. "Anyway, Shokawa used the example of Ashoka. He was an Indian Emperor. He felt so guilty about his genocidal deeds during his conquests that he turned to Buddhism. His Chakra is still seen today on the Indian flag. I think Shokawa's idealism is well-meant."

"Well, tell that to the people Ashoka killed during his invasions! I'm sure they were delighted he turned to Buddhism out of guilt!"

"Yeah, but he was raised to be a conqueror. He could have done that all of his life, but he saw the error of his ways enabling him to make a difference. I think he likes the idea that darkness can become light. It's inspirational."

"Well, Shokawa and I will just agree to disagree on that one!"

The cab turns right onto St. Nicholas Avenue.

"Listen, lady, I know it's none of my business," interrupts the cabbie once more, "but my brother really is a great guy. I know you don't wanna involve the police and dialling 911 has a habit of doing that. Perhaps you'd feel a bit safer if I gave you his direct mobile number. You know, just in case."

"Mum, it can't hurt. Shokawa says there are no intergalactic trials. All trials are dealt with locally. Maybe being able to put Dent in prison will be the safest option. We don't have to phone until we have Polly somewhere safe."

Elizabeth hums and haws for a second.

"Okay, give it to me," she finally concedes.

"Here we are, St. Nicholas Park." The driver pulls over. He reverses the cab into a parking space and switches off the engine.

"Okay, my brother's name is Todd, eh, Officer Todd Flannigan. Tell him Mike gave you this number. Explain your situation, he'll know what to do."

"Okay, thank you so much," smiles Elizabeth. "You know, New Yorkers really are the most decent people I've ever met."

"We like to be called 'solid'. You know, dependable, always lookin' out for each other. You don't have to be born here, lotta folks aren't, I mean does Flannigan sound like a Lenape name to you?"

"No, it doesn't," Elizabeth chuckles.

"Okay folks, that's $145," announces the cabbie, pointing to the meter.

Elizabeth digs into her purse.

"Here's $200, you keep the change."

"Oh, that is TOO much. Thank you guys. Hey, you have a great day and I hope it all works out for you! You and your space alien!"

It's difficult to determine if he was being sarcastic. Maybe not, after all, Flash Gordon played for the New York Jets. Perhaps he's grown up with the concept of aliens in his life.

As the group wave goodbye to their new buddy, they turn around and walk up the steps into the public gardens of St. Nicholas Park. It's a beautiful little strolling area, not too big, but long and on a bit of a slope. There is an abundance of trees surrounding the park, but they won't be able to secretly bring in Shokawa due to the sheer numbers of dog walkers and kids on bikes. To be honest, at this stage, that's the least of their worries.

"Come on, let's call the big guns in," Jack announces, walking over to a park bench.

The group trot over with Momo at their side. He overtakes them to examine the contents of a trash can.

Barnaby sits down on a bench, closes his eyes and pictures the lily. Once again it is floating on the water before sinking into the light and being replaced with the debating chamber of the Council of Twelve.

Shokawa is there.

The last time he had met him Shokawa was wearing his debating robes, almost as ancient Greek in style as the building that surrounds them. Now he is back in full body armour, the same medieval suit he was wearing the very first time they met.

"Welcome, Barnaby. Has the time come?"

"Yes, Shokawa. I have seen Polly, she is in danger. We think Kallick has placed a trap over the house, so we have travelled to a location near to Polly."

"Good. I will join you now." Shokawa tightens a strap on his hand.

Barnaby opens his eyes to find the rest of the group staring at him.

"Ah Jesus!" he shrieks in fright.

"Sorry, darling, we were just intrigued."

"That's fine Mum, but please guys, remember to give me some space in future!"

"Is he coming?" asks Jack.

"Any second…" Barnaby doesn't get to finish his sentence, as the ground rumbles beneath their feet and Shokawa emerges from a flash of light into the park.

Around them people are watching the storm clouds gathering overhead, assuming they are the source of the noise and illumination. Two ten-year-old African American kids on bikes, stand motionless. Their jaws are hanging open, eyes fixed on Shokawa.

"Our uncle!" yells Jack. "He's a waiter at Medieval Times!"

"Uh-uh, he's a space alien. I saw him walk through that wormhole," replies one of the boys.

"Hehe, there's no kidding you, huh?" Jack chuckles.

"Come on, let's get moving, I don't want Polly spending another second in that place," commands Barnaby, grabbing Shokawa and closing his eyes.

Shokawa pushes Barnaby's hand away.

"Patience. First, we must perform the reconnaissance."

"Oh yeah, good idea."

Both he and Shokawa close their eyes.

Lily, light, sub-level eight. They are right back in front of Polly, who hasn't been moved. She smiles as she senses his presence.

Next to Barnaby, Shokawa appears.

"Hey, we can see each other in remote state? Cool!"

"Yes," explains Shokawa. "It is like a world within a world. We share this space but cannot be seen. Those strong with the crystal's power can feel us, those strongest can see us. We must avoid Kallick."

"Look, Polly senses us." Barnaby points to his friend in the chair.

"Yes. I see this," observes Shokawa, looking into her eyes.

"So what do we do, just leap in and get her?" Barnaby asks, his tolerance waning.

"Once more, you forget your patience. You must stop to use your mind. Think things through. Look, only two guards inside the room. It is too easy."

"Do you think Kallick has set a trap?"

"Most definitely."

"So what do we do now?"

"We must go the least expected route. Through the front door."

"Through the front door?" shrieks Barnaby.

Shokawa instantly disappears. Barnaby opens his eyes to witness Shokawa already walking up the path in the direction of the research facility.

"Mum, we can't get Polly out by jumping, we'll be going in the front door instead!"

"The front door? Is he mad?" Elizabeth chases after Barnaby who is trying to catch up with Shokawa.

Jack glances at Marsha.

"Well, I'm not staying here and missing all the fun!"

"Yeah, me neither," agrees Marsha.

"Come on Momo!" she commands, pulling his head out of the trash can. She runs after Jack who is now in hot pursuit of Elizabeth and the others.

"Wait for me!" yells Uncle Finch, as he brings up the rear.

At the head of the group, Shokawa reaches the top of the hill and runs straight across the road. An oncoming car has to brake heavily to avoid him. Just as it starts to move off, Barnaby and the rest of the group sprint across the street in quick succession. The irate driver sounds the horn as once again he is forced to slam on the brakes. Bringing up the rear, Uncle Finch raises his hand in a friendly gesture on the way past. The resulting signal from the driver is not so polite. Barnaby finally catches up with Shokawa.

'What's the plan here?" gasps Barnaby.

"Knock everything down, knock everyone over!" replies Shokawa as they reach the top of a set of stairs that lead into the research complex.

"Sounds like a good plan!" Barnaby declares.

Rounding the corner, they can see a group of armed guards congregated outside the entrance to the facility. Before they have the opportunity to acknowledge Barnaby and Shokawa, they are lifted into the air and thrown through a wormhole.

"Excellent work, Barnaby!" remarks Shokawa, impressed at his young pupil's growing abilities.

"Oh my God, did you see that!?" yells Jack as he rounds the corner with Elizabeth and Marsha.

"That was our Barnaby!" Elizabeth shrieks with delight. She holds out her arms and halts Marsha and Jack in their tracks.

"This is where we back-off!" she exclaims.

"Awwww," groans Jack, dismayed that he's not going to get to see all the action.

"Come on, let's go over here behind these trees and wait for them coming out."

As Shokawa and Barnaby reach the entrance, Shokawa raises his hands. The entire glass and metal structure tears itself from its hinges and shatters across the pathway, revealing a group of startled guards inside.

"Enough running, Barnaby. Now we take our time. Kallick is here somewhere and we must be cautious."

As the first guard raises his gun it flies from his fingers and out of the entranceway. Confused, he looks down at his hands before he is dragged across the floor, past Shokawa and Barnaby and off down the pathway, screaming as he goes. The other guards inside are frozen to the spot as Shokawa walks forward and addresses them.

"All those who wish no harm to come to them may leave now. Drop your weapons and exit the building!"

Another guard lifts up his gun, but this time Shokawa decides to make more of an example of him. Once again, the weapon flies from his hand, except this time the guard in question doesn't simply slide out of the building. Instead Shokawa has him thrown twenty feet into the air, only to come crashing back down to the ground, with what will likely be several broken bones.

No one else is stupid enough to test Shokawa again and so each one of them instantly drops their weapons.

"Now leave!" commands Shokawa, as he stands still and holds his arm out towards the door. Initially the guards begin to walk, but quickly burst into a run as Shokawa raises a warning hand.

As the last of them exit the atrium, Shokawa attends to the injured guard. Kneeling beside him, he places both his hands on the guard's chest and closes his eyes. This is one Barnaby has NOT witnessed before.

The guard shrieks in pain for a few seconds and then stops squirming, realising that something miraculous has happened. Slowly, he gets to his feet, rubbing where his injuries had been.

"How? How did you do that?" he asks in astonishment.

"Go," orders Shokawa, "Get a real job!"

The guard runs off, glad to be alive and seriously considering visiting a jobcentre.

"Okay, let's go," announces Barnaby, moving toward the security gate.

'Wait!" Shokawa blocks his path. "Do you feel it?"

"Feel what?" asks Barnaby.

The atrium is completely silent.

"Take your time. Let the excitement leave you. Let it expel quickly. Focus."

Barnaby stands motionless. His eyes are closed and he is trying to allow his heartbeat to return to normal, breathing deeply as he had been taught by Shokawa only yesterday.

"When at rest, you will sense it."

Barnaby feels calm. Rest has come to him. Then a cold tingling starts to creep across his body.

"Yes, I feel something!"

"A presence?"

"Something menacing. My instincts tell me something is not right."

"It centres around a being," Shokawa adds, his eyes closed, seeking the truth.

"It's like an individual. Like a smell, but not a smell. Like a soul, but distinguishable."

"Yes, that soul is Kallick. He is here. What can you tell me about him?"

Barnaby pauses a moment longer.

"He means harm. It's a sensation I have, as if this soul lies in wait. It's like watching a lion creep across a desert towards its prey. The same feeling of trepidation, as if I'm on high alert, like the antelope he stalks."

"Good, you are very aware. This is usually slow to come to students. You have learned quicker than I have ever seen."

Barnaby gives a little smile.

"Remember, ego is not welcome in a Moderator. Humble is the state of mind you must attain."

"It's still just a bit overwhelming. Little old me, with these powers!"

"You are not old."

"Oh, you really need to learn about expressions and metaphors."

Shokawa looks at Barnaby, who grins back.

"You tease," replies Shokawa.

"Hehe, just keen to keep the mood light."

Shokawa smiles back and approaches the security gate.

Chapter 21
The showdown

Standing by the row of trees, Elizabeth is getting twitchy.

"Shouldn't they be out by now?" she queries.

"Nah, you're just being a mum," replies Jack "They only went in a moment ago. The last of those security guys have only just run around the corner onto the main road!"

"I think I'm going to ring that guy," says Elizabeth, looking at her phone.

"The cabbie's brother?" Jack asks.

"Yes. If a few of those guys were to arrive now, who would know? Nobody knows we're here. I think I'd feel safer with some backup."

"We have an alien that moves stuff with his mind. I don't think we need backup!"

"I just want to see that snake in prison. That won't happen without cops."

"Okay, but tell him to, I dunno, meet us here. No charging in the front door and arriving with swarms of flashing blue and red lights, for Polly's sake," cautions Jack.

Elizabeth taps at the most recent entry and lifts the phone to her ear. A few seconds go by before the number is answered by Officer Todd Flannigan.

"Hello, yes, my name is Elizabeth Brown and I was given your number by your brother, Mike?"

***

Shokawa waves his hands across the security gate and the door parts. The sound of crunching metal and cracking glass suggests it didn't really want to open. The pair walk through towards the elevators.

"The sensation is getting stronger!" says Barnaby.

"He calls to us. He wants us to confront him."

"Are you nervous?" asks Barnaby.

"Nerves keep you alive. With a lack of nerves, stupid mistakes are made."

Barnaby calls the lift. The door opens instantly.

"I'm scared, Shokawa."

"Good," comes the reply as he steps in. Barnaby nervously joins him and presses the button for sub-level Eight. The doors close.

'It's an odd feeling,' thinks Barnaby, 'descending in a lift to confront an alien warlord to the tune of *The Girl from Ipanema*. Even worse is that this tune will be stuck in my head for the whole battle. Why could it not have been Metallica or something inspirational?'

They reach their floor and the doors open. Shokawa walks out into the corridor, only to be confronted by a hail of bullets.

He is unsure what statement Kallick is attempting to make as he knows that bullets can't hurt him. Perhaps Kallick is allowing Dent to see how pathetic these medieval guns are. Each cartridge falls to the ground in front of Shokawa, producing an almost soothing sound of steel rain.

Shokawa glances over at Barnaby, shakes his head and tuts. Barnaby laughs out loud. It's hilarious how, even in this circumstance, a bit of comedy can lighten the mood.

Shokawa bows his head, sighs and then clicks his fingers. All Barnaby can see is a black blur of about ten security personnel flying past the lift and into the wall to his left. There is a massive thumping noise, mixed with the odd crunch and then the sound of the unconscious bodies piling onto the floor.

At this point, Barnaby steps out and turns right along the corridor to stand alongside Shokawa. At the end of the hallway stands Lord Kallick. He is blocking the entrance to the room where Polly resides. His head almost touches the ceiling and his black cloak lies open revealing the armour underneath, silver and black metal with leather and steel fastenings. Behind him stands Dent, dressed in a black suit and tie, looking about as menacing as a newborn kitten compared to Kallick.

"Shokawa! It has been a while!" shouts Kallick in a deep, broken voice.

"Indeed it has, Kallick."

"And what is this you have with you?"

"This is Barnaby. He seeks his friend."

"Ah, the girl. Is it love little one?" asks Kallick as an evil grin broadens across his face.

"That would be none of your business!" cries Barnaby. "Now let her go!"

"And why would we do that?" Dent roars. "I don't appear to be holding a crystal!"

"Bring her out and then we'll discuss crystals!" demands Barnaby.

"That, dear boy, is not going to happen!" answers Dent, getting more agitated by the second.

"Then we must proceed by force," declares Shokawa, giving his final ultimatum.

"So be it." Kallick raises his hands.

Shokawa grabs Barnaby and throws him into the lift. Simultaneously a torrent of deep red fire spreads through the corridor, the very particles seemingly igniting in the atmosphere.

Shokawa spreads out his arms and pushes back against the power of the red flames. His counteracting force emanates from him in a blue cloud of fire that seems to reactivate the particles that Kallick has attempted to destroy. Light, it seems, is trumping dark.

Barnaby peeks his head around the lift door and can see Shokawa walking up the corridor, pushing hard against the destructive rain from Kallick's hands. He keeps going, pushing and pushing against Kallick until their hands are almost touching. It's at this point that Kallick turns and grabs Shokawa by the shoulder. The force knocks Dent off his feet. Shokawa spins completely around, seizing Kallick and bouncing him off the concrete wall. It crumbles as he hits it. Both giants are now entangled together, thrusting each other against the walls and ceiling in turns. The corridor gradually fills with dust and the smell of plaster. Finally, the pair are locked together by each other's hands, driving each other back and forth, their strength equally matched. The kinetic power building up against the opposing force is allowing sparks to rain down from their hands. This has to give way at some point. Shokawa gives one mighty roar and spins Kallick around in the air. He releases him, allowing the evil giant to travel the length of the hallway and smash against the wall to Barnaby's left. Dazed, Kallick attempts to peel himself from the plaster. Shokawa is already there. He lifts Kallick and propels him around into the second lift shaft. He crashes through the metal doors, so only his foot is protruding.

"Get Polly now," yells Shokawa as he grabs Kallick's foot.

Barnaby looks down the corridor and can see Dent through the haze of dust, tapping away at the security lock to the room where Polly is imprisoned. He sprints past Shokawa who is now tearing away at the remains of the lift door to gain better access to his stunned nemesis. Dent looks over his shoulder and sees Barnaby approaching. He taps the last few numbers and the door hisses open. He races inside, with Barnaby in hot pursuit. Kallick, in the meantime, has managed to free himself. He is now hurtling up the elevator shaft to regain his composure and continue the fight. He bursts through the lift door on ground level and races into the centre of the atrium. Shokawa follows him and the two stand face-to-face once more. He knows that Kallick likes to prattle on in these circumstances, which allows them both time to grab a quick rest.

"Well Shokawa, here you are, trying to save another pathetic planet," says Kallick, pacing back and forth.

"Not pathetic. It needs hope, but it is not pathetic. This will be a hard fight for you."

Shokawa runs at Kallick, but just as his fist bears down on Kallick's face, his adversary disappears through a wormhole.

'Coward," mutters Shokawa to himself.

***

Outside, Elizabeth is pacing back and forward.
"Where are they?"

"Give them time!" insists Jack.

"Oh I feel sick to my core," cries Elizabeth. "Why did I agree to let Barnaby go in there?"

"The same Barnaby that can throw people through wormholes, without even touching them? I wouldn't worry Mrs B!" Jack remarks.

Then Marsha spots four crouched figures moving toward them from the main gate. They are dressed in police uniforms.

"Hey, look!" she shouts, pointing in their direction.

"Mrs Brown?"

"Officer Flanigan?"

"At your service. So what's the situation now? Has anyone spoken to the kidnappers?"

"No, and it's only one kidnapper."

"Okay, so has there been a ransom demand or what?"

"Um, sort of. He wants to swap the girl for a crystal we have in our possession."

"A crystal? A precious crystal?"

"I don't know about the dollar value, but it possesses a unique source of power and Mr Dent wants to weaponize it."

"Wait, Mr Dent? Darius Dent?"

"Yes, he's the one holding poor Polly to ransom."

"Wow. This is big!" replies Officer Flannigan. "So what's the latest state of play? Is he expecting someone to go discuss this ransom with him?"

"Well, here's where it gets a bit weird. You see, my son Barnaby is already in the building with the crystal."

"You sent your son in? How old is he?"

"He's fifteen."

"Wait, fifteen!? You sent a fifteen-year-old boy into a hostage situation?"

"Oh, yes, but he's not alone. He has help."

"Help? From who?" quizzes Officer Flannigan.

"Emmmm," says Elizabeth, chuckling nervously, "I can't believe I'm going to say this out loud, but he's with a Brukashi warrior called Shokawa. He's, um, shall we say, special?"

"What do you mean special? Like Special Forces? And what's a Brukashi warrior?"

Elizabeth screws her face up, almost too embarrassed to talk.

"He comes from a planet called Koyakashi and he can, like, move stuff with his mind."

Officer Flannigan stares at Elizabeth, his face not flinching for around five seconds.

"Okay boys, stand down, just a couple of junkies and their kids!"

Officer Flannigan starts to move away.

"No, no, Officer, I know it sounds crazy, I hear myself say it and I want the ground to swallow me up, but it's true!"

"How do you know it's true?"

"Because, he, um, took us, um, to his, um, home planet, and, um…"

"Okay Mrs Brown, I'm going to have to check your purse for illegal substances." Officer Flannigan grabs

Elizabeth's bag. "Has this purse been in the possession of anyone other than yourself over the past twenty-four hours?"

"No, but..."

"And could anyone have given you any kind of medication, legal or otherwise over the past twenty-four hours?"

"Not that I'm aware of."

"Okay, we're going to have to take you down to the station. We're going to have to ask you some ques..."

"But, no, what about my son and Polly?"

"I'll get one of my men to go and speak to the staff at the facility. In the meantime, you're coming with me." Flannigan seizes Elizabeth by the arm.

"Hey, let go of her!" screams Jack.

***

Downstairs, Dent is racing across the room towards Polly who is still tied to the chair. He draws his sidearm and grabs her, prodding the gun into her head. Barnaby slides to a halt, about ten feet from them.

"Not another move, dear boy, or lover girl dies!"

"Are you okay, Polly?" asks Barnaby.

"Yeah, kinda."

"Now, Barnaby, you will give me the crystal."

"Okay, okay, just point the gun away from Polly."

"Crystal!" demands Dent, growing impatient.

Barnaby reaches into his pocket and produces the crystal. He holds it up for Dent to see.

"Wonderful, now toss it here!"

Barnaby closes his eyes. Outside in the gardens he can see Officer Flannigan trying to pull his mother out from behind the trees. Barnaby smiles, opens his eyes and clicks his fingers.

'How did we get outside?' asks a confused Dent.

Elizabeth spots their arrival.

"Look, Officer, there they are!"

Officer Flannigan looks over his shoulder and can see Dent, his gun pointing directly at Polly's head. Barnaby is standing ten feet in front of them.

"Well I'll be damned!" exclaims Flannigan, dropping Elizabeth and reaching for the sidearm in his holster.

"What did you do Barnaby?" screams Dent.

"Just levelled the playing field a little," Barnaby smirks as he walks towards him.

"Give me the crystal!" roars Dent, loud enough for the entire world to hear.

"Sure, here you go," says Barnaby and tosses the crystal high into the air. As it spins, Dent raises both hands up to catch it. For a few seconds it whirls and arcs its way towards him. He prepares to grab it, but as it arrives, he realises he has lost the use of his arms and the crystal bounces off of his face. Polly rushes away from Dent, her arms suddenly freed from the ropes that had tied her to the chair. She runs straight into Barnaby's arms, where he embraces her tightly. She bursts into tears of relief. Meanwhile, Flannigan has his gun trained on Dent.

"Don't move, pal!!" he shouts.

"Are you having a laugh?" yells Dent. He is still frozen in motion, his arms raised to the sky. At that point, Barnaby releases his hold over him and Dent becomes mobile again. With Polly still clinging to him, Barnaby holds out his hand and the crystal jumps up from the ground into his palm.

"Officer, there's been a big misunderstanding," pleads Dent.

"All I saw was you holding a gun to the head of that young girl and yelling for some crystal. I guess the lady's story checks out."

"What lady?" queries Dent.

"The one over there." Flannigan spins Dent around and places him in handcuffs. Across the garden, next to the trees, stands Elizabeth Brown. She waves at Dent with an enormous smile on her face.

"I honestly thought they were going to kill me," says Polly, looking deep into Barnaby's eyes.

"That was never going to happen." Barnaby strokes her face.

"I owe you my life, Barnaby. Twice!"

"I'm sure you'll find some way to repay me," he smiles. Polly leans forward and slowly moves her lips towards his, tilting her head at the last moment. To both their delights, they have finally come together to share their first real kiss.

Suddenly, behind them, there is a powerful flash of light and a rumble, as Shokawa and Kallick tumble onto the well-manicured lawn. Shokawa has Kallick by the shoulder and is repeatedly punching him in the face.

Officer Flannigan and his colleagues stand motionless. They watch this intergalactic bare-knuckle fight, even Dent who is being propped up by Flannigan.

Shokawa continues to pummel Kallick into the ground, his head moving deeper into the soil beneath the grass.

"Enough!" screams Kallick, holding his hands out in front of him.

"It will be enough when you release all veils you have placed over this planet!" Shokawa roars, as he lands another punch square in the middle of Kallick's face.

"Alright, I will remove them."

For Dent, this is wonderful to watch. 'Kallick can be defeated! That will be handy when the time comes.'

Elizabeth walks over to Officer Flannigan.

"No illegal drugs in MY purse Officer."

Flannigan turns to Elizabeth.

"This is going to be a tough one to write up! I'm sorry I doubted you, Mrs Brown. Now if you don't mind, I'd like to get this one to the station and get him booked. Is it okay for you and your family to come down as soon as possible to recount your version of events? Obviously, we can miss out all the stuff about these two guys." He nods in the direction of Shokawa and Kallick.

"Of course, Officer," replies Elizabeth.

"Hey," adds Flannigan, halting before marching Dent off to jail. "Where's your husband?"

"Florida, I think? Haven't seen him in fourteen years."

"So he's not around anymore?"

"And why would you be interested in that level of detail, Officer Flannigan?"

"Well, I'd like to hear more about these alien guys, off the record, you know?"

"And?" presses Elizabeth.

"I thought you could explain it to me over, you know, dinner?"

Flannigan shrugs and looks a bit sheepish. He's late 40's, hair starting to turn white, but still very attractive with quite the jawbone!

"Let's discuss this later shall we?" Elizabeth grins and walks off towards Barnaby. She fails to see Flannigan grab the brim of his cap and dip it slightly.

"Yes, ma'am!"

Meanwhile, Barnaby and Polly are still hugging.

"Hey, you! Get your hands off my sister!" teases Jack walking over, with an enormous grin on his face.

Polly lets Barnaby go just in time for Jack's high-five.

The two boys embrace and slap each other's backs. Simultaneously Marsha approaches Polly and gives her a big hug. As Elizabeth joins, Barnaby releases his grip on Jack and moves to her instead.

"Oh, Barnaby, I'm so proud of you!"

"Thanks, Mum. All in a day's work!" he smiles.

With Barnaby still attached, Elizabeth grabs Polly towards her also.

"And how are you, Polly?"

"Well, my finger hurts like hell, but apart from that, I'm good!"

At this point, Elizabeth releases her hold over Barnaby and focuses on Polly's finger.

"Oh, those monsters! Let's go get this fixed up. Come on, Poll." Elizabeth leads her down to where Flannigan is tucking Dent into his squad car.

"Wait, Mum, Shokawa can fix that!"

"Really"

"Oh yeah!" confirms Barnaby, as Elizabeth trots off up to Shokawa. Uncle Finch sheepishly arrives beside Jack, Marsha and Barnaby.

"Well, seems my little device has ended up causing quite the stir!"

"It certainly did, Uncle Finch. I'm glad it's all over now! Don't think I fancy travelling any time soon!"

Suddenly Barnaby remembers that Shokawa still has Kallick pinned to the ground. He rushes over to join them, just as Shokawa finishes mending Polly's finger.

Barnaby crouches down on the ground to face Kallick as Polly looks at her fingertip in amazement.

"Why do you do this? Why is it all about conquering?"

"Why do your dogs bark? Why do your fish swim? Why does your population have so many stupid individual little wars?"

"It's in his nature," interrupts Shokawa. "So many chances I gave him. Tried to show him the error of ways, but he does not heed. He is intent on his mission."

Shokawa grabs Kallick by the collar and pulls his head out of the ground. Behind him is a Kallick-shaped hole in the soil.

"So what do you do with him now?" asks Barnaby.

Shokawa waves his hand and Kallick disappears in a flash of light.

"Woah! Where did you send him?"

"Arkavia."

"Arkavia, like, his home planet Arkavia?" replies Barnaby, not quite believing his ears. "Why would you do that?"

"Every time, I beat him, he comes back. We fight, I win and I let him go. I hope one day he will get bored. Bored of never winning. It's impossible for him."

"Well maybe one day he'll work out a way to win!" shrieks Barnaby.

"He's too stupid. Look how easy it was today. We rolled through a couple of your countries. Jumped around time, smashed each other about, but always the same. Kallick fails. It has been this way for hundreds of years."

"Okay, I guess you know best."

"Yes I do," Shokawa responds.

"What now?" enquires Barnaby.

"Now? Talk to the Police. Make Dent go to prison and go to school tomorrow."

"And you?"

"I must go home now. I have a pizza recipe."

Barnaby smiles a big, broad grin, equally matched by the one on Shokawa's face.

"I will see you soon, Barnaby Brown!"

And with that Shokawa vanishes with a subtle little rumble and the mildest flash of light.

"Smooth," nods Barnaby. "Real smooth."

He wanders over to Jack and Marsha.

"Right, we better get this police statement out of the way and then let everyone go home. There's been more than enough excitement for one day!" he announces.

"Yeah and I'm starving!!" adds Marsha.

So is Barnaby. He could really go a big pile of McNorton's toast right now. Maybe he'll just settle for his new favourite. Bagels.

Chapter 22

Epilogue

Darius Dent sits in his cell. It's been six months since he was convicted of kidnapping but he's dealing well with prison life. Someone as rich as he is always able to influence people with the lure of money.

Because of this, he has secured himself the largest cell along with a desk, filing cabinet and TV. The cook has been bribed by the prison warden, to ensure Dent always has the very best, unlike the rubbish dished out to the poorer inmates.

He has another four years to serve, which was better than the original twenty that the prosecution was aiming for. There were too many discrepancies in the story, or maybe the judge was under pressure from Dent's numerous business partners. Everyone involved thought the sentence was very light, except Dent, of course. If he keeps his nose clean, he could be out in eighteen months for good behaviour, something that is actually very likely.

Of course, the internment hasn't stopped his evil plans. On his wall hangs designs of things he intends to build when he is free again. He already has his teams working on prototypes, but what he really needs are some of those crystals. That's the tough bit, as it's evident that he won't be able to get his hands on Barnaby's anymore. Not with his powers and that pesky Shokawa turning up all of the time. No, this time he needs a new approach.

As Dent lies on his bed reading, a revised strategy is forming. Not in his head, but in the air around him. Initially, it goes unnoticed, just a dimming of the light, but then faint little sparks start to ping into the room from nowhere.

Dent lowers his book, aware that something is happening.

Suddenly, with an electric crackle and a shudder of the room, Lord Kallick stands before him. The fizzing particles around him dance off of his shoulders and onto the floor.

"Well, well, if it isn't the 'Evil' Lord Kallick. Master of…, well nothing really."

"Dent," replies Kallick in his deep, rough voice. "I can understand your anger. I underestimated our opponents. Especially the little boy who overcame you."

Dent grins.

"I've been sitting here for six whole months, where the hell have you been?"

"Planning, Dent, planning."

"Well enough of this, get me out of here!"

"No."

"No?" Dent yells into Kallick's face.

"My plans are not complete," continues Kallick. "More research, more planning, more time in prison for you!"

"Why am I to remain in prison!!?" barks Dent.

"Character building, shall we say," Kallick grins.

Dent prepares to throw a punch, but his action is halted by Kallick.

"I don't have to be here, Mr Dent, but I see potential in you," remarks Kallick. He circles Dent, who although frozen to the spot, is still able to follow him with his eyes. "I'm afraid you're just going to have to trust me."

Kallick releases Dent. He glares at him before sitting back down on his prison bed.

"I spent many years in prisons. It teaches you discipline. You will thank me later."

"Oh, I'm sure I will," Dent smirks. "So if you're not here to free me, why are you here?"

Kallick pauses for a moment, motionless.

"What do you know of the Baetylus Stones, Mr Dent?"

"Never heard of them!"

"It is said, in your history, that five powerful stones fell to Earth. They endowed the holder with life bringing qualities along with gifts of strength and supernatural powers."

Dent stands up, interested.

"Four of those stones have been lost to ancient history, but one was recently found in an undisclosed location by a Professor Mathias Finch. Now, we can't get our hands on the Finch crystal. However, with some assistance, I'm sure we could locate at least one of the other four. Your planet's folklore describes where they once were."

Dent's grin grows wider than has ever been seen.

"Well Lord Kallick, that IS good news!"

Barnaby Brown will return in
Barnaby Brown and the Baetylus Stones.

About the author and Barnaby

Michael Gordon was born in Edinburgh in 1970.

Educated at Broughton High School, it was his favourite English teacher, Mr MacMillan who first turned him on to the fact that he might be able to portray a good story, comparing something he had written to Steinbeck, no less!

However, the lure of a musical career got the better of him and he spent many years as the singer for Edinburgh rock band Imperial Racing Club, along with, for a spell, fellow Edinburgh author Doug Johnstone.

His first novel, *Mark Elder - Dawn of the Robokaze,* was written to 'test the water', before embarking on something that had always lurked at the back of his mind. A time travel adventure for kids and young adults.

Barnaby Brown was born in January 2018 in Singapore, while Michael was laid up ill in his hotel room on a business trip. Originally called Barnaby Jones, the name had to be changed so as not to clash with an American detective show of the same name. On the same day, most of the other major characters of the book were born, along with concepts and a rough storyline.

The book was finally completed in August 2018, having been mostly written at his home in Hong Kong.